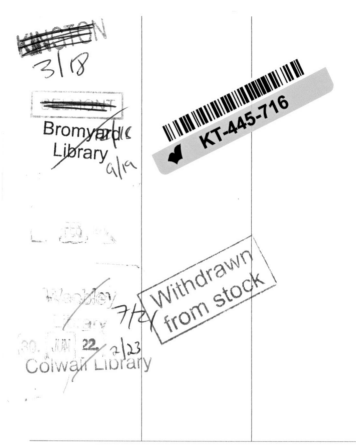
Please return/renew this item by the last date shown

**Herefordshire
Libraries**

*Herefordshire
Council*

740009761598

SPECIAL MESSAGE TO READERS

THE ULVERSCROFT FOUNDATION
(registered UK charity number 264873)
was established in 1972 to provide funds for
research, diagnosis and treatment of eye diseases.
Examples of major projects funded by
the Ulverscroft Foundation are:-

- The Children's Eye Unit at Moorfields Eye
  Hospital, London
- The Ulverscroft Children's Eye Unit at Great
  Ormond Street Hospital for Sick Children
- Funding research into eye diseases and
  treatment at the Department of Ophthalmology,
  University of Leicester
- The Ulverscroft Vision Research Group,
  Institute of Child Health
- Twin operating theatres at the Western
  Ophthalmic Hospital, London
- The Chair of Ophthalmology at the Royal
  Australian College of Ophthalmologists

You can help further the work of the Foundation
by making a donation or leaving a legacy.
Every contribution is gratefully received. If you
would like to help support the Foundation or
require further information, please contact:

THE ULVERSCROFT FOUNDATION
The Green, Bradgate Road, Anstey
Leicester LE7 7FU, England
Tel: (0116) 236 4325

website: www.foundation.ulverscroft.com

Pippa James is a full-time writer with a love of food, fashion and all things French. She is best known as Janey Louise Jones, author of the fantastically successful Princess Poppy series, with sales of over four million copies to date. Before Princess Poppy took over her life, Pippa had always intended to write contemporary fiction. *The Secret Life of Lucy Lovecake* is her debut novel.

THE SECRET LIFE OF
LUCY LOVECAKE

Daisy Delaney's life is pancake-flat. A talented baker and passionate lingerie specialist, she has wound up with no one to bake for and an unsuccessful career. But when she starts a delicious relationship with famous French author-chef Michel Amiel, everything begins to look a bit more exciting. That is, until Michel's bestselling cookbook is knocked off the top spot by newcomer Lucy Lovecake. His outdated recipes slide down the charts, while the popularity of Lucy Lovecake's new dating cookbook is rising like the perfect sponge. How can Daisy ever tell Michel that *she* is the mysterious Lucy Lovecake? And more importantly, does she even want to be with a difficult, egotistical, down-on-his-luck Frenchman just as her career is beginning to take off? Especially when she has some other very interesting offers . . .

PIPPA JAMES

◆

THE
SECRET LIFE OF
LUCY LOVECAKE

Complete and Unabridged

CHARNWOOD
Leicester

First published in Great Britain in 2017 by
Black & White Publishing Ltd
Edinburgh

First Charnwood Edition
published 2018
by arrangement with
Black & White Publishing Ltd
Edinburgh

The moral right of the author has been asserted

This novel is a work of fiction. The names, characters and incidents portrayed in it are of the author's imagination. Any resemblance to actual persons, living or dead, events or localities is entirely coincidental.

A catalogue record for this book is available from the British Library.

ISBN 978–1–4448–3571–7

Published by
F. A. Thorpe (Publishing)
Anstey, Leicestershire

Set by Words & Graphics Ltd.
Anstey, Leicestershire
Printed and bound in Great Britain by
T. J. International Ltd., Padstow, Cornwall

This book is printed on acid-free paper

1

Lovely Cake by Lovecake

'A chocolate, ginger and Chantilly cream gateau, coated with chocolate ganache, decorated with candied ginger, dipped in bitter chocolate,' I said, smoothing out my Green Kitchen apron.

Thumbs up from Bex, the director.

Phew. Sounds okay — but can I make it in public, against the clock?

'Mmmm. Ambitious *and* delicious plans from our delectable literary debutante, Daisy Delaney, author of the trending date cookbook *everyone's* tweeting about: *French Fancy*,' said the host, TV cook, Victoria Darling, radiant in a chartreuse wiggle dress, with impressively engineered balcony bodice. 'Or should I really call you 'Lucy Lovecake'?' she added.

A tinkle of tittering from the capacity crowd, seated in the largest tent at the Hay-on-Wye literary festival. The *Barclays Glenfiddich Daily Telegraph* venue was styled as the rival Green and Red Kitchens for the duration of the festival. Every day, another hotly vied culinary contest for the delectation of the ravenous audience. It was, said Hay's chief fixer, Tara, proving to be their most popular concept ever at Hay. A sell-out each and every day for three weeks. 'No more can authors just talk about books; we need tricks as well,' she said.

I feel a bit sorry for writers who write stories. What can they do at their events?

Most of the front six rows of seats were taken by journalists and bloggers, and some famous authors on complimentary tickets. I had got to know most of the media people since I'd 'joined the circus' eighteen months before in the pre-publicity for my first book. I considered some of the journalists friends, others foes, and wasn't at all sure I'd put them in the right camps.

Kitty, my flatmate, waved wildly from the middle of the audience. Next to her, Clara, my boss from the lingerie store Voluptas, where I'd dared to dream of being a published writer, as I'd scribbled amongst the silky camisoles, lace-topped stockings and fiddly suspenders. Francesca, the chaise-longue restorer from the shop next door, sat next to Clara, her pre-Raphaelite curls bouncing wildly on an emerald-green dress as she chatted excitedly. Mum and Dad were to their left, waving covertly, not wishing to draw attention.

They're a bit proud and a bit mortified, aren't they? 'Our daughter is a published author. She's a genius. But she's written about seduction. She's a hussy.'

Jessica, my friend from the baking course, was there, too, with her husband, Ted. She'd said my book saved their marriage. It was lovely to see all of them, their presence making this ludicrous situation seem a fraction more believable.

How can we be here? How can this be happening? To Daisy Delaney, Dreamer, Ditherer, and Perpetual Failure?

I had been such an ordinary young woman a year and a half ago — impoverished, directionless, depressed. Cursed, even, until *French Fancy* was released and hit the bestseller lists after a teasing feature in the Christmas edition of *Elle* magazine. It felt as if my life had turned into its own version of magic realism. There we all were, in the bookish Big Top. And who were the clowns performing that mellow June morning? Me — Daisy Delaney, lingerie-specialist-turned-author, trainee clown — and my arch-nemesis, and general toss-pot, the French writer-chef Michel Amiel. A very experienced, hard-drinking clown. The sort that makes little children scream.

At this exact point, though, he still had not turned up for the event, although he had been spotted on site. According to Tara, he was under a tree, swigging from a bottle of Veuve. She'd just come over to ask if I might be able to talk him into showing face in the Red Kitchen. Tara, with her big, veneery smile, was beginning to grate.

'Tara, there's no way. We don't *pretend* to be at loggerheads on Twitter. We really are. I haven't spoken to him for months.' *Since Valentine's Day, in fact. God, don't even think about that, Daisy.*

The organisers were pushing me to the edge, and Bex was obviously sympathetic towards me, smiling reassuringly as she went about her job, making sure that all the technical stuff would

3

happen at the right times. I was still reeling from the shock of having to compete directly with Michel in such a publicly humiliating way. I'd been expecting to be up against *Bake It* star Myles Munroe, which was worrying enough, but as Tara had said in the Green Room a bit earlier, 'This is such a fuck-up, totes sorry. Hope you're okay with going against Michel Amiel? You're a lifesaver, Daise. You're one million per cent the nicest author we've ever had.'

Yeah.

Back to Victoria. 'For those of you who have read *French Fancy*, you will know that it's an ironic, third-wave feminist look at contemporary dating, combined with the current fixation with baking and the joint effects of sexuality and cakes on seduction . . . that's what it says on my notes here anyway, folks! Some may refer to it as 'that bake and bonk book', but I never would.'

Victoria was clearly under earpiece instructions to keep things rolling while Michel Amiel was lassoed. The audience was in her thrall. As well as being invited regularly into the kitchen of Victoria Darling through our TV screens, we all felt as though we'd been through the ups and downs of her life with her too.

'And don't forget that regular updates during the contest will be posted by the Hay team on Twitter, Facebook and Instagram. Plus, an edited version of this contest will be available to view on YouTube just two hours after you leave the tent,' she said.

Bad enough doing this, but for it to be immortalised!

As Victoria read out a clutch of tweets and texts, I busied myself in the Green Kitchen, checking the oven was at 180°C, that all the appliances were working, and that my order-of-tasks list for the world's trickiest cake still made sense.

From the 'backstage' area, a stumbling Michel Amiel was led in at this point by a burly minder, who was having some difficulty keeping him upright. A huge cheer went up. The more he did wrong, the more he could do no wrong.

Bex and Tara exchanged 'thank fuck' expressions.

I got a shock when I saw him.

2

Michel

In the four months since I'd last seen Michel in the flesh, he'd changed for the worse. The pallor of his skin was like uncooked pastry and his dark eyes were sunken into his head. His hair was wilder than usual, more salt than pepper now — and his brow shone with a glaze of perspiration. His clothes had been marinaded in sweat and sploshes of alcohol. As far as we knew, he *had* slept in them.

Michel, what's happening to you?

Victoria tried to smooth things over.

'Phew! Great to have our esteemed second contestant in the Red Kitchen!' she said.

Michel gave a wave and blew a kiss to the audience.

'Always the charmer, Monsieur Amiel,' commented Victoria. 'Well, the French are known for romance, and Daisy's book is certainly intensely romantic, maybe even a little erotic,' she said. 'In fact, I'm sure there are some members of the audience disappointed to see 'Lucy Lovecake' fully clothed today!'

Peals of laughter this time, followed by some raucous remarks. 'A bit of page forty-seven, please!' called one man, which led to a bit of foot-stomping agreement.

Ah, the famous page 47.

I should respond to Victoria. My publisher, Dominic McGann, sat in the front row, willing me to sparkle. To his left, Branwell Thornton, my literary agent, who had been the first to believe in me, encouraging me to find this book inside me where other agents had dismissed my previous offerings without comment. I couldn't let Branwell down. It's just that I'd never wanted to hurt Michel professionally, or personally — and I'd managed to do both in the space of a few short months.

Come on, Delaney, Michel hates you anyway. Just play the game. Promote the book, make the money, then this will all seem like a silly hallucination of what once didn't really happen on a hot summer's day in the Welsh borders . . .

I cleared my throat. 'Ah, I never bake *in* my lingerie, Victoria. As Lucy Lovecake will tell you and page forty-seven confirms, that is best saved for serving it,' I said.

Mental note, work out what they love about page 47, and do more of that in the next book.

My opponent, now propped up on his kitchen units, busily decanting amber liquid from a hipflask into a coffee supplied by Tara, shot me a look which flash-fried my cheeks instantly. He was obviously thinking of the day he'd paid an unexpected visit to my flat on Rosehip Lane, just as I'd been taking a cake from the oven whilst wearing a corset, stockings and suspenders. I'd been experimenting for a racy crime novel which never materialised, as it happens.

Seems so long ago, but it was only eighteen

months, the very day that I got the idea for French Fancy.

'Ever the coquette,' he muttered, picked up by his microphone.

I considered a comment about just dropping the 'ette' in his case, but my parents were in the audience, plus Granny Delaney was going to watch the YouTube clip in her convent nursing home that afternoon. If the nuns allowed it. We knew that Sister Angelica had a laptop, and a Foxy Bingo habit.

Michel laughed as if he knew what I was thinking.

He's always good fun, whatever else he might be.

I hated being at loggerheads with him, almost as much as I hated him in general. I just wished I'd never met him. *But I wouldn't be standing here, in the freakish circus of minor fame, without him.*

Michel looked set for mischief. 'We could all sell piles of books if we stripped down to our panties!' he said, hiccupping.

'Knickers!' I corrected him.

This generated hoots from the crowds.

Dominic winked from the front row. I guess I'd found my Lucy Lovecake voice all right.

'They do say sex sells, but I wouldn't know,' added a pouting Victoria, getting the biggest laugh yet, and taking it well. 'Let's find out what Michel has in store for the contest. In case we should forget, this is meant to be all about the cakes!'

She tottered over to Michel's kitchen, wiggling

8

Marilyn Monroe-style, in dainty slipper-mules.

'*Qu'allez-vous faire aujourd'hui?*' she asked.

He took a slug of his coffee.

'Cherry clafoutis. *C'est tout*,' he replied.

Damn. His killer pudding.

'A classic! I love it!' said Victoria. 'A certain contrast in choice of cakes between our contestants, but I'm up for a piece of both!' She turned to the audience. 'These two writers may have a flair for cakes in common, but I think anyone with half an eye on social media will know that they never agree on anything else!'

'How can you agree with a liar?' said Michel.

He's not getting away with it.

'If some people could learn self-control and discretion, they could be trusted with the truth,' I added.

Victoria stepped in nimbly on the beat with a perfectly judged platitude. 'Well, you know what they say: the proof is in the pudding! It will be up to our talented tasters to decide on the winner — an hour from now,' she said, making her way to a round table in between the two kitchens. 'We're going to meet the judges now, but for Daisy and Michel it's almost time to start baking. The cameras will be following them around their kitchens, and no, we're not hoping for any disasters. Really we're not.' She winked. 'We all make the odd mistake, even me! God knows, that's how I've invented many a new dish.'

I had much more scope for mistakes than Michel with my ludicrously complicated cre-ation, and my rookie-ness to boot. Why, oh why, had I not just opted for a simple Victoria sponge cake or even my signature French fancies?

'You can watch the detail of these two bakers at work on the huge screens above their respective kitchens,' said Victoria.

She now turned to glance at me, then Michel. 'All the best to both of you. Daisy, Michel, you have an hour. Time to start baking. Three, two, one. Go!'

It was a relief to be able to retreat into the familiar rituals of baking. The habits of a lifetime, which had been firmed up during a course at Michel's cookery school in Primrose Hill. 'You must be a voice of authority on baking,' Dominic had said. I'd countered this; I am not trained in the way of the great bakers, the patissiers, so how can I ever be 'a voice of authority'? Trust me, he'd said.

I got on with making the two sponge cakes which I planned to layer into four discs, sandwiched together with the Chantilly cream. Measuring. Greasing. Sifting. Creaming. Blending. Whisking. Folding. I got lost in the processes. It was a very ambitious cake, with extra whisked egg whites giving the sponge an extra lightness and softness, which I felt lifted it from 'cake' to 'gateau'. The ganache was a worry, with equal proportions of cream to chocolate essential for the thick frosting effect I needed. I had rehearsed the entire process several times, with Kitty timing me in our little basement kitchen — and I knew I had not a minute to spare.

There was a fixed camera trained onto the

mixing bowls. I had strict instructions from Bex not to move them out of the 'magic box' which framed my hands at work over the bowls and mixers. There was also a young cameraman, Harry, following me around, trying his best not to get in my way. I was expected to say the odd thing to the camera, such as, 'Well, that's the cake mixture nearly ready. I'm reasonably happy with it, although I might have overdone the ginger . . . ' and other such profundities.

I could hear Michel being vocal in the Red Kitchen. He was much more interesting than I was — telling jokes, larking around for the audience. Sometimes funny, sometimes cross. His usual. I tried to block him out but couldn't help hearing the calls for: 'Champagne, please!' And 'Can this camera guy fuck off for a minute?' As well as, 'You call these eggs? Were they laid by budgies?'

Sixteen minutes into the hour and my two chocolatey, ginger sponge mixtures went into the oven for twelve minutes. I glanced over to Michel's kitchen.

He was still showing off for the crowd. Juggling eggs . . . Oops! About to drop one. Ah, just caught it! So cool.

'Shall I stone the cherries one-handed?' he said. 'I want this contest to be fair to Daisy, after all!'

He insisted that Victoria re-tie his apron at his back, with one of his arms strapped to the side of his body.

The crowd loved him. It was hard to believe this was the man who had been marched out of

11

Britain under police escort less than a year before, when French police wanted to question him about fraudulently withholding income due to his ex-girlfriend, the film star Eve Berger.

We were so close at that point . . . I can hardly believe I went to Paris with his mother to support him. As we walked by the Seine, he said he trusted me more than any other person.

I was getting things under control in the Green Kitchen. And then I allowed myself another glance across to the red. My eyes grew wide with disbelief at what I saw this time.

No!

A jug of pre-prepared clafoutis batter mixture was handed to Michel from behind the scenes.

So he's not even going to make it for real! Scoundrel.

3

The Result

One moment I'd been feeling warm and tender towards him, and now I was filled with rage. This was the dual effect he always had on me. The reason I'd decided I couldn't try any longer.

My cheeks felt hot and pink. I took a deep breath, trying to decide if I should let it go. After all, this 'show' was about entertainment. Did I really want to come over like an officious head prefect, grassing up the coolest boy in school?

Get on with your own cake, Daisy!

Once the sponges were rising quite magnificently into gentle domes, creating a delicious aroma of combined bitter cocoa and sweet ginger, I whipped the cream, adding a sprinkle of icing sugar and a dash of vanilla. I must have relaxed a bit, as I could hear Victoria for the first time in many minutes, although I'm sure she'd been talking to the judges and the crowd all along.

Paul Finch, Jane Bell and Caroline Bateman were judging, and they sat around the circular table with Victoria.

'Ah, clafoutis is one of my all-time favourites,' said Paul. 'But I'm just not sure how good Michel would look serving it up in a camisole.'

'I'll leave the camisole for the tart,' called Michel.

'Cream gateau, actually, over here,' I replied.

'More like cream tease,' he retorted to the delight of the crowd.

Time check. Half past. Focus. Ignore him now. He wants to put me off my stride. Well, I won't let him.

Now for the ganache. The rich, dark chocolate melted quickly into glossy folds. I set aside a little for dipping the ginger, then added the rest to the cream, whisking until it sat in soft peaks inside the pink ceramic bowl.

I looked at the clock.

Get a move on!

Just time to dip the crystallised ginger into the remaining silky chocolate.

Ding! The sponges were ready.

The last stage left no room for other thoughts, and I put Michel's cheating out of my mind.

I still had to slice the two cakes into four equal discs, allow to cool, and sandwich them together with Chantilly, then smother with ganache, and finally, decorate.

'You're doing really well,' Harry whispered.

I smiled, afraid to speak in case everyone heard.

It was impossible not to notice that Michel now had a beautiful young woman from the audience in his kitchen, helping with the custard sauce, a version of crème anglaise, with a dash of amaretto. His clafoutis was resting. I could smell it from the Green Kitchen. The cherries so sharp and tangy, the cooked batter so gently comforting — a perfect, winning combination.

Well, I did my best.

Soon my gateau was ready for the outer

coating of ganache. I used the palette knife to smooth, and it did look deliciously velvety. I lifted it onto a vintage glass pedestal dish — Kitty and I had found it in Pike's Antiques on Gloucester Avenue — ready for decorating.

What's the time? Help! Five minutes to go.

The candied ginger hadn't quite set, so I popped it in the freezer for two minutes to speed things up, then arranged a cluster of the chocolatey, crystallised pieces on top of the cake.

'Time's up!' called Victoria. 'Stop baking!'

'You nailed it!' said Harry. 'Looks fantastic!'

'Thanks. Phew, not a moment to spare!'

I took a breath. *Harry's right. It looks pretty good.*

I caught Dominic's eye. *Happy. Proud.* I realised my cheeks were glowing as he snapped me with his phone, then fiddled around, probably Instagram-ing an image of me and the cake. Proud, fatherly smile from Branwell. Everyone in the middle row beaming and waving.

The two efforts were carried forward to the table where the judges sat. There was a lot of photographing going on — both looked more than respectable.

Michel and I stood side by side behind the table as the judges came to taste.

He came up close to me, covering his mic. 'You smell so . . . smug.'

'You smell so . . . dirty,' I said, covering mine.

'Ah, what a lovely compliment. I know how you like dirty, Lucy Lovecake.'

'Don't mention it.'

'I messed my clafoutis up to give you a chance,' he said.

15

'You're so damn sweet.' Then under my breath. 'Or do I mean, you're a damn cheat?'

'Ha! Your fancy ways with words!'

He wobbled. *He's going to fall over.* I reached out for him. He caught my hand and stood straight again, then put his arm round me. It might have looked as if he was embracing me, in that fake, showbiz sort of way, when people wait for results and pretend to be pally, like at results time on *Strictly Come Dancing*, but, in fact, I was holding him up. I put my arm along his lower back and felt his ribs protruding. He reeked of cigarettes, wine and unwashed clothes.

I had rarely felt so nervous, as the judges tucked into the cakes.

Caroline tried my gateau first. 'Absolutely divine,' she said. 'Light, lovely flavours. The balance is sublime. The sweetened Chantilly works on a cake that is actually quite sharp and rather grown-up. Inspired.'

Paul liked it too, saying it sent his senses into overdrive — 'Or is that just page forty-seven?' — but Jane thought it a bit too complicated. 'I don't know which flavour dominates,' she said. 'They compete.'

Fair point.

They moved on to Michel's clafoutis. I knew it to be a wonderful thing — he'd made it for me once.

'Superb!' said Paul.

'Magnificent!' breathed Jane.

'Just . . . a little taste of heaven!' quipped Caroline.

Michel whispered, 'Oily suck-ups. It's average.'

Victoria ordered the judges to have a confab and pitched in to the tasting table herself, enjoying a mouthful of each.

'I'm going to stick my neck right out here,' she said. 'For me, Daisy's cake has the edge — for sheer courage alone, let alone the wonderful taste, but it's not up to me, is it?'

She approached Michel and me for our final mini-interview prior to results, as the judges nibbled on. Michel had stabilised a bit, but he was still holding on to me.

'Well, first of all, Daisy. You're new to this kind of pressure. Very well done for staying composed. There are so many distractions, it's no easy task in a location like this. How did you find it all?'

'Stressful!' I said. 'I was under my own pressure as much as anything. I think there is a perception that I am not serious about baking. It's important to me to show that I *am* very serious — and accomplished.'

Dominic had told me to max on the dedication to the primary skill as a way of countering those who thought Lucy Lovecake's book was lightweight and 'not really about cakes at all', as Penny Laws in *The Times* had said. (Well, it's not *all* about cakes, actually, I had pointed out to Dominic.)

Dominic winked in conspiratorial style from the front row, pleased with my bakery blah-blahs.

Michel was mulling my remarks.

'Well, may I just say,' said Victoria, 'that gateau is a very accomplished work. I thought it indescribably yummy.'

17

Michel was melting his bitter bile and combining with his acid tongue. *Ding!* Ready to serve: 'Amazing, so accomplished. Tell them how you became so accomplished, Daisy,' he said.

'You must be referring to the course in baking I took at your cookery school in Primrose Hill, Michel,' I said.

'That's right — a course you took 'for fun'. Meanwhile, you were secretly penning a book which you did not tell anyone about. You are accomplished in many ways — principally in the ways of deceit.'

I looked to Dominic. He now seemed concerned, but was not for intervening. I had to handle this alone, I knew that.

Brush it off lightly.

'Ah, the line between a secret and a deception — who can ever see that line?' I said. 'It's a skill to keep a secret and a sin to deceive. I kept a secret, that's all.'

Victoria decided it was time to step in.

'Now, Michel. How was it for you?'

'I had no complaints at the time. What? Oh, the baking thing? Today?'

'Yes. The baking thing.'

This time my cheeks flambéed. I tried to move away from him, but he was not letting go.

'I'm lazy,' Michel replied. 'I chose something I've done a hundred times. Maybe a thousand.'

'Well, maybe you've made it a lot because people love it so much?' said Victoria. 'Let's see what the judges say.'

Paul came over to deliver the judges' findings.

'This is all bollocks,' said Michel, whispering

18

into my ear. 'They're going to suck up to me because I'm a name in the game.'

'Paul, a tough contest today?' Victoria asked. 'I thought both cakes were divine — but that's why I could never be a judge! I'm so greedy, I love them all.'

'Yeah, it was tough to decide. One very classic, simple pudding, with a fabulous custard sauce. The balance of the flavours just right. The other, a gateau, a fabulous creation with a clever mix of notes, the sweet countered by the sharp — really, it was a triumph.'

'But that isn't telling us what we need to know,' said Victoria.

'I know, I know. And I've been elected as the bringer of the results, an unenviable job.'

I looked across at Caroline. She caught my eye briefly and looked away, with an expression of adorable apology. What a lovely woman. I knew the result at that moment.

'We decided, finally, that the clafoutis had the edge,' said Paul.

4

He Offers Me Protection

Robust applause, but not of the foot-stamping, standing-ovation variety.

Embarrassingly, a tear fell down from my eye. Michel wiped my cheek tenderly with his rough, dirty hand.

'Ah, thank you, Paul. I'm sure it was a tough call,' said Victoria. 'I'd like to thank our contestants, Daisy Delaney and Michel Amiel, our judges, Paul Finch . . . '

Michel interrupted.

'That's just nonsense,' he said, breaking away from me and finding his feet. 'I cheated. You all know that. Some girls behind the scenes passed me the batter, all pre-prepared, you know? I made them do it. I threatened not to appear if they didn't. Don't blame the girls, for goodness' sake. I am a bully, and a fraud. It was a performance, not for real. Daisy's cake is real. Very beautiful, actually. She bakes so well. I had some cake made by her before she even went on my course. It was very good. Maybe the best French fancy I've ever had.'

Victoria was *almost* lost for words. Paul, Caroline and Jane looked like they'd been slapped. The crowd was unusually quiet.

Victoria had to step in.

'Erm, well, Michel, you certainly do speak plainly, and I applaud you for that. I'm hearing in my ear that we have to disqualify your entry, I'm afraid. Rules of the game state that the food must be prepared and made in one of our kitchens inside the tent. I'm terribly sorry.'

'No, I'm sorry,' he said, making to leave the tent. 'This is all bollocks. It's a sham. I shouldn't have done it. Any of it. I don't want to be part of this charade. I'm a chef, you know? Not a performer. I'm going home to bed.'

The minder who had brought him in whisked him outside. I think everyone realised we were lucky he'd lasted the hour. There was no attempt to bring him back inside.

The judges were confused and humiliated. There was a bit of flapping at the central table. Victoria approached them and huddled in for a few minutes, joined by Bex and Tara, and Stephen Murray, the director.

Victoria obviously wasn't happy. It looked like they were going to make her announce that I was the winner now — which was preposterous. I heard her say, 'You should have picked Daisy in the first place!'

What else could they do now? There had to be a winner, but I didn't want to win by default. However, I sensed that disqualifying myself wasn't a viable option.

Inevitably, Victoria announced that I had won the cake-off after all, placing her arm around me, feeling my pain.

I cringed, puce-cheeked, humiliated.

The crowd clapped and cheered.

I went numb.

Every time Michel showed up in my life, he caused this kind of chaos. It was unforgivable. But there was this soft, honest centre to him, and he had spoken out to defend and protect me.

What I love about him is his contempt for hypocrisy.

I found myself wanting to go and look for him. To comfort him as I'd done so often before the Valentine's Day disaster.

The winding-up part of the event took forever, especially as I was the only contestant left. Victoria and the judges bantered on a while with the crowd, trying to normalise the dramatic denouement a little.

Dominic came into the Green Kitchen and hugged me, lifting me off my feet. 'You were awesome, Daisy! They loved you.'

Stephen Murray, Bex and Tara all thanked me for being a good sport and so on. *A good sport?*

'I'm so tired,' I said, turning to embrace Kitty, Clara, Francesca and my parents, quite tearful now that the pressure was off.

'You were great,' said Mum. 'Your cake was glorious. I hope we get to taste it.'

'I was taught stuff like that at Michel's cookery school,' I said. 'He's a brilliant teacher.'

Dominic stepped in. 'No, Daisy. He's a loser. He'll be lucky to be alive in a month if he carries on like this. You are brilliant, a natural. Forget about him.'

He turned to speak to Stephen, laying into him for putting me in a terrible position. 'What happened to Myles Munroe from *Bake It?*' I heard him ask.

All the voices around me swirled together. I wanted to find Michel and speak to him, to sort out this whole mess. I'd betrayed him over my book. I regretted it, but at the time I could see no other way forward.

'Daisy will be signing *French Fancy* in the bookshop tent in ten minutes,' Victoria announced. 'Find her there to have your copy personalised. And maybe get some dating advice too! Hey, I might even join the queue myself!'

It had been a good-humoured performance by Victoria and I was full of admiration for her, but I'd had enough of clowning. I couldn't concentrate. I wanted to rest my head on Michel's shoulder, sit in the sun on a riverbank with him, and forget my brief life in the circus.

But I shook myself. My life prior to the release of the book had been disastrous. I couldn't mess up this chance to turn things around for good.

Daisy, there are masses of people who want to meet you now. This is your dream come true. Focus and perform.

I pulled myself together, took off my apron, and went to freshen up my make-up in the Ladies by the Green Room. Then I made my way to the bookshop, with Branwell and Dominic at either side of me.

'Keep smiling,' said Branwell. 'They're buying up your books by the bucket load.'

I had first signed my books in Harrods, back on Valentine's Day. I still wasn't used to the idea that people would queue to meet me and have my scribble inside their book.

Crazy. I've spent my whole life being the one at the back of every queue, and now people are queueing to meet me.

Tara said it was the biggest queue of the festival. She probably said that to everyone, but there was quite a snake of people waiting patiently in the midday summer sun, wearing straw hats and sandals.

I took my seat in the bookshop and let the event begin. Soon my cheeks grew sore from grinning, and my fingers ached from scrawling my signature. Some people were adorable, saying how much they loved the recipes, and what a fun idea the book was, even though they couldn't imagine seducing with cake — or seducing at all. Other people were flattering, verging on lunacy: 'It's wonderful to meet you after following Lucy Lovecake on Twitter. You have changed my life, made me feel anything is possible. Can I have a photo with you for Instagram? You are so pretty. Where do you get your clothes? Could we meet for lunch? I have this book idea . . . '

A lot of men were in that queue, I noticed. They were good humoured, though.

'I'd be happy to share a chocolate kiss with you anytime,' said a big bruiser of a boy, probably in his twenties, referring to my chocolate meringue kisses, as recommended by Lucy Lovecake for third dates.

'Are you dating yourself?' asked one man who I suspected was in his thirties, adding: 'Asking for a friend.'

It was all in good fun, and I should have been

24

so proud, relaxed and delighted.

Dominic whispered news to me from Twitter every so often. 'People are saying that your cake demo was awesome. 'Luscious Lovecake not half-baked!' 'Amiel is a cheating old twat!' 'Go Lucy Lovecake! Love your cake!' 'Recipe for the chocolate ginger cake please!' (649 likes) 'Amiel whisked away after causing a stir!' 'Silly old toss-pot boils over.''

After signing books for two and a half hours and chatting endlessly about dating, recipes and the finer details of lingerie, I went back to the Green Room for a debrief with Tara, having made a plan to meet everyone else back at the hotel for afternoon tea.

Yeah, more cake — that's all I need.

'I'll make my own way to the hotel,' I said to Dominic as he hovered around. 'I'm going to clear my head, take a stroll.'

'You won't find him. His car is just leaving the car park,' he said, reading my lie.

'Really?' I said, looking across at the big field which served as a car park. By all accounts, it was usually like a swampy marshland, but this year it was bone dry.

'See you soon,' I said, taking off my shoes and running over to the car park.

I recognised Michel's black Mercedes, driven by one of his team, in the queue of departing vehicles. I ran towards it, willing myself to reach it before it exited through the big wooden gate. I had to say sorry.

One car drove out, and the Mercedes crept forward. Another left. Now there were only four in front. I was getting closer, pounding the grass, dropping my shoes to give me better arm propulsion.

Please let me catch him.

I was close now. They were next to go.

'Michel!' I cried. 'Wait!'

Two ladies, heading back to their car, approached me right at that moment. They introduced themselves as: 'Your biggest fans. I'm Barbara and this is my neighbour, Martha.'

They had clearly been in the audience. Martha tried to talk to me about the event.

'You were wonderful!' she said.

'Thank you. That's so kind of you,' I said, eyes fixed on the black Mercedes.

'That Frenchman is a rogue, isn't he?' she said.

'Just a bit.'

Barbara stepped forward. 'You know when you added the ginger to the sponge mixture?' she began. 'Did you add that before or after the cocoa?'

'After,' I said, watching the Mercedes edge its way through the gate.

'We were wondering if you'd come and speak at our Women's Institute meeting in Woking one week. Late autumn is best because we like to have gardening themes until then.'

'I'd love to. But I really must . . . '

I'm going to miss him. Just make your excuses and leave Barbara and Martha.

'I have my diary right here,' said Martha.

'I'm sorry, I really must dash,' I said. 'So sorry. Message me on Twitter! It'll be great to hear from you! I will definitely come. I promise!'

'We're not on Twitter,' she said.

'Well, get on it,' I called, running at full speed again.

'Cheeky little madam,' she called after me. 'That's the last of your books I'll buy.'

I made it to the wooden gate, but the car had just gone! He'd left Hay, probably in a heap in the back of his car with three bottles of champagne for company. I tried to run down the road after them, but they had gathered speed. It was hopeless.

I wiped my face and sat under a tree, thinking of our cinema trips, our kisses and our walk on the banks of the Seine. Those were moments in time. Think of the present.

Dominic is going to be so hurt about all this. I must get back to the hotel and find him.

Michel Amiel always made me behave crazily, and it had been that way from the beginning.

5

The Invitation

Eighteen Months before Hay-on-Wye

The fateful invitation had arrived very early in the new year, while I was binging on cheap chocolate, the last of the prosecco, fragrant clementines and crumbles of leftover cranberry Stilton. Until that embossed white card came through the unpolished brass letterbox of 12B Rosehip Lane, sheathed in distinctly luxurious vellum, my life was a joyless jumble of abject despair.

I'd just finished reading my Christmas book from Kitty, *The Hen Weekend*. Everyone was talking about it: the bride-to-be who booked her hen-do on an organic farm in deepest Oxfordshire. Cue moans and groans from her cool friends. But they get there in the height of a heatwave, and swim in the stream, sunbathe in the hay, have cookery lessons, line dance by night and sip strawberry wine in the barn. It was so evocative I could hardly face my reality when I finished the book.

Why am I even living in the city at all? It's so expensive and dirty and noisy and competitive. I could move out, become a milkmaid or a line dance teacher, or what about working with wild ponies? I know! I could become Amish!

There had to be a better way to live. The festive season had been as much fun as a string of broken fairy lights. Personally, I think Christmas should be at the end of January. As it is, there's far too much to do before it (dress-up parties, bonfires, Diwali and Hanukkah — and *Strictly Come Dancing*) and truly *nothing* to do after it. Except eat bizarre combinations of leftover treats (rich fruitcake with duck paté, anyone?) and search for coins in old handbags for the Food Fund. Six-week months seriously do suck. That particular year, I will admit to peeking at dodgy dating sites as well, reverse-seduced by tempting usernames such as *Nobunnyboilers, Expornstar* and *Philip-Philop*.

One Saturday morning towards the end of the holiday, I lay on the sofa in the flat, feeling hopeless. Nothing was right in my life. Nothing at all. Firstly, I was fuming about those pretty retro lingerie designs I'd sent off to Eve's Secret Garden on spec back in the February. I'd never heard back, but had seen clear aspects of those same designs incorporated in their Christmas range for Debenhams. Serpents!

This was all especially annoying as my ex, Tom Percy, was busily developing a range of fashion and household items for John Lewis, and word was he'd soon have his own brand. *Still a tosser, though. Trading off connections he made when dating Princess Elisha Von Hapsburg. Snake.*

Secondly, I was completely broke — nothing out of the ordinary about that, but I was at the scrabbling-around-for-crumbs stage. And thirdly, my book about the history of lingerie hadn't been taken on by one single literary agent in all of London. I had *everything* crossed for the solitary agency I had yet to hear back from, Branwell Thornton. One of the best. Possibly *the* best.

Please, God, may no news be good news.

I was cheered when Kitty and I discovered that very interesting invitation in the first post of January. We'd been holed up in the Primrose Hill basement since the epic snowfall of New Year's Eve, with the slightly sinister skeleton of our Christmas tree still posing at our basement window.

London was royally iced with a thick layer of deep snow, so Kitty and I had gone into semi-hibernation mode, hunkered down in our underground burrow, unable to get flights out of town. We played board games and made do. Kitty's boyfriend, Charlie Baxter, was away 'on business' for the whole holiday season, giving vent to my bigamy theory, and I wasn't for discounting polygamy either.

We were so fed up by this point we'd even broken into a sealed box of books labelled 'Banned Books', found in the back of a dusty cupboard behind the Brigadier's cherry-wood dresser. So far, we had worked our way through *Brave New World*, *Slaughterhouse Five*, *The Metamorphosis*, *Lady Chatterley's Lover* and *The Satanic Verses*.

There had even been a moment of dashed hope when Kitty thought she'd found a tin of syrup in there. Damn! Varnish!

I knew I should get up from the sofa that

Saturday morning to shower and dress. I had any number of silk kimonos in my collection of vintage silk sensations; however, I was wearing Grandpa Delaney's tartan dressing gown, with sheepskin boots and a fake fur hat, and if anyone had dropped by . . .

A rectangular sponge cake was rising gently, soon to be divided into French fancies for Prim & Proper, the teashop Kitty managed. It was due to reopen for new year business the very next day. Even though Kitty was the baking expert and had taught me all she knew, I did make quite a lot of cakes for the shop as a sideline, and to help Kitty out. Charlie, also the owner, was such a brute, expecting Kitty to run the place, produce lovely cakes and stay late for special duties. The hours she worked!

I was going back to my main job the following Tuesday. I tried not to think of it too much. I hadn't expected, five years after graduating in fashion and textiles, to be working in a tiny lingerie boutique, Voluptas, on a cobbled back lane of Primrose Hill. You'd think it might be a place to meet eligible men, wouldn't you? But the only men who came in were: a) happily married, b) happily having an affair or c) sleazy sex pests.

Voluptas was half of a shop, in fact. The other side of the sweet, double-fronted Victorian shop was owned by a chaise-longue restorer, Francesca Blunt. The Misses Davenport (Lavinia and Araminta) had, apparently, run the whole premises as a gown and hat emporium in Edwardian times. I loved to pore over the old photographs of the shop in its heyday.

It wasn't the most random place for me to work. I had written a dissertation on the evolution of the bra for my finals at Edinburgh College of Art, and I could tell you everything about corsetry, from whalebones to burlesque. But I wanted a life where I could wear that stuff, and live my life in the big world, in Paris, Rome, New York, Shanghai. I'd bought some gorgeous little slips of silk over the past few years, starting in the Tom Percy days, but they were folded neatly in a drawer.

As for my role in the shop, I was good at my job and took a pride in it, of course. The provenance of every sexy slither in that shop was known to me: the pastel French knickers and matching lace-trimmed camisoles, the spaghetti-strapped teasing teddies, the rosebud-adorned bustiers, the satin corsets with a hundred devilish hooks, the flimsy silk stockings and lacy suspenders with their impossible fasteners.

But I was so bored. If it wasn't for secretly writing my book behind the counter over a two-year period and practising my dance moves to music, I'd have been in therapy. We had an old gramophone player and I played records constantly. I liked to try out my moves for jive, salsa, ballroom and disco. Sometimes Clara danced too, and occasionally Francesca, and if we could possibly get away with it, we'd lure James Jolly over from his place on the other side of the street. He had a gift shop for gentlemen — luxury leather items, bits of cashmere, hip flasks, and playing cards. He was quite a mover, even at sixty-five. An expert on all matters cha-cha-cha.

There was no denying I had been hoping for a little book deal for quite some time. So far, I'd had no luck — not even a glimmer of hope. One of the few plus points of the Christmas holiday shutdown was that the painful but steady arrival of rejection e-mails from literary agents had ceased, and I could pretend that the eponymous Branwell Thornton was going to fall in love with *A Brief History of Briefs (& Other Underwear)* and would write to say as much in due course.

Sorry. That invitation!

As I deliberated on showering and dressing, quite a pile of old-fashioned mail dropped behind the front door with a resounding thud.

'I'll get it, Kitty,' I said, nosy by nature.

'Thanks,' she replied, engrossed in breakfast and a book.

Scooping up the mail, nothing seemed of particular interest initially. Mostly junk — voucher deals for the local supermarket, plus a few delayed Christmas cards from exotic lands, bank statements and bills. There was one letter for me. I recognised the writing on the envelope straight away. Addressed to my parents' house and forwarded to me by my mother, as usual:

From the hand of Tom Percy.

I put that in the pocket of my dressing gown.

There was still that one rich vanilla, vellum envelope which looked promising; franked, not stamped, and addressed to our flatmate, Pippa, who owned the flat. (Actually, her grandfather with the penchant for banned books did.)

Pippa Cavendish
12B Rosehip Lane
Primrose Hill, London, NW3 4TX

I held it between my fingers, considering the possible contents.

6

Shanghai Shenanigans

'A ball, perhaps,' I said, as Kitty munched on a granola concoction from Savannah's Wholefoods whilst reading *Kiss Chase*, a book she'd got for Christmas from her brother. It was a manual for men about what women really want, written by a man. *How does he know?*

Soft pink rollers in Kitty's coal-black hair framed her exquisite little face as she looked up.

'Sent by the office of Prince Charming?'

'Possibly,' I said.

'I told you: Harry's mine!' said Kitty.

'For as long as he has some hair, I'm first dibs.'

'Whomsoever the slipper fits . . . '

I was longing to dance freely on a proper dance floor, not the postage-stamp space in the shop or the little bit of room around my bed. A ball would be just perfect. I was a bit worried it might be a personal wedding invitation for Pippa, so I flipped the envelope over. The stamp of the V&A.

Oh, interesting . . . not too personal, I'm guessing.

'Is it for Pippa?' said Kitty, always a stickler for convention.

'The envelope says so, but I sense it's for sharing.'

'You steaming it?'

'Why not?'

She set the kettle to boil.

Pippa was in Verbier until who knew when, in a chalet, which evidenced by her Instagram account was more of a luxury mansion. I checked the last message from her on my phone: *Lots of snow, met up with Jamie 'Sex God' Patterson . . . missing you . . . nah, not really. Please forward bills for me and any other official stuff (except parking fines) to Grandpa: Brigadier Charlie Cavendish, 3 Charles Square, London W1J 7ET. Be cosy, babes. Gramps is going fucking crazy about my fines, and he mentioned raising the rent. Sos. Love ya loads. X*

The envelope steamed open quite easily and I eased out the card.

Copperplate writing!

It was indeed an invitation — but not to a ball.

Never mind.

It was for the launch of a new exhibition. *There MIGHT be dancing!* Pippa always asked us to those anyway, so I didn't feel *too* guilty. I'd never have steamed open a love note or a court summons or anything like that. (She *was* particularly unlucky in all matters parking and car-related.) She wouldn't mind us going to a party as her fashion ambassadors. We had all loved the parties for the famous wedding dresses and Alexander McQueen's Savage Beauty.

Kitty came over to read the details. 'Oh! *Miss Wong! Shanghai-Paris of the Thirties.* Cool as. What'll we wear, Daisy?'

36

'eBay, Kitty. Look for cocktail wear, possibly cheongsams? Tiny satin shoes, bijou evening box bags with silver clasps. Orchid hair-clips. That sort of thing.'

'Can we actually afford new outfits?' said Kitty.

'Good point. I might have to sell something.'

'The petty-cash tin at the teashop owes me £45,' Kitty offered.

'Perfect!'

'Okay, I'll claim that. And we could possibly take a tiny look in Pippa's wardrobe, couldn't we?' asked Kitty.

'Yes, she would want us to.'

'You mean expect us to?' said Kitty.

'Yes, that too.'

★ ★ ★

It was nice to have something to look forward to, but I was getting tired of short-term highs. I needed some radical changes in my life. As I fluffed up the buttercream for the French fancies, I admitted to myself that if this year didn't fare better than the last, I might have to quit London for good and seek out that bucolic life from *The Hen Weekend*.

You should never have come here for a man anyway, Daisy Delaney. Read the letter.

But I didn't. I put it in the box with all the others. It always took me a few days before I could look at them.

Why would you keep sending letters to someone who never replies?

7

The Party

I was *longing* for January payday, but at least thinking about the party (hair, nails, outfit, shoes, bag, lipstick, F-R-O-C-K) was a distraction from thoughts of pauper's prison, complete with meals of watery broth and rough gruel, and toothless, violent inmates who particularly despise fallen princess types.

On the Friday of the V&A launch party, I took the afternoon off work. Clara, who owned Voluptas, was very fair to work for. I did some favours for her, such as telling little fibs to her investment banker husband. Nothing serious: 'Oh, Phil, she left here about an hour ago, but the traffic's very bad.' When she was, in fact, applying Lancôme's Black Tulip to her lips right in front of me, following a lengthy gossip and dance session with Francesca Blunt and James Jolly. And Clara did favours back. She said it was fine to take the afternoon off before the big fancy party, and that she was jealous that I was invited. *Ahem.*

I took ages to get ready, piling my long blonde hair up in a loose 'effortless' chignon (seven attempts) and approximating a china-doll face to go with the black silk cheongsam I'd picked up for £4. At about 6pm, I bounded out of the flat in a mad rush with flushed cheeks *(No! They're supposed to be china-doll white!)* and feelings of self-loathing. A curvy blonde in a size zero cheongsam? I always look much better in my imaginings. *If only the diet had worked.*

I crossed London by tube, jumping off at South Kensington — well, hobbling, so tight was the dress. I was ashamed to be running late, while Kitty had already sent a text to say she was almost there. She was coming from a meeting with Charlie in the Bloomsbury area, where he was eyeing up another opportunity. She said she had changed for the party in the lavish, multi-mirrored powder room of the St Pancras Renaissance Hotel.

Nearly there!

I shuffled along Cromwell Road in the eBay cheongsam, red-velvet swing coat and trusty tattered trainers, taking short strides due to straining side seams. The enticing darkness of the January evening was decorated by delicate frosty sparkles on sandstone façades, while beacons of electric light shone at wantonly undressed windows.

The glorious, curved arch at the top of the V&A steps was now in sight. I negotiated the stairs daintily.

'You're in a hurry,' said a steward, holding open the door. Welcoming warm air leaked from inside the building.

A reply would require energy best directed at my footwear; a nod and smile sufficed as I pulled off my trainers, then fished in my shoulder bag for my satin kitten heels and embroidered

Shanghai cocktail bag. As I changed shoes hurriedly, losing balance at least once, I looked around for Kitty in the entrance area.

I turned to the friendly steward.

'Erm, does this dress look okay?' I asked.

'What criteria am I using?'

I paused. 'General aesthetics?'

'You're having an operation?'

'Ha!'

'If I was twenty years younger . . . ' he said.

'Just twenty?'

'Cheeky!'

'Really, thank you!'

A little spray of *Miss Dior*.

'Daisy! There you are!' Kitty's voice.

'Kitty! Wow. The dress is a dream! You look beautiful.' She'd found a classy evening dress in Pippa's wardrobe, while mine was tight and tarty. I felt like going home when I saw her, looking so elegant and demure.

'You're going to be a magnet in that one,' said Kitty. 'You can leave your coat and stuff in the cloakroom. I'll show you.'

'Enjoy the evening, ladies,' said the steward.

'Thank you!' we chorused as we clickety-clacked across the tiled floor. Traditional Chinese music played softly from the ornate balcony above us, merging with the low buzz of people mingling. I looked up to see strings of cherry-red lanterns garlanded with blossom branches across the balcony, while exquisitely decorated fans dangled daintily from the balustrades.

With my coat safely deposited, we teetered up the steps to the first-floor gathering. Welcoming us was a sign that read: *Miss Wong's Wardrobe: Shanghai-Paris Fashion of the Thirties*. Gazing at the glass-encased exhibits of exotic silk cheongsams, clasped box bags, tiny satin slippers and exotic orchid hairclips, I was transported to a glorious era when girlish glamour was a given. Even the underwear was elegant and dainty.

'Oh, Kitty! I wish life was like this now.'

'Snap. It's so romantic to dress up.'

Satin-clad girls with porcelain cheeks and ruby love-heart lips tiptoed around. Each balanced either abundant silver platters of dumplings, all adorned with mango flower art, or endless glasses of pink gin fizz.

We each took a drink and began to identify some stars.

'Poppy Cavanaugh!' said Kitty, flashing her eyes to five o'clock.

The young model wore a daring creation formed from a few grey chiffon scarves. Next to her, a pillar-box-lipped Florence Maddox, classic in black crêpe, golden curls bouncing on her narrow shoulders.

I noticed Ella Woods, looking gaunt but chic in one of her own navy shifts, posing with a frosted-pink pout beside portly Sir Eddie Macdonald, fashion king.

'Do you see that girl from *Bake It* looking all voluptuous in violet over there?' I asked Kitty, but her eyes were elsewhere.

8

The Frenchman

I followed her gaze.

How could it be? Yes, it certainly was.

BEAU BONAS!

He was our number three hottest guy. We'd seen every movie he'd ever starred in. He wasn't far from us, chatting to some suits, who in normal circumstances would have been of some interest.

'Let's shuffle over that way,' I said.

It was about an eight-step manoeuvre, by the looks of it. We edged nearer by degrees. We were close to him, so close we could hear his voice. Not clear words, but the timbre of it. While American accents sound so natural in movies, they always stand out in the middle of London.

Giddy from that closeness, I took a sip from my glass and tottered dizzily on my kitten heels for a moment, somehow listing to the left, knocking into the back of a broad man. He turned round sharply — and crossly.

Scary beast. I'm sure I've seen him on TV.

'Oh, I'm so sorry!' I said.

No obvious response from him, eyebrows knitted.

'Oops,' whispered Kitty. 'He's annoyed!'

'It's that grumpy French chef, Michel Amiel!'

I said. 'He's always annoyed.'

'Oh yeah, we saw him on the *Saturday Kitchen* programme.'

He towered over me, scowling, while a beautiful woman at his side, wearing a charcoal coat dress, looked me up and down. Very quickly, I recognised her as the actress Eve Berger; I'd seen her in *Les Aventuriers* the previous year.

Two famous French people scowling at me . . . what to do?

I did what my mother taught me to do in difficult situations. I held out my hand, smiled and introduced myself: 'Daisy Delaney, good to meet you! And this is Kitty Chang.'

Amiel and the girlfriend smiled weakly.

'Michel Amiel,' he said with a heavy French accent.

Now, the actress. 'Eve . . . Berger,' she said frostily, adding the surname as if the first name should have been enough.

We all shook hands.

There was an awkward silence. I didn't want to say anything fawning, and besides, Kitty and I were still desperately trying to track Beau. He'd moved already. *Trust me to bump into this pair of Gallic ghouls mid-mission, losing sight of the target.*

'The canapés *do* look delicious,' I said, taking a little prawn dim sum from a passing tray.

Monsieur Amiel stared at the pretty platters as they wafted past. 'Why does everyone piss around with mangos these days?'

'Ssshhh!' I said. 'You have to call them

43

'girlgos' now. It's a directive from the Commission for Sexual Equality.'

'In fact,' said Kitty, very gravely, 'they really should, in fairness, be called 'girlcomes.''

Kitty and I almost fell off our shoes — again, in my case.

Michel Amiel looked at us disparagingly.

I scanned the room for BB. No sign.

'What do you think of the exhibition?' I asked, reluctantly giving up on Beau for the time being.

'Rather shallow,' he said, Eve Berger nodding earnestly at his side. 'A missed opportunity to explore the socioeconomic relationship between Paris and Shanghai in the Thirties.'

You what?

'You do know this is a museum of *decorative* arts?' I said, looking at Kitty with an expression conveying: *Wanker.*

Eve Berger's arched eyebrow suggested she was cranking up for action.

'I am reminded of Henry Moore,' she began with barely a trace of French accent in her brittle voice. 'Between the beauty of expression and power of expression, there is a difference of function. You know, the first aims at pleasing the senses, while the second has a spiritual vitality more moving and deeper than the senses.'

Oh, wow. So, you're clever.

'Well, as Sir Roy Strong so famously said, 'The V&A is really just a very big handbag'.' (I remembered that from a chat we'd had with a curator at the Wedding Dresses launch).

I sipped what seemed to be my second cocktail. We'd lost track of Beau Bonas for this deeply annoying duo?

They reflected quietly on the handbag thing, so I seized the silence.

What's that famous Ruskin quote again? Think, Daisy, you know this from A-level art.

I felt a little lightheaded, but wasn't so tipsy that I couldn't think straight.

'I prefer Ruskin to Moore,' I said boldly before I really *had* recalled the full quote. I dredged it up from the murky depths of my back brain.

The three H's?

I spoke very deliberately. ' "Fine art is that in which the hand, the head and the heart go together".'

Kitty smiled proudly. *Thank-fuck-you-got-that-right* was her nuanced expression.

Monsieur Amiel grabbed a glass ungraciously from a floating tray.

The Awkward Couple grew more awkward, but, joy, suddenly I caught a glimpse of Beau near the exhibits.

'Would you excuse us?' I said. 'I've just noticed someone.'

Amiel followed my gaze.

9

Le Dancing

Kitty and I set off for the exhibition area. The warm, creeping anaesthesia of the pink gin fizz was clearly taking effect as we chatted amiably to various strangers we bumped into on the way. Everyone was craning to see BB, who was wearing the greatest suit — *or is it just that he has the greatest body?*

But Beau kept us on our toes, working the room faster than he'd signed up for *The Gangster 2*.

Where is he now, for fuck's sake?

The drinks flowed, the music changed to pop and the evening loosened up as the lights went down. Kitty had forsaken Beau and was chatting happily to an Oriental rug expert from the museum, who had admired her dress. Handsome enough, but a man who knows his rugs for a living?

But anyone is better than Charlie. Go, Kitty!

I decided to go to the powder room to touch up my Rosebud-red Dior lipstick and check out my dress.

I swivelled through the yabbering throngs and was deciding on the best direction to take, fantasising that I'd bump into BB, when I became aware of someone walking close to the

46

right of me, but still slightly behind me.

I turned round.

And jumped in fright, clutching my throat.

It was the infuriating French guy, Michel Amiel.

'I'm that scary?' he asked, chuckling.

'Yes.'

'Did you get to chat to Bonas?'

'No. Not yet. Alas.'

'That might be because my girlfriend is pigging him.'

'Huh? Oh, you mean 'hogging'?'

'Yes. She knows him. They were in a film together. I left them to it. You know, in-jokes from a movie you weren't part of.'

'Not that funny?'

He nodded.

We stood silently for a few moments.

'You want to dance?' he asked.

YMCA was playing.

'Sure. Why not?' I replied.

I realised that he was just using me to annoy Eve, and I was a bit upset that my lipstick would have to wait, but a dance seemed like a fun idea, so we made our way over to the busy dance floor. There were scores of people garlanded around its edges. We pressed through conversations to left and right. Finally, we squeezed our way onto the wooden-floored square.

'You know the actions?' I asked.

'Actions?'

'YMCA.' I showed him.

'No. We're not in kindergarten.'

'Oh, go on. I'll teach you. You have to do it.'

He gave me a 'oh, go on then' look.

He was hopeless. 'That's not even a 'Y'!' I complained.

'Oh, so we're supposed to mime the letters? *C'est ridicule!*'

The evening took on that magical quality, where the lights began to glow quite hypnotically, and I knew that my cheeks were flushed a warm pink despite my earlier attempts to look pale and interesting. My eyes were wider, sparklier and crazier than in the cold of morning, and everything was ten times funnier than in reality. I giggled so much that I toppled over again, and he caught me heroically.

'I must admit, jiving is my absolute speciality,' he said as the band struck up with 'Crazy Little Thing Called Love.'

I threw back my head and laughed some more.

'Don't be rude,' he said, seeming very insulted.

'Okay. Are you quite sure you can jive?' I asked.

But before the jiving began, beautiful Eve Berger returned, blushing and excited. They vanished into the crowd without so much as a goodbye.

10

The E-mail Exchange

All weekend I daydreamed about Beau Bonas. He would most likely be living in a rented house in Primrose Hill, and I'd bump into him when shopping (with leftover euros, buttons and farthings) at Mrs Taylor's corner store, which in my imaginings was a lot like Nellie Oleson's store in *Little House on the Prairie*. He'd say, 'I saw you at the party but I just couldn't get to you.' I'd say, 'Really? I'm afraid I didn't notice you.' He'd say, 'That's disappointing.' I'd say, 'I've just baked a cake . . . '

I was still hoping I'd hear good news by e-mail about my book. I had googled Branwell Thornton so many times I'd convinced myself I knew him.

He'll need a few days back at his desk before he writes to would-be authors about submissions.

Monday morning began badly: in the *Metro* I picked up in Prim & Proper there was a photograph of Beau Bonas at Heathrow, bound for JFK, having an altercation with a photographer. The reveries had been so real I was disappointed that he'd left London without saying goodbye. I picked up a coffee and chocolate-filled croissant as compensation — just one of each, as Clara wasn't expected in until later.

I was in Voluptas nibbling the pastry and

49

bidding on eBay for a Chantilly lace 1930s teddy (I had authority to make purchases up to £200) when my phone vibrated.

That's an e-mail shudder. Probably Groupon. I must unsubscribe to all pointless organisations. False hope is killing me.

But it wasn't Groupon. It was a message from one Branwell Thornton.

Is this a hallucination?

I gulped, swallowed, choked. *Please may this be it!*

From: Branwell Thornton
Cc: Bea Gibson
Subject: Submission

Dear Daisy,
A Brief History of Briefs (& Other Underwear)
Thank you for the above-mentioned submission which I read over the holiday period with interest. While your knowledge of lingerie is impressive and your writing style rather charming, the history angle has, alas, been done before. (1000 Dessous et al). I don't feel that I could sell this concept as it is, I'm afraid to say. The market for non-fiction is very niche-driven, admittedly, but I can't see this working commercially. Sorry, I realise you have worked hard on this submission, and I wish you well with it elsewhere.
You might want to consider fictionalising the content in some way.
Best wishes,
Branwell

My last hope. Dashed. Tears pricked in the corners of my eyes, and my face crumpled like a paper bag.

Where would I go if I didn't live in London? What would I do? My head throbbed with thoughts, my heart raced in panic. It was irrational to feel that my world had ended with that e-mail from the last of the agents, but stupidly I had placed all my hope in the fact that he was taking so long to get back to me — 'No news is good news' and all that. *No, it really isn't.*

Francesca's back shop adjoined ours and when the linking door was open, we could walk quite easily between the two places. She popped through to see what the sobbing was all about. I showed her the message.

'Oh, not the 'slow no',' she said. 'I fucking hate that. So rude. False hope.'

'I don't know what to try next, Francesca. That book took two years to write.'

'But it's not wasted,' she said. 'Really, it's not. You can build on that. Turn it into something else. Come on, let's think this through calmly.'

She read the e-mail, which was still on the screen.

'He does say to consider fictionalising it. Maybe your current book is just the research for a future bestseller. Come on, I know it's January, and I know you're broke, but don't lose spirit. Fight for your book, Daisy. You must!'

Francesca had to get back to a Liberty print creation next door. 'There's a Russian battleaxe coming to view it at two o'clock. I'll need to

51

push on, but come and get me if you need me.'

'Thank you, Francesca!' I answered. 'Appreciate it so much!'

'You've done it for me before. Let me know how it all goes.' Her pre-Raphaelite red curls bobbed out of sight as she went down to her basement workroom on the other side of the door.

Francesca was right. I had to fight. I knew it. But I didn't know where to start.

I played one of my favourite old recordings, Ella Fitzgerald's 'All the Things You Are', a nice little foxtrot number, and reread the message from Branwell.

What would most people do in response to such a message? Ignore it? Reply politely? Or, maybe, challenge it?

When I stopped to think, I considered that it was very decent of *the* famous Branwell Thornton to write to me in person. Most of the other agencies had sent a generic three-line message from personal assistants. I decided to compose a reply.

Be bold but not pushy. Show self-belief but not self-importance.

I wrote him the following e-mail:

From: Daisy Delaney
To: Branwell Thornton
Subject: Re: Submission

Dear Branwell
Thank you for your message. Disappointing though it is, I do accept your professional opinion totally,

52

and *I would like to thank you for such a person-alised response. It really helps to know that it's not the writing but market conditions that are the problem. Also, the generic rejections are very depressing. So, many thanks.*

I do think I have a unique area of expertise and I could, as you say, put it to use in a fiction work. I will give that some thought and if any-thing springs to mind, would it be acceptable to get back to you for your opinion once again? I hope that wouldn't be troublesome and I cer-tainly won't send too many 'half-baked' things.
Yours sincerely
Daisy Delaney

I pressed 'send' without too much procrastina-tion. I knew that dithering would lead to a 'delete' situation. A customer came in, so in the mirror surrounded by palest pink pearly seashells, glued on by Clara's gorgeous little daughter, Tashi, I checked my eyes for smudged mascara and went through to the front of the shop.

It wasn't a bad day for trade: I sold two sets of wedding underwear and an embroidered satin robe. The robe was exquisite, white duchesse satin with red poppies and cobalt cornflowers stitched near the shoulders. It was £480.

Who are these people who can buy stuff like this in January? Or in any month of the year?

When I went through to check on e-mails during a lull, I found that a further e-mail had arrived from Branwell.

I allowed my heart to soar. *It doesn't matter*

what it says. The simple fact is that he has messaged me twice in one day. I love this man.

From: Branwell Thornton
Cc: Bea Gibson
Subject: Re: Re: Submission

Dear Daisy,
It's very nice to receive such a balanced reply. Thanks. You'd be amazed at how often such messages sent out by me elicit returns along the lines of: 'If you're so smart, write your own book' and words to that effect! They may have a point!

My instinct is that there is something about your knowledge base that is book-worthy. This is something we should explore together, because I like the way you operate and I think I can work with you. That's a very important factor.

Would you be interested in accompanying me to a book awards evening — The Laphroaigs — on the evening of 15th February? It might be inspirational for you and let you see which books are currently well received. If this is of any interest to you, please arrange with my assistant, Bea Gibson, who is copied in here. I have attached a list of the shortlisted books.
Yours,
Branwell

11

An Intriguing Development

Read it again, Daisy.

Utter disbelief. Could it be a joke from one of my friends? But it certainly was his e-mail address. Was one of London's top literary agents *really* inviting me to a literary awards function as his guest? I read it over and over. Yes, it seemed he was. And I had something 'book-worthy' inside me.

This could be the breakthrough moment. Not conclusive, but a definite shift in position.

I was fluttery, excited, possibly hysterical. Trying to research the awards, I kept pressing the wrong buttons on my keyboard. Finally, a link to the event came up. Very fancy. To be held at Claridge's, with a full dinner and champagne. *What will I wear? I must look magnificent!*

Next, I read the attached shortlist:

The Laphroaig Literary Awards, Claridge's, 15th February 7 pm

Literary Fiction:
The Ribbon by Leonie Roberts
Death and Other Hobbies by Ian Bassett
Symphonium by Jan-Luc Morreaux

Biography:
Cicero, Orator: Life & Times by David Welsh
Nicolaus Copernicus: Sun, Moon and Stars
    by Sally Finch
Otto von Bismarck by Rebecca Snow

Culinary:
Bake Roast Grill by Rory Bridges
Classic Cuisine 6 by Michel Amiel
Soup to Nuts by Edie Greene

Crime:
Forensica by Alana Dunn
The Candlestick in the Dining Room by
    Herb Gutteridge
Buried Deep by Brian Jackson

Catching sight of his name amidst the Culinary genre, I thought, *Oh God — that bloody Frenchman! Is there no escaping him?*

I waited for a respectable amount of time, tinkering around with satin teddies, googling Branwell Thornton a dozen times, doing fifty sit-ups behind the counter. In the middle of the afternoon, I messaged Bea Gibson, accepting the kind invitation. Clara didn't materialise at all that day, so I had to go through to see Francesca to share my joy.

'Well done, Daisy!' she said, hugging me.

'It was you. You inspired me!'

'No, this is all about you. The work you do is never wasted. You know what that golfer guy said: The harder I work, the luckier I get.'

I bounced along the street on the way home, stopping for lots of tapas things (which were reduced) at the supermarket. And a bunch of cut-price rosebuds.

Now let's get the flat sorted out.

Back at the flat, there was no sign of Kitty, so I activated my feelgood playlist, starting with Toploader's 'Dancing in the Moonlight', and put the flowers in water. Next, I started cleaning like a maniac: squooshing environmentally friendly spray, mopping wooden floors with steaming hot water, cleaning the oven. After that, I set to work on making a fabulous dinner for us: stuffed olives, chorizo sautéed in red wine, ham and cheese croquettes, and calamari with capers. I'd seen a TED talk by Mihaly Csikszentmihalyi all about creative 'flow' being the secret to happiness. A trigger is what's needed. The e-mail from Branwell Thornton had triggered my 'flow' in a big way; I was seriously whooshing along now like a glacier in a thaw.

By the time Kitty arrived back from the teashop, however, I was spent. 'Wow, this all looks lovely,' she said, as I lay flumped out on the sofa with a glass of Rioja.

'I had a burst of energy, Kitty. It passed over, thank God. How was your day?'

'Not so bad. Yours?'

'Got some lovely news today, actually.'

'Tell!'

I waited for Kitty to fill a glass and join me on the sofa. I passed her my phone, the screen showing the Branwell e-mail thread.

She read it speedily. A squeal of delight.

'Oh! WOW! Fantastic! He wants to find a book in you!' She hugged me. 'So proud of you.'

'I'm about to burst with excitement, Kitty. But I really need inspiration about what sort of book to write. It's my first real chance to get published.'

Kitty thought for a while. 'What about something to rival this *Kiss Chase* book?' she said, picking it up from the table and passing it to me. 'Tell it from the girls' side?'

I considered this.

'Nice idea, Kitty. But what do I know about seduction?'

'Well, maybe you're just going to have to seduce someone.'

'Beau Bonas and Prince Harry elude me.'

'Maybe there's someone else . . . '

'I wish.'

Who? The dating sites were disaster areas, and sometimes it felt like everyone on the streets of London was part of a couple. Tom Percy had done so much harm when he went off with that princess. But I had to start thinking positively — about men, my book, *everything*.

★ ★ ★

Feeling temporarily in control of my life next morning, I went out for a run before showering, and then ate some quite sawdusty muesli before setting off for Voluptas nice and early. Striding along the high street in a teal Miss Sixty lambswool mini-dress, cherry fur jacket, and knee-length boots, I felt invincible. My hair was piled up in a full top knot, and my lips frosted with Maybelline's First Blossom. My luck had turned. I was going to be one of the successful people.

Beau's out of town. But, hey, Charlie Grosvenor might have taken up residence in Primrose Hill . . .

As I got near my left turn into Hedgerow Lane, I noticed a commotion on the high street, right next to the Blink! beauty parlour, where I'd once had my eyebrows threaded. A man was high up on a ladder, painting a new sign above the double-fronted shop which had previously been a bridal shop called Anastasia. A queue of women were chattering, clearly waiting for the doors to open.

What's going on? This is a bit of a hullabaloo for a Tuesday morning.

I crossed the street to investigate.

The sign writer had chalked out the words: *French Cookery School* on a plum-coloured background, and was filling in the letters with lush gold-leaf paint. A sandwich board on the pavement declared: *Limited places, sign up today for: French Sauces, Classic Patisserie 1&2, Family Cuisine or Fusion Fun. Discount for Early Birds!*

The real housewives of Primrose Hill arrived in their droves. Imagine the dinner party embarrassment if one wasn't booked on a course!

Still, it looked very impressive from what I could see. I peered in the window and saw a lovely reception area, where a vintage chandelier lit up the rich, plummy walls. Behind the desk was a slightly flustered girl, booting her computer, literally, as far as I could make out. All quite interesting, but it was time for me to hurry along to work.

12

Clara's Sister

Clara was already in the shop, complaining of the early start as her car had gone in for repairs and Phil had dropped her off.

'A whole day in here, Daisy!' she exclaimed.

'Bad luck! So, what's happening?'

'Not much. If you wouldn't mind changing round the window display — anything you fancy — I'll get the lattes?' she said.

'Sure. Anything new arrived?'

'Oh yes, actually! This lovely Twenties silk nightie — just back from dry cleaning — is rather gorgeous,' she said, offering it over in an embossed box lined with pale lavender tissue paper.

'Nice. Provenance?'

'Hever Castle, home of Anne Boleyn. Belonged to Madeleine Astor, wife of John Jacob. American heiress. *Titanic* survivor. Doesn't get better, Daisy.'

'I'll say!'

She wrapped a velvet cape around her shoulders and flew out the door, her stylish bob ruffling in the draught. I busied myself, emptying the window of an assortment of bras, then draped the nightdress in there instead.

When Clara came back with the coffees, she was carrying a heavy-looking bag, and was bursting with news.

'Just wait until you hear this!'

I could guess, but said, 'What? Spill!'

'There's a new cookery school!' she announced.

She loved to convey news, so: 'Oh, really? Where?'

'Next to Blink! Didn't you notice on the way past? I went inside. Love the sound of Fusion Fun — but there's no availability until March, can you believe?' she said, setting down the lattes on the glass counter.

'I wonder who owns it?'

'Wonder no more. I know *everything!* It's owned by sexy Michel Amiel, no less! Why do you think the ladies are going crazy to get involved? He's apparently renting a big house on Elsworthy Road — along with his perky little pixie, you know, that actress . . . '

Michel Amiel? YMCA Michel Amiel? Living a few streets away and opening a cookery school here in Prim Hill?

It was my daydream gone wrong.

Clara emptied the contents of the heavy bag to reveal a full set of cookery books — *Classic Cuisine 1–5* by Michel Amiel.

'Gosh. How much for those?' I asked.

'On a deal. £150!'

'Bargain!' I said.

'You look a bit stunned by all this,' replied Clara, sipping on her warming drink daintily, preserving her cupid-bow lips, painted to perfection.

'Erm. A bit, yeah. I met him at that party at the V&A the other week. I didn't realise why he was in town . . . that it was relatively permanent.

And so close to home.'

'Ah, so you've met him. You should have told me all this! Lucky you. And? Hot?'

Hot?

'Well, he got my blood boiling, if that counts.'

'Ha! He's French — what do you expect?'

She flicked through the cookery books. 'I've always wanted these. He's so masterful.'

I had to admit, they were beautifully produced hardback books. Very old-school, nothing too glitzy. No images of anyone licking spoons or ornate, overly frosted cupcakes. Just simple jackets showing classic fare, with elegant font displaying his name and the titles *Classic Cuisine 1, Classic Cuisine 2,* and so on.

'I might have a look at those later,' I said.

'Sure, of course. I'll leave them here for a few days. You know I never cook.'

Clara occasionally spoke fondly of Georgie, who seemingly did all the things at home that bored Clara, including school runs and cooking.

Clara was on a roll now. 'And it's not just the cookery school. He's opening a restaurant in the high street too — Brasserie Rose. Named after his elderly mother. Isn't that sweet? My friend Aine was saying that his mother is living here too. She goes everywhere with him, apparently!'

'That's cute, I suppose. I wonder how Eve Berger likes that? He didn't seem the sentimental type to me.'

I wonder why he's suddenly London-based?

Clara babbled on about the various cookery courses, as she added a hefty price label to the nightie. There followed a heated phone call with her sister Annabel, which was nothing unusual. Clara took it in the back shop, but it was impossible not to hear.

'It's not your turn to have the villa in August!' said Clara. 'I've promised it to our good friends, Sarah and Tom Armitage, and she's just had a monstrous viral thing. I always have dibs on August, Annabel. That's a fact.'

Silence. Clara sighing.

'Well, you have it then if you feel it should be alternate years, but just because you can boss everyone around in your office, don't try doing that with me!'

Silence again.

Clara came back through to the front.

'My bloody sister! She's so fucking condescending.'

I didn't know what to say.

'She tries to boss her family around as she does at the magazine. Well, I'm not taking that from her!'

'Quite right.'

'We all know she got the Oxford degree, and edits *Elle* magazine. She looks down on me, her little sister who sells knickers for a living. Huh! There's no way we agreed to alternate Augusts for the French villa. My mother would have put her straight, but she's so out of it. Poor Mummy.'

'Sounds a bit like *Devil Wears Prada* on that magazine?'

'A bit, yes! She's really very nice, and I'm proud of her, but that's not the point. Sometimes I hate her, and I was so looking forward to going with the Armitages this year, and it saves a fortune on accommodation elsewhere. Things are very tight for Phil at work right now. Very tight indeed.'

Clara did not give the impression that anything was remotely tight, by normal standards. There was the Queen Anne manor house towards Windsor, ponies for Tashi, quad bikes for the boys, and acres of land. Georgie and a few others to help out. Clara bought endless handbags and thought nothing of spending £1,000 at a spa for the day. She lived in another world entirely, but that didn't bother me. Clara, undoubtedly, had a big, warm heart.

I wonder why she says things are tight for Phil at work?

I knew he was an investment banker but didn't know what that involved. Anyway, by lunchtime, Clara felt a bit tired after all the cookery school excitement so went home by cab and train instead of waiting for Phil.

'Feel free to use the cookery books, sweetheart,' she said as she applied her lipstick, looking into a gorgeous little art deco compact mirror.

'Thank you. See you tomorrow, Clara.'

'Yes, bye for now.'

She flew out the door, leaving a sense that the place was empty.

13

Vital Research

I took a look at the cookery books. Sauces, soups, methods of stock-making. Ways with meat, ways with vegetables, ways with potatoes. Pies, tarts, fruits . . . cakes, pastries, mousses, madeleines. All the fundamentals simply explained, the words peppered with photos of Michel Amiel in action, the whole effect rather alluring somehow.

I decided to try out a couple of the recipes later. Meanwhile, I opened my laptop and found myself researching Michel Amiel.

Oh! Look at all this!

The official line from his website, Wikipedia page and sycophant fan page: *France's most important living chef and culinary author, an inspiration to legions of chefs. A cook who writes, or a writer who cooks? Michel Amiel is so talented in both areas that it's hard to know his métier.*

However, such kind words were at odds with other items like: 'Another Court Case for Michel Amiel' and ''He was a beast to work for,' says his former employee.' Tribunal cases, driving offences, even a breach of the peace. There were press articles relating to tax evasion, employing illegal immigrants, quarrelling with models in fancy restaurants, and plenty accounts of him being horribly rude to journalists when he was clearly supposed to be promoting his books.

There were a number of photographs of Amiel looking ill tempered, fierce and occasionally psychotic. One publicity shot showed him brandishing a meat cleaver, sporting a blood-spattered apron, a chunk of dead cow before him. It made me shudder.

There was one particular article which caught my eye. I clicked 'translate'. A more thoughtful, measured piece by well-known French writer Albert Noir:

★ ★ ★

What Has Happened to Amiel?

I've known Michel Amiel since he first came into the public eye over fifteen years ago. We were friends for many years, drinking buddies and weekend companions. I've spent many a Sunday in a coma in his Paris apartment, which is rather a pity, as it really is quite gorgeous.

Fame came to him at a tender age, and we know that can be a curse. But I didn't expect him to make such a spectacular mess of the fame game — or that we would fall out so dramatically.

It's two years since we spoke last. It was a pointless fight. Perhaps I tried to rein him in, talk him down from the roof, so to speak. I miss him, sure, but that Michel, the person he has become, I wouldn't want him back in my life. He became pathetic, drunken and vile. Spiteful too, ungracious about the successes of others. How much success does one man need?

How sad that he's ruined a good friendship, I thought.

But this wasn't getting on with my own life. I closed him down and opened a Word document, desperately thinking of ideas for another take on my book. If Branwell Thornton was prepared to host me at the awards, and believe in me, I wanted to have some fresh ideas for him.

Underwear tycoon fiction — inspirational character? Lady Lily Carter-type protagonist? No. Rags to riches is too clichéd. Angle: heroine is a doctor who designs beautiful bras which are also good for women's health. Makes a fortune, but is torn between her business and her medical ethics.

Feminism and lingerie: objectification and bra-burning . . . do women wear it for men? Do third-wave feminists use sexuality to outwit men? Why did second-wave feminists take against the bra so violently?

Sex sells: From Nell Gwynn to Madonna — décolletage and ambition. Would you 'go low' for promotion? Would you risk general anaesthetic for larger breasts? If breasts are for feeding babies, why do we make them the centre of sexual allure?

I was just contemplating the charms of girl-next-door versus siren when I was interrupted by the door chime of the shop's front door. I swished through the velvet curtain to the front shop as though going on stage in a show. As Clara always said, a sale required a performance.

'Hello!' I said. 'How can I help you?'

The customer was a bride-to-be who had fallen in love with the Edwardian nightie in the window, despite the cool £325 ticket.

'I've been on quite a spending spree today,' she said with a flick of her professionally blow-dried three tones of blonde hair.

'Oh?'

'Yes, I ordered the invitations at Smythson, bought Heidi Klein swimsuits for the honeymoon, and just signed up for a cookery course — £1,250!'

Ah, that cookery school again.

'Not cheap . . . '

'I know, but Monsieur Amiel said I'd be able to hold a first-class dinner party after I've completed it.'

'You met him in person?'

'Yes, he was working the queue. He says he'll be teaching some of the classes himself! He's seriously the sexiest man on the planet.'

He is?

'Don't let your fiancée hear that!' I warned.

'Oh, now that I've got hold of his credit card, the fun's gone out of *him!*'

Poor man!

'Amiel is naughty — it's obvious,' she said.

Is that what women see in him? Badness.

14

The Annoying Customer

After the bride left, I went back to my half-baked book ideas, then made a pot of Earl Grey tea, which tinkled into a china rosebud teacup, and I allowed myself to imagine that the new James Bond had dropped into the shop, looking for a sleeper agent. All of a sudden, everything was fun and anything was possible.

★ ★ ★

I had not felt so optimistic in years, and continued to jog through the streets of Primrose Hill each morning, eat spelt porridge from Savannah's Wholefoods, think positive thoughts, and mull over book ideas. There were frustrations along the way. I would think I had a bestselling idea, then find it was already out there when I Google-searched.

On other occasions, I wrote screeds of fictional words about a medical lingerie entrepreneur called Dr Sophia Fox, only to decide it was all facile nonsense and delete it. (The chief problem was my lack of medical knowledge.)

I really do hope I'm capable of being a writer because it is a whole lot harder than it looks.

The ideas were less than the half of it, and just

because I could make things up this time, it still had to be based on facts.

I was, by turns, thrilled and terrified at the prospect of the awards event. I remember feeling that my biggest fear was that this period of heightened hope and excitement would end without progress. I had the strongest imaginable sense of urgency. My life had to change. My job had to change. Yes, I knew I could climb the ladder in retail, using my specialist lingerie knowledge, but if I were to take on a very stressful day job like that, in John Lewis or Victoria's Secret, or even Rigby and Peller, I felt sure the writing dream would evaporate in the distraction and exhaustion of wage-slave daily life.

One afternoon towards the end of January, I was in the back area of Voluptas, contemplating a sewing job, with Nat King Cole's 'Cachito' playing in the background as I tried out my cha-cha-cha.

Must get some work done, Delaney!

We always had surplus stock in the back, often awaiting minor repairs. In many ways, it was more intriguing back there than in the main shop. The lingerie hung on rails in a colour-coded scheme, from white through to ivory and cream, then onto nude, beige, blush, dove grey and mocha, shifting to shell pink, pastel peach, dusky pink and powder blue, turquoise, eau-de-nil, as well as soft lilac. Black and red items had a 'hot' zone of their own. Clara didn't much like to display the hot stuff, but we had regular customers who asked for the racier numbers.

I had a plan. I cha-cha-ed my way over to the

70

shabby purple-velvet, buttoned armchair, which we'd got from Francesca. I sat down, threaded a needle, and began to stitch a tiny ribbon-bow back into place on a pretty lace bra (Sixties), getting quite lost in the task, making the smallest, neatest stitches with nimble fingers.

It took me a few moments to realise that the doorbell chime had sounded. I got up reluctantly and went through to welcome the visitor, a wide smile on my face, still holding the lacy little bra and the needle and cotton.

There was a vaguely familiar smell of aftershave, or expensive man-soap, as I did a furtive cha-cha swish through the velvet curtains. On the other side, I froze. *How could this be happening?*

Monsieur Amiel.

I blushed.

He looked surprised.

Does he remember me?

'Hello, how can I help you?' I said, hedging bets.

'I'm browsing, thank you.' He looked at things for a few minutes, while I stood still.

'I know you from somewhere?' he said, not looking at me.

'The V&A.' I signed YMCA.

A nod.

He then looked at me intensely for what seemed like ages. I was uneasy under his stare.

'So, I'll leave you to browse,' I said.

'Thanks. Someone in the pub was telling me all about this place.'

'Ah. Very British already. 'Pub,'' I teased.

'Yes, I'll give you your 'pubs'.'

'Oh, you will, will you? What will you not give us?' I questioned.

'Your food.'

'Is that so?'

He looked at some of the basques. 'I've come to London to sort out your food.'

'How gracious you are,' I mocked.

'Anything you recommend here?' he asked.

'That depends on what you like. Or what she likes.'

He made no reply.

I felt a bit spare. 'I'll be through in the back if you need me.'

I finished the sewing job and began writing a fancy label for the newly repaired bra. I wondered if he'd managed to leave very quietly, because I heard nothing of him as I carried on working: *1960s lace bra from 10 Berkeley Square. 36C. Belonged to Lady Lydia Spencer. Worn at her wedding at Westminster Abbey.*

I looked up to find Michel standing in the doorway between the front and back shop, holding back the velvet curtain, watching me intently.

I was startled. 'Oh, hi. You found something you like?'

'I did,' he replied.

'That's good.'

'How will I know that the lady in question will like it?'

'If you know her well, you are the best judge of that.'

'Could I just ask your opinion?' he asked.

'Yes, of course. I'll come right through.'

I followed him. He held up a very cute bustier, in a rosebud silk fabric — one of my favourites. 'I love that one,' I said.

He nodded. Looking at the bustier, looking at me.

I thought for a terrifying moment he was going to ask me to try it on.

He paused, then said: 'But do you think a sophisticated woman would like it?'

I did not miss a beat. 'More to the point, would a sophisticated woman like you?'

He choked, silently.

'I think I'll leave it,' he said, replacing it on the rail.

Eventually, he picked out a white teddy that was to his liking.

'Let me wrap it up for you.' *And tape up your mouth with this sellotape!*

I wrapped it without saying a word, working expertly, as he watched.

'Very nice,' he said.

He paid and left, again without a proper goodbye.

15

The Book Awards

Waiting for the awards night was akin to anticipating Christmas as a six-year-old. At least payday happened on the way, so I was able to buy some new make-up, have my eyebrows threaded, and get some new silk stockings.

Fifteenth February. *At last!* I was due to meet Branwell at Claridge's at 6.45pm. I started getting ready at four o'clock, having left work early after negotiating an early start in lieu.

It wasn't a full black-tie event and, style-wise, I didn't want to look like a complete try-hard. But not too grungy or edgy either. I piled my hair up in a chignon and used some low-key make-up — Bobbi Brown Apricot Blush and Mac Watermelon Liplast and of course, lots of retro eyeliner by Lancôme in Velvet Brown. After drawing a blank in Pippa's wardrobe, I had borrowed a dress from Clara.

'You need to look like a world-famous author,' she'd said, producing this wondrous frock from her palace in the shires. It was a proper wiggle dress. Made from dark green fine jersey, with a very nipped-in waist, long sleeves and a simple boat neckline. I thought it looked good with some hot-pink suede heels I'd picked up in Oxfam. I remembered what Grace Kelly said:

'Your dresses should be tight enough to show you're a woman and loose enough to show you're a lady.'

I think I was pushing my lady luck with that green dress.

I had made a batch of pancakes, a tray of tiffin, two banana loaves and a red-velvet cake for Prim & Proper in order to fund a taxi to and from Claridge's, and when it arrived I thought I might explode with excitement.

In the back of the cab, I began to imagine I really was an international bestselling author:

The photographers called out to me: 'Hey, Daisy Delaney, when's the next book out?'

'Daisy! You look great!'

'This way, Daisy!'

'Daisy, they're saying your latest novel is the fastest-selling book of all time.'

'Daisy, did you know you've outsold Michel Amiel and you're the number one bestselling author?'

'Fifteen quid, love,' said the driver.

I giggled as reality interrupted my reverie.

'Oh, that was quick,' I said.

'My wife always says the same thing!' the driver joked.

I laughed.

'You were miles away. Something fancy, is it, by the looks of you?' he wondered.

'Yeah, a book thing.'

'You a writer?'

'No, but I'd like to be,' I admitted.

'As long as you want it bad enough, love . . . '

I nodded. 'Exactly.'

When I got out of the cab, there was a battery of flashes up ahead. The canopy of the hotel was studded with pretty lights and, from what I could see, known authors were posing for press photographers on the steps as they went in. I teetered towards the entrance, and as I did so, I glanced over to see who was being snapped.

At first, it was short-listed thriller writer Brian Jackson and his wife. They turned to go inside. Next up, cookery writer Edie Greene. I waited and saw Michel Amiel arrive, posing in a designer suit, with Eve Berger at his side, looking exquisite in a black body-con dress. I was a bit startled to see them together.

I just can't see her in the white teddy . . .

I snuck into the hotel, looking around for Branwell. I'd sent him a small photo as an attachment, whereas I knew how he looked from his website. I felt very insignificant, all the more so due to coming down from the dream sequence in the cab. Invisible little me. I could melt away from this glamorous scene and not a soul would notice. Surely there was some mistake. Was I really supposed to be here?

'Daisy?' said a male voice from behind. I swung round.

The great agent himself.

'Branwell, nice to meet you!' I said, offering my hand.

'Pleasure's all mine,' he replied, shaking my hand firmly. He had a voice like God's, booming and yet velvety at the same time. 'You look lovely! Let's get to the bar, my dear.'

As we walked through the foyer, everyone

stopped to say hello. Branwell Thornton was quite the magnet in the publishing world.

He pointed out important people as we walked.

'Most of these successful people are crime writers,' he explained. 'Everybody loves crime, that's the thing, Daisy. That's where the serious money lies. And readers never tire of it. Maybe they tire of a particular detective, but never the subject matter, you know?'

I nodded, not revealing my dislike of crime stories, unless they involve nice period clothes and lashings of red lipstick, Agatha Christie-style. Posh murder I can just about take.

But what about lingerie and classy crime combined? Silk camisoles and revolvers. Could work, actually.

There was no time to mull over creative ideas once in the bar area, as Branwell commanded the bar, passed me a chilled Kir Royale, and began to introduce me to some of the authors who were going to be at our table for the evening. There was a pleasant-faced sports journalist-turned-author who wrote about sporting scandals, especially to do with gambling and match rigging. (That stuff can't be true?) And a sophisticated lady with a chignon, apparently a modern-day Georgette Heyer, firmly in the Regency-rom bodice-ripper category.

'Those women can make piles of cash,' whispered Branwell. 'Producing a novel a year for an adult lifetime, all of them doing a bit more than okay in a few languages. The odd thing to television. That works as a model. At least it used to, before the obsession with Top Tens.'

Next up was an ex-soldier called Gary Hopper. 'That's not me real name, darlin',' he'd said. 'If I told you I'd have to 'old you prisoner in my cave-side lair for the next twenty-five years an' make you do fifty press-ups a day.'

Everyone was buying drinks for Branwell, which he threw down his neck with one flick of the wrist.

I was mid-chat with Gary Hopper, secret agent extraordinaire with the biggest mouth in Britain (yet somehow quite a sexy man), who was telling me about his selfless, single-handed humanitarian work for the education of girls in Afghanistan (getting smoother), when Michel Amiel and Eve Berger arrived in the bar with a silent fanfare. They were accompanied by a nervous-looking gooseberry of a man who, according to Branwell, was Michel's Parisian manager, Auguste Flaubert. As a sea of people parted biblically to clear a path to the bar for them, they charged past us ungraciously. No sooner had Michel Amiel received his drinks than he was clearly complaining about the standard of them to the poor young barman.

'Tosser,' said Gary loudly.

Agree. What is worse than people in positions of power talking down to those who serve them? Nothing.

Branwell leaned in: 'Quite possibly the most obnoxious man in the business. But, pains me to say it, a world-class cookery writer. Deserves his success, handles it badly.'

Branwell gadded off to chat to yet another

author who had arrived — a woman with drawn-on eyebrows who wrote all about massage parlours.

I wonder how she researches that stuff?

Gary glanced over to the French trio and shook his head.

'Bloody hate men like that.'

'He's a horrible man,' I said.

'You know him?' asked Gary, sounding surprised.

'Slightly. Met him at a party, then he came into my shop. His new cookery school isn't far away, worst luck.'

'You have a shop?'

'It's not mine. I work there,' I explained quickly.

'What do you sell?'

'Guess.'

He looked me up and down.

'It's gotta be classy, I reckon. Is it them pottery mugs and jugs wif polka dots on them?'

'Nope, try again.'

'Cakes! Fancy little cakes with more icing than cake? Went out with a skinny girl once who could make one last a month.'

'Also wrong!' I giggled. *Why am I encouraging this man?*

'Shoes and 'andbags?'

I shook my head.

'You're goin' to have to tell me. I'm intrigued now.'

'One last guess,' I said, looking at him flirtily.

'Knickers.'

I gasped. 'That's right. Lingerie.'

His eyes widened. 'Thought so. Makes sense.'

'Does it?'

'Yeah, there's something quietly racy about you,' he informed me.

I laughed. 'I have an academic specialism in bras, is all.'

'Sure you do.'

Gary moved in a bit closer. 'About this lingerie shop . . . '

16

The Frenchman's Revenge

But before I could say 'silk stockings', someone jostled into me and my Kir Royale cascaded over the glass, a blackcurrant splosh narrowly missing my green dress.

I swung round.

Quelle surprise!

'Ha! This time you've bumped into me!' I said, seeing Michel Amiel standing there, Eve Berger at his side.

There was a pause. He looked at me menacingly, which made Gary put his arm round me.

'Watch what you're doin', mate,' he said with a muttered, 'Fucking French klutz.'

Michel Amiel recognised me, for sure. As did Eve. But from him, only this: 'Sorry, do I know you?'

As much as I wanted to slap that arrogant French face — which was not even handsome in the normal sense, with its overly large nose and madman eyes, and its Picasso asymmetry — I resisted and took another tack.

'Ah, I'm sorry too. I thought you were someone I knew,' I said, turning my back on them abruptly, then saying very loudly to Gary Hopper: 'About the basques . . . '

'Tell me more.'

But Branwell was rounding up his flock. 'Everyone in my gang, time to go to our table!' he announced.

I glanced over my shoulder as I left the bar, and it looked as if Michel Amiel and Eve were squabbling, as Auguste Flaubert watched helplessly, still gooseberry-like.

Gary looked at Auguste. 'That poor guy's like a spare prick at a party,' he said. He was full of old-fashioned expressions, clichés and terrible puns and jokes — I just knew he'd be capable of saying, 'Done that, been there. Got the T-shirt,' but I liked him.

Branwell led the way to our table. It was circular, covered in dazzling white linen with lots of little candles in glass pots, and posies of pretty gypsophila dotted here and there. I was seated with Gary on one side and Branwell on the other.

Gary was underwhelmed by the food: 'A fish should be a fish, not a fucking mousse, surely?' 'A medallion of beef? A garland of green beans? That's two things that should be worn round your neck, innit? Twats.'

The more wine I drank, the funnier I found Gary. As coffee was served, Belinda Seton, the host for the evening, who presented *Fully Booked* on BBC2, came onto the platform. She looked stunning. Demure. Intellectual but human. Sexy but girl-next-door. *How does she do it?*

However, we were all distracted by a terrible debacle in the central aisle of the hall. Raised voices, chairs flying, followed by a deathly hush.

I knew before I looked over.

Michel Amiel, making his way to his table in the style of a rampaging bull. I hadn't realised that Team Amiel had stayed in the bar while we'd been eating dinner. Auguste Flaubert trotted after him with a look of abject apology-cum-terror on his earnest face. I craned my neck to see where Eve was, but she wasn't there. Finally, Michel sat down.

Back to beauteous Belinda . . .

Well, that's a silver dress to die for — strappy, floaty, elegant. Caroline Castigliano, I'm sure.

As the literary part of the evening unfurled, I glanced across occasionally to Amiel's table. He was drinking massive amounts of champagne and was variously slumped over the table or gesticulating madly at anyone who walked by.

If he was anyone else, he'd have been ejected by now.

Belinda was in full flow, explaining the order of events.

'There will be discussions between the authors and various expert academics relating to their genre, which is really rather thrilling for us. I'd like to begin by welcoming Dr Sayed Farouk to the platform, a specialist in the revival Gothic synergy novel,' she said. 'He'll be interviewing Jean-Luc Morreaux.'

Dr Farouk spoke eloquently enough: 'The juxtaposition of formal and informal language echoes the Gothic hero's dichotomous take on reality. Was that planned, or just a stroke of genius?' he mused. And so he went on. And on.

Gary took a pen from his inside pocket and wrote on his napkin: *WTF?*

I took the napkin and pen and wrote: *WTFF?*

He replied: *FFS!*

Ever since I'd mentioned lingerie, Gary had become a devoted fan.

Branwell looked on, almost amused, but I pulled myself together. I was there to learn about the publishing world, not flirt with former soldiers.

Ah great, we're going to hear from the author now. Let's get some reality injected into proceedings.

The light shone on Jean-Luc Morreaux.

He was a flimsy man in his thirties with a really big, brain-shaped head, which seemed much too weighty for his body.

'It was an almost existential experience, writing it,' said the author. 'The Gothic milieu has its own energy and demons.'

Dr Farouk nodded earnestly, almost shaking his own head off.

Gary tried footsie. Meanwhile, I could see Michel Amiel agitating from the corner of my eye.

17

Sour Grapes

'Let's get on to the pie-makers!' Michel called out.

Part of me had to agree.

'Looks like your ex-'friend' might be thrown out,' whispered Gary.

'He's no friend of mine.' I took the pen and napkin, writing: TWAT.

For the next half-hour, Michel heckled intermittently, then he slumped back in his seat, seemingly snoring at one point.

There was a pause in official proceedings.

'I feel like punching his lights out myself,' said Gary.

'Please don't,' said Branwell. 'He's like this every year. All part of the show.'

When the culinary awards moment eventually came, pop-star-turned-actress-turned-cook Annie Jones appeared on stage in a wonderful sparkling black gown, with demure roll-collar and a hip-hugging bias.

'Good evening,' she said in her delightful caramel voice. 'Let me get straight to business. The winner in the culinary category is . . . ' She seemed to take an age to open the envelope. Then the results card fell, and she couldn't bend in her dress, so Belinda came to the rescue amid much giggling.

'My apologies,' said Ms Jones. 'The winner is — Rory Bridges for *Bake Roast Grill!* Well done, Rory!'

There was a burst of applause which nearly masked Michel Amiel's cursing and swearing, mostly in French. Rory kissed his wife and made his way to the platform, bounding there in a mid-blue suit and open-collared white shirt.

He kissed Annie Jones in the style of a slobbering Labrador.

'Cheers for this, folks. I get a lot of help with my books and I'm really proud of the whole team . . . '

Amiel was now making his way to the stage in a drunken swagger.

The security team was slow to react. Amiel was on the steps now, just feet away from Rory Bridges.

'You don't even write the books!' shouted Amiel.

'Whoa, sunshine,' said Rory. 'Where did he come from?'

The security team was zooming in on Michel Amiel now as Rory was taken back to his seat from the other side of the platform.

'He's definitely going to get thrown out,' I said.

'Serves him right.' Gary snorted. 'Sore loser.'

The bouncers grabbed Amiel and pulled him off the platform. As he was hauled past our table, he saw me and made a bid for freedom, saying: 'She knows me, it's Daisy. Daisy, who sells the lace suspenders. Leave me with her. She'll look after me.'

All eyes were upon me.

18

A Friend in Need . . .

The security team looked to me for a response. I hated Michel Amiel. He had ignored me earlier, humiliated me. He was an embarrassing mess. I owed him nothing.

'Don't even consider it,' said Gary.

But I felt so sorry for Michel Amiel in that split second.

I stood up and said, 'Yes, I know him. He can sit here. Bring some coffee, perhaps?'

They let go of him. He veered towards me. 'Thank you,' he said.

An extra chair was put at our table. He sat down, slumped and fell asleep. Monsieur Flaubert, who was a frazzled heap by this point, thanked me emphatically and announced that he was leaving.

Everything settled down, and I plied Michel Amiel with coffee when he woke from time to time.

'You gotta be crazy,' said Gary. 'He was proper ignorant to you in the bar before.'

I shrugged. 'He's harmless really.'

I spent the rest of the evening talking between Gary and Michel; a surreal mix of mockney and Franglais. A couple of hours and four cups of coffee later, Michel was more sensible.

'Thank you for this,' he said as the event wound up. 'I won't forget it.'

'You owe me one, Monsieur Amiel,' I responded.

'I do. Take me home, Daisy.'

'I don't know why I'm even helping you.'

I said goodnight to Branwell, Gary and the rest of the guests at the table.

'Be careful with him, Daisy,' warned Branwell.

'I will. And thanks for a wonderful evening.'

'You're welcome. I hope it's been inspiring for you.'

'Very much so. I'll be in touch,' I assured him, kissing his cheek.

'Yes, do that. A couple of years from now and you'll be on the shortlist.'

'Ha, I doubt that. Didn't notice a section on knickers,' I joked.

Gary hovered around, waiting to say goodnight.

'It's been so nice meeting you,' I said, kissing him on both cheeks.

'Pleasure. Where's that shop you work in?'

'Primrose Hill. Voluptas.'

He winked.

Was that wise of me?

Michel walked in zigzags. Fortunately, there were lots of cabs waiting outside the hotel, and we managed to get one straight away.

'What's your address?' I asked him as the driver waited for instructions.

'Elsworthy Road,' he said. 'But get the driver to go to your house first.'

We said nothing during the cab ride, sitting at

opposite sides of the back seat. I presumed he was dozing. When we got to Rosehip Lane, he couldn't find his wallet, so I paid the driver generously and jumped out, explaining that Michel should be taken to Elsworthy Road.

Michel leaned out of the cab as it pulled away. 'Thank you.'

I waved as I began to go down the steps into the flat. 'Sleep well!'

I let myself in, warmed some milk which I poured into my favourite mug — dotty, in fact, which made me think of Gary Hopper.

I need to find a man soon. I'm at that dangerous stage. When nutty ex-SAS men seem so cute . . .

I flopped on my bed and took off my pink shoes, amazed I had worn them for so long. After taking off my make-up and putting on my Victorian nightie, I got under my duvet, nestling until I found a comfortable spot.

The Laphroaigs — what a night. I want to be part of that bookish world. Yes, it's vain and pretentious. But it's also magical and exciting. I really do need a killer book. Maybe I should turn to crime fiction? But would someone have to die? I want to write about life not death.

I fell asleep feeling that I knew exactly what I wanted but not how to get it. That was what I had to figure out next.

19

The Lingerie

Frustration set in quite deeply after the awards evening. I still didn't have my book idea, much as the evening had been an exciting eye-opener to the industry. Crime just wasn't my thing. I seemed to be as confused as ever about direction, and I wrote and discarded paragraph after paragraph. *I can't write about something I don't understand. Surely ex-cops should write about crime? And lingerie experts about lingerie?*

I received a message from Branwell a few days after the event:

From: Branwell Thornton
To: Daisy Delaney
Subject: Awards Ceremony

Dear Daisy,
Well, that was quite a party! Hope you got home safely. It was very kind of you to look after M. Amiel. I hope he appreciates it.
Did the evening kick-start any creative processes? Or perhaps, more likely, put you off the industry for life?
Let me know if you have any brainwaves, large or small!

Yours,
Branwell

I didn't want to say that I was getting nowhere so (crazily) I e-mailed back like this:

From: Daisy Delaney
To: Branwell Thornton
Subject: Re: Awards Ceremony

Dear Branwell
Thank you so much for taking me to the event. I really enjoyed it and did get home in one piece. As a matter of fact, I have had an idea. Give me a couple of weeks, and I will get something over to you.
All best wishes,
Daisy

As soon as I pressed 'send', I regretted it.
  What if you can't think of anything, you muppet?

★ ★ ★

I took the Friday afternoon off work the following week, searching for literary inspiration. Time was running out. I pottered in the flat, penniless as ever, longing for the February pay cheque. I played Louis Armstrong's 'We Have All the Time in the World', brewed fresh coffee and was baking a sponge for French fancies for Prim & Proper's weekend trade.
  I'd learned so much about baking from Kitty

since we became flatmates two years before. She had the most amazing skills for creating cakes, which she'd acquired at the West London Cookery School. She'd paid for the course herself after working flat-out in London hotel kitchens for three years. That was before we met. I told her she could easily be a model as she was so beautiful, but she took the hard route through life.

There had been a worrying phone call from Pippa's grandpa, the Brigadier, to say he would be over later 'to discuss the rent'. Pippa had warned me about this.

Please don't say he's going to put it up. I'm not ready to become a milkmaid in the country just yet.

I glanced at the oven timer. Eight minutes left for the cake. My brain was working overtime. I only had a week left before I must reveal my brilliant new idea to Branwell. But there was no brilliant new idea!

For fuck's sake, you are a moron, Delaney!

I decided to go and try on some of the underwear I'd bought over the years of working in Voluptas, Louis playing in the background. I was desperate for inspiration.

I went through to my bedroom and opened the drawer tentatively.

Is this a good idea?

For one thing, it was freezing in the flat, and for another, I had no idea in what way the underwear might inspire me.

Try the crime and food and sex angles. Branwell said they were the money makers.

There was an assortment of items. After taking my clothes off, I chose a black silk and lace corset and put it on, fastening the tiny hooks, then attaching some silk stockings.

Bloody hell. This is a lot like hard work!

I stepped into some fancy mules Clara had given me as a gift after I'd helped at a weekend vintage fair at Earls Court one time.

I was posing about in front of my big vintage mirror — I suppose I didn't look too bad, a lot of curves and soft white flesh against the black silk — when PING! *Oh fuck, the cake's ready!*

I tottered through to the kitchen, grabbed some oven gloves and pulled down the oven door when: KNOCK KNOCK!

Oh my flipping goodness, who's knocking on the window?

I turned round on my heel and stared in disbelief.

It did not seem possible.

Michel Amiel was staring in. I froze to the spot.

He looked at me strangely. Why?

Oh, of course. You're baking in a basque, Daisy Delaney.

'Give me a minute!' I called.

'Do you have company?' he called back.

'No.'

Great, that's even weirder of me.

20

The Brigadier

He waited. Staring. I grabbed an apron, tied it round myself, took the cake from the oven, placed it on a rack, then walked backwards through to my bedroom, as I wasn't completely sure I'd look respectable from behind. I grabbed a kimono, tied it firmly, brushed my hair and took some breaths.

I opened the front door breathlessly. Michel entered the flat, where the scent of warm sponge cake mingled with the aroma of deep embarrassment.

'Hi,' I said.

'Hi.' He produced a tiny posy of flowers from behind his back. 'I was a twit at the awards. I'm sorry.'

'I think you mean 'twat.''

'Is that like 'arse'?'

'Not quite. Would you like some tea?'

'That would be nice.'

I busied around in the kitchen, while he sat on the tapestry slipper chair which Pippa had brought from her granny's place on her mother's side, Harebell Hall. According to Pippa, it was a 'run-down old dump', but Kitty and I googled it and it looked pretty palatial.

I threw together a version of French fancies,

with some jam and icing. I realised the kimono was hanging off my shoulders and coming undone, so I tied it back together, tightly.

'Don't let me forget that I have the cab money for you too,' said Michel. 'I never did find my wallet.'

'Oh, I would've needed a cab anyway . . . What a pain for you — you had to get duplicate cards?'

'Ah, *oui*. Happens all the time.'

He chatted about how disastrous he was with money, plans, personal effects — really selling himself hard.

With the tea and cake served, I sat opposite him on the little Lloyd loom chair.

He looked at me intently.

'Nice song?' he said.

'Yes, I like to dance around here at times.'

'Show me.'

'I'd need a partner.'

He stood up.

I laughed, then realised he was serious. 'Okay. Sway your hips in time to the music.'

'How is that?' he asked.

'Terrible. But never mind. Now, I'm going to twirl out to the side, and when I twirl back in towards you, you catch me with your left arm.'

He started to get into the rhythm of the music and did a little spin himself, knocking over the (drained) china teapot in the process.

SMASH!

'Oh fuck,' hissed Michel. 'I'm sorry — your cute little teapot. I am a clumsy-clot. I just can't dance.'

'Don't worry!' I assured. 'You were actually doing well there.'

'I was?'

'Definitely. But perhaps that's enough progress for one day,' I decided.

'Yes, I think so. I owe you a teapot now. An excuse to come back.'

'Well, maybe one day if you see a nice one. No rush. We have others.'

He seemed tense. We sat down again.

'How's the cookery school going?' I asked.

'Good, actually. That's the only thing that is.'

'Oh?'

He took a mouthful of the fancy. 'This is actually wonderful,' he murmured.

'Thanks. You were saying?'

'Things going wrong with the books all over the place. As you saw the other night.'

'Well, you're still at the top of the pile. You can't win every award going. Don't be a baby.'

'But the sales are dropping, Daisy. I need to get things sorted out in my head. Too much of the booze, you know. And the court cases. I'm going to be bankrupt if I'm not careful,' he confessed.

'But you sell masses of books!'

'I know. But we don't make as much from them as you'd think. We need the sponsor deals, the kitchenware, the public appearances. You see, we had this huge financial disaster with a line of foodstuffs in a supermarket chain in France. Turns out people like my books, but not my endless jars of sauce and salad dressings. That's why I'm in London. The cookery schools. The

96

restaurant chain. It's all Auguste's idea. Rebrand me abroad! Take me out of the nest I shit in.'

This is a lot of information.

I reflected on his financial situation. 'It must be hard, everyone thinking you're wealthy.'

'Yes. Do you know, I have to get approval from my accountant to make purchases over £300? I'm treated like a moron.' He shook his head, as though disbelieving his own situation.

In a strange way, we were both equally impoverished. That surprised me.

'I guess things are never as they seem,' I said.

'True. Who would have thought that you spend Friday afternoons baking cakes in lingerie?'

'I don't usually.' I blushed.

'Sorry, I'm embarrassing you. I just wanted to say thank you properly. Soberly.'

'Consider it done. Pretty flowers. I'm easily pleased.'

He looked so calm and sensible, sitting there, smiling at me shyly. Who knew what might happen next.

As it was, I jumped in the air with another loud knock on the window. A big, cheery face looking in, pipe in mouth, with Santa Claus hair. *Of course. The Brigadier! About the rent.*

He burst in with his usual rush of energy and good humour, dressed in his tweed jacket and green cords.

'Daisy, how are you?' boomed Pippa's grandpa, looking at my get-up, then glancing at Michel.

Michel stood to leave. 'I should go. See you some other time.'

'Yeah.' I answered. 'Thanks for the flowers.'

97

'Oh, I almost forgot,' said Michel. 'The cash!'

He handed the cab money over in an envelope.

I saw him to the door.

'Daisy?' he said.

'Yes?'

'May I ask you a question?'

'You may. I may not answer it,' I said.

'Why were you at the awards ceremony anyway?'

I swallowed hard. I've often wondered how differently this whole story would have been if I'd just told the truth at this point. But somehow, I didn't want him to know that I was an aspiring author — what if I was never published? How embarrassing would that be?

'It's okay — you don't wish to say,' he said, turning to go.

'No, it's not a problem,' I replied, thinking up a story. 'I was invited there by an author — Gary Hopper, an SAS guy.'

'Ah, right,' he said. 'The guy at the table. Is he your boyfriend?'

'Not exactly.'

'Do you have a boyfriend?'

The Brigadier harrumphed at this point.

'Please excuse me,' I said. 'I really must — '

'Yes, of course. See you around,' said Michel.

After Michel had left, the Brigadier turned to me.

'I say, Daisy,' he remarked, looking quite blatantly now at my kimono and the envelope of cash in my hand, then glancing at the retreating Frenchman. 'Are you resorting to this kind of thing to meet the rent payments? A nice girl like you?'

How embarrassing! He thinks . . .

'I, erm, well,' I began. 'It's not how it looks.'

He sat down and I brought some tea and cake to him.

'We can go easy on payments, you know.'

'Give me a minute, please. I need to change. I was just playing at dress-up when he arrived.'

'Right you are,' he said. Then, under his breath, 'Girls nowadays.'

I went off to my room and pulled on a huge polo and jeans.

We each enjoyed a nice little cake (my second) and said no more about the rent.

'You and Kitty keep this place very nicely,' he said. 'But I don't want the place to get a bad name. See if you can straighten yourself out, will you?'

He clearly wasn't sure about what he'd witnessed, and I didn't think that any amount of further explanation was necessarily going to have an effect.

I nodded, feeling ashamed for appearing like a prostitute, and even more ashamed that I didn't deny it properly.

As I looked across at the Brigadier, I remember thinking, *I must get out of this mess. I will become financially strong, independent and prosperous. This humiliation has to end.*

21

Turning Point

It was a relief when the Brigadier left, with the rest of the fancies wrapped and placed in a Quality Street tin, and a vast pile of Pippa's mail. He kissed me goodbye and told me: 'Be a good girl. You're a pretty girl. You don't need to do that. Especially with seedy old French chefs.'

So, he had recognised Michel Amiel.

'It's not what you — '

'Never complain, never explain!' he boomed, banging the door shut behind him.

I needed a lie down after all that. I pulled down the blind on the kitchen window and made my way to the sofa.

My face turned as pink as a rose for at least fifteen minutes. I thought about my desperate situation. *The solution lies in your own mind. Only you can change your life. You have a chance with Branwell. A glimmer of hope. The answers are inside you.*

As I lay on the sofa, I could still see the look in Michel's eyes as I stood icing the cake in the lingerie, with the kimono hanging off my shoulders. What was it? Amusement? Not exactly. More than that. He melted in front of me, became defenceless. Was he enchanted, even?

That look. I know what it was.

The realisation hit me like an explosion in my brain.

Desire.

The humiliation of the afternoon subsided and I smiled at the unscripted, accidental-ness of the whole crazy scene. And then it came to me. The book. An idea for my book. It seemed so obvious I didn't know why I hadn't thought of it sooner.

Food and lingerie. The perfect recipe for seduction.

This is how to get men in your thrall.

All that melting, beating, blending, creaming, baking and icing. Carried out in a variety of delicious little lace numbers from Voluptas. Topped off with dating tips and lessons in love. This would be more than a rival for *Kiss Chase*. What if I could think of a cake or a meal to suit romantic occasions? First date? First kiss? Sixth Date Sex? I began to make notes on my laptop.

Think of other big romantic occasions . . .

Christmas, First Sunday lunch party, country cottage weekend, flat-warming, meet the in-laws, engagement party? *This could be great fun.* Tarts, crumpets, pies, cupcakes, honeymoon-buns, fancies . . . hey, I could call it *French Fancy*.

I almost messaged Branwell instantly, but, no, that would be rash as I still had a week, so decided to start writing first. In fact, I couldn't stop the flow of ideas.

22

The First Draft

The ingredients of the book combined together quickly. I headed up the chapters:

First Date
First Lunch
First Picnic
First Kiss
Sixth Date Sex
IN LOVE
Country Cottage
Christmas
Party!
Flat Warming
In-laws to Tea
Surprise Him!
Six-Month Snap
Make-up Tricks
Anniversary
Engagement
Wedding

I didn't even look up from my laptop when Kitty came in from work.

'Hi, Kitty! You okay?'

'Yeah. You've got 'flow'?' she asked.

'Yes, sorry. Something came to me. A lot of

things, actually. A whole pile of ideas.'

'Cool!'

Kitty pottered around, boiling the kettle, taking milk from the fridge. She made a pot of tea for us and produced some dainty sandwiches on an antique, fluted plate, then sat at the table, checking her phone.

'Oh. Nice flowers,' she commented.

'From Michel Amiel.'

'I see. He came here with them, or sent them?'

'Came here,' I said.

'Bloody hell.'

'What?'

'That's interesting.'

'Yeah, well. That's the least of it,' I revealed.

'Meaning?'

'I was wearing nothing but a corset and stockings when he arrived — I was trying to get inspiration for a lingerie crime novel whilst baking a cake.'

'Death by sponge cake? How terrifying! Suffocation? Choking? Or poison?'

'God knows what I was thinking, Kitty. Anyway, I covered up with a kimono, welcomed him here, and we had quite a good time, actually. Dancing a little, eating fancies, talking about life. And then Pippa's grandpa arrived to discuss putting up the rent — while Michel was here.'

'Flipping hell! The rent's going up?'

'Not any more. I'll explain. Michel gave me cash for the cab we got after the awards thing — remember I had to pay for it as he lost his wallet?'

'Yes, I sort of remember that.'

'And now I'm pretty sure the Brigadier thinks I'm working as a whore out of financial desperation!' I made a noise between a giggle and a sob.

Hoots from Kitty. 'That's too funny! I wonder if he'll mention it to Pippa.'

'It's hilarious. But on the upside, he's leaving the rent as it is. Just so long as I curb the prostitution on his premises!'

'God, I just go out to work for the day . . . '

'I'd love to tell you more, but I am possessed by my literary voice.'

'Ha! You literary types! Your 'voice', darling! I'll get the details later. Carry on with your lingerie crime novel. Strangled by suspenders whilst eating a strawberry tart?'

'No, it's not that any more. Michel gave me an idea. Another idea.'

'No! You seduced him!?' cried Kitty.

I paused for effect.

'No. But I really do think I quite possibly could have done.'

'Wow. Daisy! What's going on? This year is so different from last already.'

'Something *is* different. The year is not different. *I* am different. And I'm just getting started.'

Apart from giving me Twitter updates now and again about our hottest men 1 to 10, which were soliloquised rather than addressed to me, Kitty just floated around, bringing me from time to time a bowl of fluffy scrambled eggs, a fruit salad in a cut-glass bowl, and a ramekin dish filled with cashew nuts.

This is work? I was having so much fun. The author voice just bubbled up from somewhere, as though it had been waiting for this moment.

Sixth-Month Snap — Raspberry Chocolate Cake to the Rescue . . .

SURPRISE HIM! The six-month snap happens to us all. You know how it is, the first flush of romance is being replaced by a wave of apathy, a spate of rows and a plague of raucous, rival hen and stag weekends. He's more excited about his season ticket and games console than the prospect of cosy weekends together. On the one hand, he's a great big disappointment all of a sudden. You believed that he really did love opera and ballet, but, shockingly, it was lies to get you into bed! But on the other hand, you still like him loads and need to get him to look at you like that first night all over again. What's a girl to do?

This requires a SHOCK strategy! He thinks you're the girl next door with the white T-shirt bras and matching knickers? He thinks wrong! Dress in something you've never worn for him before, a vampish red silk and lace push-up bra, with silk stockings and killer heels — and bake him this luscious chocolate cake creation, topped with crushed raspberries and delicately whipped Chantilly cream. He will look at you in a whole new light . . .

23

French Fancy

I whipped up twenty thousand words over the weekend. My first literary offering, written in the shop and declined by all, had taken me over two years to write. *How can this be forming so quickly? Does that mean it's rubbish?*

I had in mind a line I'd once read in a magazine: 'Louisa M. Allcott wrote *Little Women* in the space of a few weeks as she needed the money.' I'd always thought that a book must take years and years to write if it was to be good. But that phrase gave me hope. I researched the topic of fast-penned hits. *Casino Royale* by Ian Fleming. *The Prime of Miss Jean Brodie* by Muriel Spark. *A Clockwork Orange* by Anthony Burgess. *Come on, Daisy. Speed might be a good thing when it comes to books.*

Of course, *French Fancy* was going to be no *Little Women!* But the principle seemed to help me.

Nothing else matters. Only this book. These words. This creation. Branwell will love it. A publisher will love it. Readers will love it. It will change my life.

I slept for just a few hours on Saturday night, even then handwriting notes on the pad by my bedside during the night and dreaming ideas as I slept. Back to my laptop in the morning, a bowl of muesli in hand.

Sunday sped by. In the evening, I felt ready to evaluate my work.

Please may this not be gibberish when I read it back.

I lit a lavender and vanilla candle in my room, washed my face with cool water and brushed my hair. I hadn't realised that my head was aching where my hair was caught in a tight band, and my neck and shoulders were in tight, angry knots.

Read it, Daisy. See how it sounds.

I was nervous about reading my words, afraid I wouldn't like it.

Opening the laptop, I lay on my bed, propped up on three pillows.

French Fancy by Daisy Delaney

I stopped for a moment.

Daisy Delaney? Does that sound right? Do I really want people to know this is my book? Maybe I should call myself something else? Yes, think of a nom de plume, Daisy!

I wrote down all the words associated with the book. Cake, Love. Love, Cake. *What about Miss Lovecake? Or Lydia Lovecake? Lucy! Lucy Lovecake sounds young and fun and fresh. Written by Lucy Lovecake. Perfect. She sounds a bit naughty, fun, feminine.*

French Fancy by Lucy Lovecake.

It was decided.

When I read it all back, I was struck by the fact that it didn't sound like my thoughts at all. I liked it. It had me gripped, as though I hadn't

107

written it. Crazily, I didn't always know what was coming next. How could that be?

It could be a vanity thing that I like it so much. I must get another opinion before I send this to Branwell.

I hardly knew where the content had come from, then reflected that I had experienced a lot of dating vicariously through girlfriends, TV shows, films, and novels and it was clearly all stored in my mind. All that secret watching of *Sex in the City* and *Gossip Girl* in my teens had obviously led to Lovecake.

Of course, I'd had some dating fun with Tom Percy. Before it all went horribly wrong. We'd been quite the glamorous couple to watch in our last year at art school.

24

The Letter

I was feeling buoyant after the read-through of *French Fancy* so decided to read the new letter from Tom. I went to the drawer and opened the envelope carefully.

16 Banbury Avenue
Islington
T: 07842666547

Dear Daisy
I don't know if you get these letters, but I will keep writing to you at your parents' address in the hope that one day you will write back. I also hope that one day you will forgive me and will see these letters as a testimony to my never-ending love for you. I have to live with my regrets.
*   Someone on Facebook said you work in a lingerie store, but she wouldn't say where? Much as I can see you in such a shop, I do hope that your own beautiful designs have been picked up and that next thing we know, there will be the Daisy Delaney range of bridal lingerie. I'll never forget you in that slip of silk we bought in Paris. You are always in my thoughts.*
*   I would love to know what you're doing, even though I know you won't tell me where you live. What harm is there in updating me? Please do consider it.*

Next summer, I am launching a range of swimwear and shoes, and a few bits of bedding for John Lewis. Can you believe it? Remember how rude our tutor Anna MacDonald always was about my swimwear designs? I'll be sending her a selection! That's if she still works at the art college in Edinburgh. Can you believe it's over five years since we both arrived in London? Funny how you tend to think things will be as you left them . . . they never are. No doubt you have changed too. As for me? I am quieter, more reflective. I suppose my carefree days are gone, with how I behaved. I am ashamed.

I hope your mum and dad are okay. I have some news for you. My grandmother died. Do you remember meeting her at the graduation lunch at the Prestonfield House Hotel? She gave me such a hard time about hurting you. She was dead right. I was a fool. I regret everything, and wish I could make it right.

I'd like to invite you to my range launch party in the summer, as my personal guest. It's on 5th August at Liberty's. I will send the details and I'll be looking for you there.

Love you always,
Tom

Too late, Tom Percy. Mere words. You can't stop trying because for once you didn't get your own way. You wanted me back, but I had gone forever. It's a personal challenge to you now — to bring me back into your life. To hurt me again? Well, enjoy your launch. Enjoy your life. I am writing a book. One day, I'll be having a launch party of my own.

Somehow the thought of surprising Tom Percy

with my racy book really motivated me. He had been so cruel to me. Made me feel like a naive country girl lacking in sophistication. Well, I suppose I was, compared to Princess Elisha Von Hapsburg! She was descended from the French royal family; her father claimed he was the rightful heir to the French throne. He started chasing a life with dukes, earls, countesses and royals. I couldn't compete. I became quieter and more subdued. He found me changed, he said. 'I have changed because you have,' I explained. We rowed. I cried, became 'pathetic'. It was over.

The worst sort of betrayal, I always thought — for status, not love. Of course, it hadn't lasted. The endless round of European balls and house parties. Tom wasn't really like that, but his ambition was a powerful, Macbeth-style force within him. And he did meet all sorts of designers and celebrities during his royal days, and was happy to trade off connections through the princess. People said he dumped her after a ball at the Crillon Hotel in Paris. Who knows? Next thing I read, she was dating a Chelsea footballer.

When I was feeling very sorry for myself, I wondered if that was the way to play life. The Tom Percy way. To use people who are useful, for short or long periods, then move on, taking all that you've gained with you.

The way to play life is my own way. That's what I'm doing.

I gave the sample text to Kitty to read late on the Sunday night. While she snuggled up on the sofa with my laptop, I went for a hot bath to ease my aching shoulders. The odd thing was that I wasn't even nervous of what she'd think. I knew it was right.

25

The Wait

'Well?' I said, as I stood in the hallway in my fleecy robe, combing my wet hair, peering into the sitting area.

Kitty said nothing but got up, came towards me and flung her arms around me. 'It's going to sell millions of copies. I mean it. It's fun, different, relevant. I love it!'

'Oh, Kitty. You're so biased, but thank you anyway. It means a lot to me that you love it. It really does. Can you check the recipes for me?'

'Sure. I can even help you to create brand new recipes especially for the book.'

'Great. I will not forget all your support.'

If this is ever published, I will dedicate it to Kitty. And help her escape.

I was exhausted but took my time over the cover letter to Branwell.

From: Daisy Delaney
To: Branwell Thornton
Subject: Submission 2

Hi Branwell
How are you? I am attaching some words which came to me after a recent (potentially) amorous encounter. I've called it French Fancy. It is

written by 'Lucy Lovecake'. It's about dating and cakes and lingerie. It's about seduction and the delicious games we play in love. I hope you like it. Most of all, I want it to be fun.

I've been thinking about the national obsession with baking. We have somehow entered the third wave of feminism where women want to have traditional skills. Not for everyday use; not like our great-grandmothers who baked on Mondays and Thursdays as one of their many responsibilities. But rather, something we do for leisure. Of course, men bake cakes too. As for the lingerie tips — we know that sex sells, don't we? But it's more to do with style and allure and the sensuousness of silk against your skin. And dating dilemmas are perennial, so we have a bit of everything in there, don't you agree?

I very much look forward to hearing what you think!

All best wishes,

Daisy (Lucy Lovecake!)

I flumped in an exhausted heap after this.

Following a deep sleep, all too short, I got up for work on the Monday morning, trying not to feel that my days working in a boring routine were numbered.

I don't have a book deal. Even if I get a deal, it will take months, maybe years, for the book to get to the shops. Then it will take ages for the shops to pay the publishers . . .

Real life was going to carry on for a while, alas. Maybe forever more.

I hardly dared look at my e-mails because I

was going to be so disappointed if Branwell didn't get back. I unsubscribed to scores of messagers because I couldn't bear the false hope of the pointless ping.

But after I'd opened the shop and done my morning jobs, which involved replying to messages on Voluptas's social media sites and a quick dust and mop, I had a furtive look at my personal e-mails.

Yes!

There was something in from Branwell already!

My heart raced.

Brace yourself, Daisy.

I could hardly look, but summoned the courage. Damn, it was an auto message, saying that he was on holiday for the next two weeks!

Shit, why do people have to go on holiday? It's so self-indulgent! Just when I get my inspiration too.

I busied myself around the shop that week, deep-cleaning, reorganising, papering one wall with a roll of vintage paper I'd found in Francesca's place. At other times, I browsed on the internet for outfits for my book launch party at the Ritz, or maybe the Orangery at Kensington Palace? I put all thoughts of hearing from Branwell out of my mind. Clara breezed in and out at the start of the week, but on the Wednesday flew off to New York with her husband, who was due to sign a merger deal between his family banking firm, Standings, and the Bank of New York.

'That sounds exciting!' I said.

'Yes and no.'

'Why 'no'?'

'He's really anxious about it. Feels a traitor to his great-grandfather who started Standings.'

'I can imagine. Money isn't everything, though.'

'Too true. I've told him that. If he'd rather run it as a small concern, why not?' she said.

'And what did he say to that?'

'He said I don't understand all the factors. Which patently I don't.'

'What will you do in New York?' I asked.

'I'm going to go to a few vintage clothing auctions. You know how many old-money families have heritage in New York. The Forbes, the Astors, the Roosevelts, the Lowells. I might just pick up a little something with great provenance. We could do with some new items to get people talking.'

'That would be wonderful,' I said. 'Any fancy social events? Can you get all dressed up?'

'Well, when the deal is signed, we're supposed to be going to Eleven Madison Park. I'm sure that will be quite fancy.'

'Sounds it. Madison anything sounds it. You will be the belle of the ball.'

It was true. Clara had luminous skin, expressive dark blue eyes, slender limbs, exquisite hands, and elegant poise.

'Ha! So kind, but I'll just wait for the jibes about my 'British teeth'. Gosh, I think there are two that are slightly differently sizes! Heavens!'

Clara said her goodbyes — never a fast operation — which involved taking leave of

116

Francesca, and James Jolly too. Eventually, she was gone and I felt lonely without her chatter.

I checked Voluptas's Facebook page.

A couple of new likes — and a new message.

Gary Hopper, secret agent, from the book awards, had found us on Facebook!

I opened the message: 'I met Daisy Delaney recently, I believe she works here? Can you give her my number: 07654 222 133.'

Ah, the power of the lace.

I looked at Gary's page.

Gary jumping from an aeroplane with a parachute. Gary in a diver's suit. Gary in ski mode. Gary in a pin-striped suit. In a summer-weight beige suit. Gary clearly *was* James Bond. He was the most ostentatious secret agent on record.

26

Flow

I slept well that week, and I often dreamt of a time when I had not a worry in the world. I lay beneath a tree in a park, with sun-dappled grass to either side, dotted with daisies.

An amazing development on Thursday morning. I was in the back shop, lining drawers in a distressed antique dresser with orange-blossom scented papers, when an e-mail popped in. I dashed over to the laptop. From the great man himself! Branwell Thornton had messaged me.

I clicked on the message so many times that it took ages to open. Cursing myself, I took deep breaths and waited for all to be revealed.

From: Branwell Thornton
To: Daisy Delaney
Cc: Bea Gibson
Subject: Re: Submission 2

Dear Daisy,
Well, this is a first. I have never sent an e-mail from my annual holiday before — to an unpublished author anyway. I had to contact you to say that I LOVE the manuscript you sent over. I absolutely adore it. I think it will do very well. Can I ask you to do the following before my return:

Talk about other romantic settings, maybe log cabins, beach houses, possibly even romantic cities and venues of the world?

Think about some 'scripted' anecdotal stuff. You know the sort of thing: 'When Kate met Jamie, she said there was an immediate attraction, but both were unsure, until . . . ' etc.

I'd like to get this out to the big publishing houses as soon as possible. I'll try a couple of small publishers too, as our insurance policy. I was thinking of Glass & Co. and Bluebells — they did 'The Hen Weekend'. Check all of them out. We need to discuss if we'd grant TV and film rights. I'll get Bea to arrange a meeting for when I'm back. How does that sound?

Well done, Daisy. I'm feeling really excited about this! Well, it's time for another piña colada.

Yours,

Branwell

I got up from the little desk in the back shop and clasped my hands to my face. I paced around. Re-read the message. Forgot to breathe. Then took deep breaths. It was the most exhilarating moment of my life. *Branwell Thornton loves my book!*

'Francesca!'

She came running. 'Is this good or bad?' she asked. 'I can't take much more of this, Daisy!'

'Read this,' I said, pointing to the screen.

Her eyes eagerly swept over the e-mail. When she looked back to me, her expression was a mix of pride and sadness. 'Oh, Daisy. I'm going to miss you when you leave here.'

★ ★ ★

I was living in a permanent state of excitement and, of course, FLOW after that. This was annoying for others, according to Francesca next door. As well as busying away on the changes suggested by Branwell, I had rearranged everything in the shop several times. I'd washed the skirting boards, re-labelled all stock and set up a website for selling items to a wider audience.

At the weekend, there was a call on my mobile from Clara.

'Hey, Clara, are you still in New York?'

'Yes.' A little, quiet voice. Not like Clara at all.

'Are you okay?'

'Not exactly, Daisy.'

'What's the matter? Can I help?'

'It's Philip.'

'What about him?'

'His deal. It didn't happen. They did some last-minute due diligence. Said Standings isn't even solvent. No deal. No cash.'

'So, surely he can just run it as before? Isn't that what he wanted, deep down?' I said.

'It's not that simple.'

'I'm sure it's not.'

'You see, this due diligence done by the Bank of New York has unearthed something even Philip didn't know about. Someone on his team has been trading illegally . . . ' Her voice faltered.

'Oh no! Oh Clara. It's okay. It'll be okay. It's only money.'

'It's really not okay, Daisy. Turns out we're bankrupt.'

27

Prim & Proper

When Clara returned to the shop the next week, she was quite altered.

'I have said to Philip that I will make economies,' she explained.

'Such as?'

'I'm going to make my own juices! I've bought a NutriBullet.'

'Good. Save money, get healthy. That's a bogof.'

'Yes. And also, I'm axing my weekly laser facial at Gunters.' Her voice caught over the word 'Gunters'. It meant a lot to her, the laser facial.

'I see. Well, a lot of people swear by Nivea cream.'

She rolled her eyes. 'Plus — and I hope you can help me with this — I'm going to see if this place can make a proper profit for once. We'll introduce some contemporary lines. Some Ultimo. Some Eve's Secret Garden.'

Eve's Secret Garden! How unbearable it would be to see echoes of my own designs here in the shop!

'Anything but Eve's. I don't trust them,' I said.

'Okay, well, we need items which sell at high-end high street prices. We need to boost turnover. Generate sales, and web sales too.'

'I'm ahead of you there. I set up a little website while you were away!' I revealed.

'Did you really? Thank you, Daisy. And this place looks immaculate. I'm really going to need you. We'll turn this around. I'll call in favours with Annabel and all the magazine editors she knows. Although most detest her. I'm going to ask Francesca if we can take over the whole frontage again. Maybe start some bridalwear.'

It was wonderful to see Clara so fired up. The calamity had brought out the businesswoman in her, in theory at least. Time would tell if she could really up her game, but I had seldom seen her eyes so alive. I didn't have the heart to tell her about my great e-mail. No need to give her extra things to worry about. I tipped off Francesca to keep my news on the down-low too.

★　★　★

One morning the following week, about eleven o'clock, Clara sent me out on a banking errand.

'There's no rush to get back,' said Clara. 'I've got some phone calls to make. Can you just deliver this to the front desk at HSBC, please?'

'What are you up to, Mrs Standing?'

'Wheeling and dealing, all in a day's work.'

That was the unbelievable thing, Clara *was* actually working full days now. I'd seen a card on her desk, detailing a Leo Packard, SME business consultant, and I knew she'd made an appointment about a bank loan at the local HSBC.

I hope she knows what she's doing.

'Okay, I'll drop by on Kitty while I'm out, if that's fine with you?'

'Sure. Take your time.'

As well as being concerned about Clara's situation, I couldn't stop worrying about Kitty these days, knowing how unhappy she was at work, and with the way Charlie was carrying on. I pulled my white fun fur jacket about me as I went along the high street. The chill wind of winter was still in the air, even though the compacted snow had thawed and given way to some tiny signs of spring, such as clumps of sweet snowdrops and clusters of golden crocus.

I handed the letter into the bank for Clara and was just slipping into Prim & Proper when I heard someone calling my name from the pavement on the other side of the road. My heart fluttered as I turned round. It was Michel Amiel. I waved, and gestured that I was going inside. He came across and followed me in.

'Long time, we don't see,' he said.

'Yes, how's tricks?'

'Excuse me?'

'How's life?'

'Good, in some ways,' he said. 'Shall we have coffee?' He nodded towards a free table at the window.

'Sure, as long as it's quick. I'm working. Technically.'

Kitty came bounding over to greet us.

'Daisy!' she said, hugging me.

'Hey, Kitty! I just don't get to see enough of you. Had to drop by. Been a while . . . '

123

'Yes, breakfast was ages ago. Glad you did.'
She looked at Michel.

'Oh sorry, this is Michel Amiel. You remember, from the Shanghai party at the V&A? We just bumped into each other — yet again.'

'Hi!' she said.

'I remember you,' said Michel. 'Both of you. Obsessing with Beau Bonas, yes?'

She laughed. 'He's so last month. That fracas at Heathrow. Ugly.'

'Right. I'd never do a fracas, I'm sure,' said Michel, all faux-innocence.

We laughed and chatted until there was a shout from the kitchen. It was Charlie.

'Oi, Kitty! Get back in here. There are four orders waiting.'

'Oh God! I'll fall behind. Excuse me,' she said. 'I'll be back to take your order in a moment.'

Michel rolled his eyes towards the kitchen.

'I know. He's a beast.'

'I suppose I am too. But only when someone is as strong and nasty as I am. He's exploiting his power. I don't like to see that. She should leave,' advised Michel.

I agreed.

We sat down and I took off my coat, feeling rather boring this time in a black ribbed polo and black jeans. I couldn't even remember if I was wearing make-up. I glanced at myself in the big gilt mirror. Just eyeliner, but my hair, though technically in desperate need of a wash, looked rather cool in a messy Bardot sort of way, or so I convinced myself anyway.

Kitty came to take our order. Two Americanos

and two *pasteis de nata*.

'With cinnamon,' Michel and I said at once.

Our eyes met momentarily.

'All good at the cookery school?' I asked.

'Yes, more or less. A few teething problems,' he said, 'but no lack of takers. I think we picked the right district. This place is at the aspirational end of aspirational.'

'Yes, I'd agree with that,' I replied. 'Don't know what I'm doing living here. And what about your books?'

'Bad. Auguste says my latest draft is execrable. I'm rewriting it. That's something I've never done before. But listen to me, boring on about things that are of no interest to you.'

I smiled. *Better not focus too much on book things or I might end up divulging about my e-mail.*

He looked at me with his intense, dark eyes. 'How have you been? Selling much lace?'

'Quite a lot. It always picks up for the spring bridal season. Can't complain. Clara, who owns the shop, has ordered a lot of new stock. You should check it out,' I suggested.

'I might do that. You enjoy your work?'

'Yes, I do. It's a good environment. I have a very nice boss. I can suit myself, really. Of course, in time, I'd like to do other stuff, but for now . . .'

There was no point in prattling on about my milkmaid plans if nothing were to come of my book.

'Your accent is not from London?'

'No, that's right. I'm Irish.'

'So why did you come here?'

I paused.

'I'm sorry,' he said. 'I'm being very nosy. Forgive me. I'm curious.'

'It's okay. I came here for love. But it didn't work out.'

'Ah, does it ever?'

'I hope that one day it will.'

He nodded. It was in my mind to ask about Eve Berger, but I thought better of it. However, he brought the subject up.

'I'm having a few romances problems myself right now,' he said.

'Oh? I'm sorry to hear that.'

'Yes, well. Life is complicated. Sometimes it gets so bad that it's better when it's over.'

'Certainly.'

'I got too involved with her — included her in some publishing matters. Big mistake,' he revealed.

'Really?'

I was longing to hear all about publishing matters of any description, but restrained myself.

I sipped the coffee and ate the custard tart, which was creamy and delicious, its smallness being the only problem.

There was an unspoken subject hanging in the air.

'About that day you dropped round,' I mentioned, squirming. 'I'm so sorry about that. I can't quite believe how ridiculous it all was! It would be too far-fetched for a film!'

'Don't apologise. You looked rather amazing. Unforgettable, in fact.'

'How embarrassing. I was trying on some things I'd bought in the shop to see how they fitted. I didn't expect . . . '

'Yes. Obviously. I was somehow relieved to learn that you were alone.'

'Relieved?'

'I mean I would have been jealous of the man, had there been one.'

'Ah. I'm going to take that as a compliment.'

'Please do.'

I blushed. 'Well, I should be getting back to the shop.'

'Sure. Let me get the bill.'

'Thanks. Bye for now,' I said, standing to leave.

'Goodbye. It was nice to see you, Daisy.'

We stood looking at each other a bit goofily. I blushed as I took in his soulful dark eyes, chiselled cheekbones and strong jawline. He didn't look so ugly any more. His hair was still wild, but it looked clean, and I could smell that sandalwood fragrance again, the one which had lingered in the shop after he left.

'I really must dash!' I said at last, tearing myself away.

'Yes, maybe I'll pop by again. To the shop,' he suggested.

'Right, okay. That would be nice. Whenever.'

'Yes, whenever I can.'

'Okay, so, bye.' I leant towards him, kissing his cheeks.

I looked in on Kitty, who was totally flustered in the kitchen, so I blew her a kiss and left.

'Bye, darlin,' called Charlie from his desk.

Oh, fuck off.

As I sprinted out and past the window, Michel was definitely staring at me.

Not one of our Top Ten, but not as bad as I first thought, I suppose.

28

Edited

I didn't have much time to think about ageing French chefs with complicated movie star (ex?) girlfriends because Branwell got back in touch straight after his holiday. He called me. How novel was that?

'Daisy Delaney!' he cried.

I held the phone away from my ear — that big, God-like voice.

'Branwell! Nice to hear from you.'

'What? You sound far away,' he complained.

I had no choice but to bring the handset closer.

'Is that better?' I asked.

'Yes. Much.'

'So, do you have any thoughts?' I asked.

'Well, well, well,' he replied.

'What does that mean?'

'The manuscript is sounding fantastic, Daisy. I'm going to send it over to you with a few tiny suggestions on the tracker software system. Just write on the script, don't worry about all the lines and bubbles and boxes.'

What's he even talking about?

'Great. I'll work on it straight away.' *I hope.*

'It's an absolute winner, Daisy. I've already spoken to a few trusted editors, who love the sound of it. They're just waiting for the submission! Woo-hoo! Jump on the Book Train, we're going to heaven!'

'We are?' *He really is God.*

'Well, at least to King's Cross. Hodder & Stoughton on Euston Road want to take a look. They're part of the Hachette group — MAS-SIVE. Clementine Clancy there thinks it sounds just what she's after! That's what we want, an editor who wants to champion it, make it her breakthrough book as well. Build her talent-spotting reputation on it. I haven't been this excited in ages.'

I was shaking with excitement myself, but I felt that it was all still speculation and that perhaps some caution would have been a good thing in an experienced agent towards an inexperienced author. But Branwell didn't do understatement, and I supposed that was why he was so infectious and successful.

'Well, I don't want us to get our hopes up too soon,' I said.

'Oh, very head prefect. But I like that approach, Daisy Delaney. It's true: nobody ever knows how something will go. Not even a genius such as myself. But you do get a gut feeling after forty years in the game. The next thing is that we'll be asked to publisher meetings to chat it over. Used to be called the Beauty Parade — before that sort of phrase could land you in prison — meaning, you pick who you like best, not the other way around. For their part, they'll want to see that you're marketable.'

'Oh. And am I?'

'I think they'll be happy with your marketability!' he asserted.

'Do you really think so? It's such a shame that I've got my winter body right now. I'm so much more presentable in summer. There's something about candles and fairy lights that leads me to believe that cellulite doesn't matter so much. I'll have to get to the gym, and step up the running. And get my roots done, maybe eyebrow threading — '

'I'll leave that stuff over to you,' interrupted Branwell, obviously quickly losing interest in the small detail of my life. 'I prefer to think women just wake up looking wonderful.'

'And we do, after twelve beauty treatments the day before.'

★ ★ ★

When his suggested changes came over by e-mail, I was instantly confused by the editing software, as I'd expected.

I scanned the many bubbles of comments down the right side of each page.

'*Try another word for romance here. Overuse.*'

'*Add more adjectives, make this more alluring, consider figurative expressions . . .* '

'*You move out of voice here, sounds like you're being disapproving rather than decadent all of a sudden. Stay in Lucy Lovecake character.*'

'*Try to add some anecdotes and characters here. 'When Toby first met Hannah . . .* ''

131

'Think about ways of describing the cakes. What about some puns/double entendres? There's a lot to be said about buns with cherries on top!'

I immediately set about making the changes, but I found I didn't agree about the buns and the cherries.

Can I disagree with God? Do I want a book in the shops which does not say what I wanted to say? Be bold, Daisy.

I sent him a message:

From: Daisy Delaney
To: Branwell Thornton
Subject: Re: Re: Submission 2

Hi Branwell
Thanks for the suggested changes, most of which I agree will improve the script. However, I don't agree about the puns and double entendres. I think it might be a male/female divide thing here. I don't want it to sound smutty and sleazy, like those holiday postcards. Just romantic and a bit playful. I will try to add some humour. Hope that sounds okay with you? I should get this back to you in a day or two.
Best regards,
Daisy

I hesitated before pressing 'send'.

What am I thinking? Just into a potential career as an author and think I know better than forty-years-in-the-game Branwell Thornton?

I took some breaths.

132

But if I don't say what I really think, and the book is rejected all over London, then I will blame it on my inability to make it my own.

I pressed 'send' before any further deliberations.

I just hope he's not exaggerating about the potential of this because I'm going to be devastated if I don't get asked to meet any publishers!

I'd already worked out from the awards evening that there was quite a lot of exaggeration and fakery in the industry. I figured it was to inspire you to keep on writing — until nobody wanted that writing, and then the compliments would dry up.

I felt uneasy as I waited for Branwell to reply, anxious that I might come over as arrogant, or difficult, or even disrespectful.

I didn't hear a thing that day.

He thinks I'm a diva! He's reconsidering. I'm a twit.

I discussed it with Kitty. 'Should I message him and say sorry for challenging his ideas?'

'Absolutely not. What I always think,' she said, 'is that when you really, really want something to happen, you should try to behave as naturally as possible, because that sort of heightened, panicky, intense behaviour can really kill things off, even if they were fine before.'

Wise.

All of the next day, I heard nothing from Branwell.

He's a busy man. I'll hear soon.

He's a busy man, he doesn't need little

know-alls correcting him.

I got so cranky that I sat at night researching publishing, writers, the stories behind books being published. I decided to Google:

Famous books which were rejected at first:
Gone With the Wind by Margaret Mitchell
The Diary of a Young Girl by Anne Frank
The Spy Who Came in From the Cold by
   John Le Carré
The Tale of Peter Rabbit by Beatrix Potter
Little Women by Louisa May Alcott (told:
   'Stick to teaching')
The Jungle Book by Rudyard Kipling
Animal Farm by George Orwell

I was comforted by this. *But what's happened to Branwell?*

29

Approval

I sent the finished manuscript back to Branwell, having included most of the changes he'd suggested. A whole week went by and not a word from him.

He's had a heart attack. He's not getting any younger. Maybe I should call the office.

And then the message came, on the eighth day.

From: Branwell Thornton
To: Daisy Delaney
Subject: Re: Re: Submission 2

Hi Daisy,
Really sorry it's taken me some time to get back to you. We had some problems in the office with regard to London Book Fair. All very tedious. Arguments about book jackets, payment squabbles regarding appearances by some of my authors. Sorted now.
So, the changes you made. Fantastic! And of course, you are quite right not to include the smutty postcard references I suggested. What do I know? I am not a cool young lady-about-town. If you ever need to take issue with an editor — that is exactly the way to do it. Not too

forceful, but measured, considered, respectful.

So, well done to you. All ship-shape and I have been able to send it out reasonably widely! How thrilling is that? And scary! I've listed the houses below and mentioned why I've chosen them. There are, of course, other places, but I think this is a good start, and I have based my choices on conversations, so everything crossed, but don't expect to hear from me for a week or three, okay?

Kindest Regards,
Branwell

List of Houses — *French Fancy* by Lucy Lovecake

Lennox-Cooper — big, generally good author care, can get lost in the system though.

Transworld — very commercial.

Hodder & Stoughton — talented editors.

Ebury — this imprint is a relative newcomer to fiction, mostly non, but some nice stuff in that stable . . . take a look.

Avon Books — this is technically part of HarperCollins, very romance-led.

Penguin Random House — lots of literary imprints, but some very commercial fiction too.

Macmillan — commercial as they come!

Glass & Co — small but good. Lately rave reviews for Cowboys and Engines, and Dancer.

Bluebells — teeny-tiny, might not be here next year, but check out their amazing one-off bestseller, The Hen Weekend.

I did my research. It was incredible to me that Branwell would even think of sending my work to these great places. I went to all the charity shops in Prim Hill and gathered up a pile of novels from the various publishing houses mentioned.

All of these writers would have been unknown and unpublished at one point. Keep believing it can happen.

There were some glorious books. As for *The Hen Weekend*, I'd already read and adored it. It was hilarious, sweet, inspiring, all that line dancing and strawberry wine. I decided to look up Bluebells, who had published it.

Sounds so pretty! I wonder where they are based?

30

A Little Slice of Perfect

Bluebells
A boutique publishing house in rural Oxford-shire which is the brain child of former rock star Dominic McGann, of The Rockits. Based in a barn in his organic farm, Higgledy Piggledy Hens, he says: 'I have plans to publish just two books per year, but to offer a special service to authors, to spot talent, to nurture talent, and to cater for a discerning public. I intend to hit the mass market through social media platforms, but to deliver books which are crafted lovingly in the organic tradition.'

So far the uproariously funny The Hen Weekend has sold over half a million copies worldwide, and is currently being translated into another five languages. Bluebells is about to release The Nightingale's Tale, a story of 'the beauty of birdsong in the pain of grief'.

McGann says that each title produced will be hand-picked by him, and that submissions are welcome. All will be read and considered. For those of you wondering how a rock star can suddenly publish books, Dominic spent five years in New York working for Knopf Doubleday before returning to the county of his birth.

There was a gallery of photographs: a beautiful sandstone manor house. A yard of happy hens. A cool barn-cum-publishing house. Fields of dancing bluebells. The jacket of *The Hen Weekend*. Some sort of staff party, unclear if Dominic McGann was in the frame.

Imagine being published by a rock star! Imagine being published by Penguin Random House! Just imagine being published.

I tried not to think of the whole publishing thing every minute of every day. Tried and failed. I was so obsessed with checking messages that during Sunday lunch in the local pub the weekend after the submissions were made, Kitty confiscated my phone.

We were sitting on two big leather armchairs by a crackling log fire in the Duke & Duck.

'I want to talk to you,' Kitty said after my phone was safely tucked up in her bag.

'About what?'

'Things.'

'Do you mean things in general, or one thing in particular?' I asked.

'The latter.'

'Oh, is everything okay?'

'Not really. It's Charlie.'

It was always Charlie.

'What's happened?'

'I found him with another girl. From the Hammersmith branch. She was over for training. They were in the stockroom. Canoodling — and more.'

She was tearful.

'Oh, Kitty! I'm sorry! The swine!'

139

'It's my own fault. We haven't been getting on, and I really do want to end it, but I need another job first.'

'Have you applied for anything?'

'I started yesterday. I've sent off six application forms already,' she announced.

'That's great. You're bound to get something else. You don't feel like you could just break it off but still work together?'

She shook her head. 'Charlie doesn't break things off. He just adds another girl to the harem, and gets more stressed and horrid every time he does that.'

'He was a bit off-ish that day I was in chatting to Michel. Does he always talk to you like that?'

'Mostly. Sometimes he's very sweet and charming. That really throws me.'

'You've got to get out of there. The sweet and charming thing is probably just when he wants something.'

She nodded. 'Exactly.'

She went to hand my phone back to me.

'Keep it. Let's order lunch,' I said.

31

The Photograph

As we chatted, our roast chicken feasts arrived. Tender meat, covered in delicious light gravy, served with crispy roast potatoes, creamy mash, glazed carrots, honeyed parsnips, green beans and cranberry sauce. I declined the apple crumble and custard, just in case I was called into the board room of Lennox-Cooper come Tuesday to discuss whether I would accept an advance of £50,000. Didn't want them to think I was a total splodge.

That might suggest that all this baking makes you squidgy. Which it does, if you eat it all.

Two glasses of white and I was starting to feel really relaxed.

'Thanks for taking my phone,' I said. 'I'm feeling happy.'

We saw some board games on a shelf and had a game of Monopoly. I managed to buy Euston Road.

'That's where Hodder & Stoughton have offices! Branwell says I'll be going there for a meeting!'

'That would be great!' Kitty exclaimed. 'I'm so delighted for you.'

I suddenly heard myself sounding like my seventeen-year-old self. I'd been approached in

Dublin airport once by a model agency 'scout'. I called my mother immediately afterwards: 'He says I'll be famous. I just need to pay £500 for a portfolio of photographs, then I'll get jobs all over London, Europe and America!'

Was I being delusional? I didn't think so. Branwell wasn't some backstreet chancer. He had all sorts of brilliant authors on his books. Yet I did sound like an impressionable ingénue over this.

Daisy Delaney, you need to toughen up and accept that the world is a big, bad place. And that people sometimes make promises they can't keep.

'Shall we read the Sunday papers?' suggested Kitty, spotting them across the lounge after the Monopoly was over.

'Sure, that sounds good. I haven't read a proper paper newspaper in a hundred years.'

A quick look through the tabloids; nothing of interest in there. How could it be that although I hadn't read a Sunday tabloid in eight years, Eddie Goldsmith's love life still prevailed? Still deceiving with the nanny, but a new nanny. I picked up one of the *Sunday Times* supplements, the style one, filled with features about scary sounding beauty treatments, the sort loved by Clara. Laser facelifts! Injectable wrinkle fillers? No thanks! Also, fashion tips galore — lime and violet would be big in the summer, as well as a return to hot pants — and society parties. But no hats at weddings, girls. As I flicked through, there was a section on film reviews and premieres. I turned the page.

An image startled me. I don't know why I was so shocked, really. But I was. A spread featuring the premiere of *Love on the Rocks*. I'd heard of it, vaguely. I knew that Eve Berger was starring. Apparently, the premiere had been held in London the previous week.

I gulped and felt a lump in my throat.

Michel Amiel and Eve Berger posed together at the recent showing in The Curzon, Leicester Square. They looked very handsome, and very happy, intertwined, smiling. She so delicate and winsome, he so strong and protective of her, bear paw around her tiny waist.

I read the blurb under the picture: 'France's hottest couple, celebrity chef Michel Amiel and the exquisitely beautiful film star Eve Berger, stepped out at Leicester Square last Wednesday . . . '

Last Wednesday? He was busy telling me it was all off just a few days ago. I believed him.

'You okay, Daisy?' said Kitty.

I showed her the photograph.

'It might be an old one?'

'It's not.'

'Well, you think he's an arse anyway, don't you?'

'Yeah. He certainly is.'

But I was a bit less relaxed after that.

32

Country Drive

A sprinkle of rain turned to driving torrents as Branwell and I travelled north from London to Bluebells in the village of Honeycomb, Oxfordshire. We were in Branwell's classic dark green Range Rover, with the satnav directing us.

'This is the proper landscape for this big bad boy,' I said. 'Not your city hops.'

'I suppose.'

My agent looked utterly dapper: elegant suit, designer shirt, silk tie, handmade shoes. Meanwhile, I had decided on a floral tea dress with a vintage cardigan (almost scruffy but just veered to smart) and pretty blue shoes with a heel. Branwell was normally chatty, but today he was not in the cheeriest of moods. A lot of sighing, tutting, harrumphing. Enraged by a confused sheep crossing the road, furious at being stuck behind a trundling tractor, much mumbling — 'Couldn't they just straighten out these bends and twists? It's not Roman Britain any more.'

'Did you bring wellies?' I asked.

'No. Who takes wellies to a business meeting?'

'Country folk, country ways.'

'So, did you bring wellies, Princess Smarty-pants?'

'I brought my Joules wellibobs, if you must know,' I said.

'You think it's going to be dirty?'

'It's in the countryside, and doesn't the website say it's on a chicken farm, so, common sense? But then, I'm a farmer's daughter.'

'I'm sure it will be a proper set-up with an office which happens to be on a country estate, all very slick. Paved,' he told himself.

'It says the publishing offices are in a barn. I don't think it's going to be like a stately home, you know.'

'Are you trying to get me to turn back to London? I'm actually allergic to the great outdoors. There's too much sky and grass. I'm not used to it.'

He put the wipers on super fast.

'Well, I think it's really exciting,' I said, 'heading out of the city for a business meeting. It's the reverse of what usually happens!'

'Yes, isn't it very charming, driving through sheets of pelting rain to a place with virtually no publishing history, which might be more suited to wellies and a boiler suit than traditional business dress.'

'Well, you planted the whole Bluebells idea in my mind . . .'

'Yes, as a backup. As a plan Z. The thing is, Daisy,' he said, 'rural boutique publishers are all well and good, but everything is done on a shoestring. And it's not as if we don't have some interest from the big ones. We've had great meetings in London. My other clients would kill for such meetings.'

I looked out of the window, silent for a minute. It was true that we had been at two publisher meetings in London already, which had both gone well. Branwell was feeling confident of an offer to publish from at least one of those, and such was his relationship with certain editors, he clearly knew that was going to happen.

As I thought, my gaze drifted to the weather outside. It was a pity about the rain, and that it was the tail end of winter, really. Maybe if the sun had been shining and the hedgerows bejewelled with exquisite wildflowers, then he would have enjoyed our jaunt away from the metropolis. We'd reached the chocolate box village of Marsh Riding.

'To be perfectly honest,' he continued, 'we shouldn't be wasting our time on this. What experience does this guy have? *The Hen Weekend* might be a one-hit wonder.'

I found myself immediately defensive. 'Dominic McGann was well thought of at Doubleday in New York. And you said that the big publishers were a bunch of hard-up 'tightwads' these days — when it comes to untried new things, at least.'

'Yes, but they are tightwads with clout. With international connections, relationships with retailers, foreign publishers, offices in other cities, heritage. You need for this book to sell in the US as well. In China. Europe. The world. Otherwise, you won't make money, and that's that. You do want to make money?'

'Of course.'

'Well, let's see this as an indulgence. I don't want you to seriously consider *French Fancy*

146

finding a home at Bluebells, okay?'

'I promise I'll be realistic.'

'Pah!' We barrelled along the country roads silently for a few miles.

'Are we running late?' I said.

'No, we have plenty of time.'

'Well, why are you driving so fast?'

'It's this car. It wants to go fast.'

'Relax. Does the countryside always make you nervous?'

'Sometimes. I don't have a good track record with animals.'

33

Bluebells

A hand-painted sign dangling from a post by the roadside read: Bluebells. There was a vast, magnificent twig sculpture of a chicken at the double gates. We turned into the driveway and a large notice stated: Higgledy-Piggledy Farm — Free-range chickens & Henhouse eggs here.

'Hens okay with you?' I said.

'A chicken farm that publishes books,' mumbled Branwell. 'I've heard of the scratchings of a demented hen . . . '

'Well, they did publish *The Hen Weekend*.'

'True.'

'Hope they don't pay in chicken feed,' I quipped.

'You're over-egging it.'

'Boom. Boom.'

The twisting driveway seemed very dark on that pouring, wet morning, overhung with bony branches from trees on both sides, but as a semblance of daylight resumed at the far end of the drive, a small neo-classical manor house came into view.

'This place looks nice,' I said, recognising it from the website.

'Not bad, I suppose,' Branwell conceded.

On the steps leading up to the door stood a

handsome man with a mop of dark hair, wearing jeans, wellies, and a cosy, patterned sweater. He leant on a big umbrella and, on noticing the car, began to wave.

'That must be our man,' said Branwell. 'In what way is that a suitable outfit for a business meeting, eh?' By which he clearly meant, 'Oh damn it, I am ludicrously overdressed.'

'I suppose that must be Dominic McGann.' In fact, I knew it was, courtesy of Google.

As we pulled up, he moved out of tableau and took great lurching strides towards us.

I tried to jump out of the car before it had fully stopped.

'Whoa, don't act so keen,' said Branwell.

After making a second, more sedate exit from the Range Rover, I saw that the man was younger than he seemed in photographs, perhaps about thirty-five.

'Dominic McGann,' he said, offering his hand. 'You must be Daisy. Great to meet you.'

'How do you do?' I said.

'Love your book, I must say,' he said, opening the umbrella and holding it over my head.

Branwell then introduced himself.

'Very good of you to come all this way to see us *in situ*,' said Dominic. 'I really appreciate it.'

'Just a shame about this filthy weather,' said Branwell, looking at the great splashes of mud on his car, then coming across to share the cover of the umbrella.

'Yes, it's a bit grim. Come inside, and I'll get some coffee on the go, said Dominic, starting to lead the way towards the big house. Then he turned back round. 'Everything that's important happens in my kitchen, by the way.'

Branwell rolled his eyes and picked his feet up carefully over the wet ground leading to the house.

Dominic took us in through the front door, which opened onto a lovely square reception hall with a flagstone floor covered in fine Persian rugs. Lots of interesting paintings hung on the russet walls too. As soon as we stepped inside, a ferocious melee of barking broke out.

There was no time to explain Branwell's feelings about animals. Suddenly, four noisy dogs breenged towards us: a shaggy wolfhound, a lithe black lab puppy and two little terriers. It was impossible to know whether to protect upper body parts or feet as they circled us, pack-like, one jumping up, while another went for our ankles.

'Get them away!' cried Branwell.

'He doesn't like animals,' I added.

'Sorry. Sorry about this,' said Dominic. 'I'll get Tilly to take them away.'

Branwell let out a yelp, pointing to his foot. There was a puddle around it, and the shoe was soaked too.

'Oh no!' I said.

Banger, the young Labrador, was sinking his teeth into the bottom of Branwell's left trouser leg now.

Branwell's eyes almost popped out of his head with a mix of rage and fear. He yanked his leg furiously away from the dog.

'I'm afraid he thinks it's a tug-of-war game,'

explained Dominic. 'Let me see if I can get him to let go.'

'If you wouldn't mind,' said Branwell.

Dominic bent down to cajole Banger, who eventually did let go, though he took a piece of Saville Row trouser leg with him.

34

The Kitchen

A pretty young woman, Tilly, came to round up the dogs, and we all tried not to stare at Branwell's partially exposed left leg.

'Oh my goodness, I am SO sorry,' said Dominic. 'I will replace them, of course. Why don't you borrow something of mine?'

Branwell considered this for quite some time, in such a way that it seemed likely smoke might soon billow from his ears, then finally agreed.

Tilly reappeared and ushered me into the cosiest of farmhouse kitchens, complete with a central table made from reclaimed wood. A couple of hens toasted their bottoms by the log-burning stove.

Tilly seemed very frazzled. She went into the fridge and produced what looked like a baby's bottle, which she put into the microwave. While it heated, she boiled the kettle for coffee and cut up a large and slightly skew-whiff walnut cake.

'Poor Dom,' she said.

'Puppies!' I said.

'Yeah.'

I recalled bottle-feeding lambs for Dad when he was busy on the farm. I didn't like to imagine what Branwell would make of the hens on his return, so instead I looked around the bright room. It was fully glazed on side, affording a lovely view of a walled garden about to bloom. I then took in the fabulous assortment of cluttered china, glass and pottery on an old dresser. There wasn't much chat coming from Tilly.

'Do you work here full-time?' I asked her.

'No.'

'Ah, do you have another job as well?'

'No.'

Ah, right. That'll be that, then.

A few minutes later, Branwell came sheepishly into the kitchen, now wearing jeans, a cashmere jumper and novelty slippers — in the form of two hedgehogs.

'In for a penny,' he said, shrugging his shoulders. 'I've embraced country life.'

I stifled some giggles. He sat in an armchair by the stove and while Dominic prepared coffee, I pulled up chairs alongside Branwell. He did a double-take when he noticed the hens.

'That's Hattie and Marigold,' said Dominic. 'They're getting on a bit and they like the heat.'

'Know the feeling,' muttered Branwell.

Dominic handed us mugs of steaming coffee and slabs of appetising, oozily iced walnut cake in napkins.

'Well now,' said Branwell after a bite of cake and a sip of rich, black coffee. 'Your website says this is a publishing business?'

'And so it is,' said Dominic with a smirk. 'Right you are.'

Dominic clearly did not feel the need to justify himself too much, but he began to explain as a courtesy. 'I employ a local manager to run the hen and eggs side of things here. I've been in publishing for about eight years. Used to be in a rock band, The Rockits? You might have heard of us?'

We nodded. Of course we had heard of them.

'We did okay, not bad really. Not as well as our manager, but we all came out of it with a bit to invest. I worked in New York, in publishing, then I met my wife and bought this place. My circumstances changed quite suddenly a couple of years ago, and I decided to start the publishing company. *The Hen Weekend* did rather well, and I thought, well maybe I can do more of this . . . You know, it's sold six hundred thousand copies, and we're having to reprint every week.'

Branwell was softening. 'Yes, safe to say I probably wouldn't be sitting here in hedgehog slippers if it wasn't for *The Hen Weekend*,' he said. 'I can see you understand our demographic and that's very important. But what if *Hen Weekend* was a fluke? It does happen. Like the one-hit band. Nobody knows how it was done or how to do it again?'

'Well, I must defend myself there,' said Dominic, retaining his cool charm but stepping up a gear in assertiveness. 'We put a great deal of thought into the marketing of that book. Our thinking was that it would appeal to the market slightly older than its protagonists, and we were dead right. The idea that a bride-to-be plans a hen weekend based round looking after hens, and they stumble upon a stash of strawberry wine and dance in the moonlight, telling stories and doing dares. We knew it would appeal to the organic market, but it's also commercial enough to appeal to city girls looking for something escapist. It wasn't an accidental success by any means, I can assure you.'

Branwell listened intently.

Dominic continued. 'Publishing is a changing industry and bears no resemblance to how it once was. It's all about social media, strategic reviews, celebrity reviews, blogs, vlogs, below-the-line marketing. I know everything about that. I was a specialist in that in New York.'

I nodded enthusiastically.

'Look, Dominic,' said Branwell. 'That all sounds very well and good. But this place seems pretty damned chaotic. I'm here to protect my client, advise her wisely. She has a great book here. Interest elsewhere. What team do you have in place to handle it?'

'Most of it is outsourced. The designs and layouts are done by freelancers, all exchanged by e-mail. There's Tilly. She's going to Oxford to read English. She does a bit of reading and helps me in general. And an editor called Barbara works Tuesdays and Thursdays. I do all the social media stuff. I plan to expand.'

It was clearly an impassioned plea, but even I was starting to wonder about the set-up. There was something about Tilly I didn't like. She'd disappeared, thank goodness, because she was putting me off.

We chatted on a while, long enough for me to think that Branwell saw something worthwhile in the meeting. *Or is he just enjoying that second slice of walnut cake?*

Dominic was very impressive on technology, and Branwell soaked up information about algorithms as I busily wrote notes on my iPad.

I looked up and caught sight of Tilly, looking frantic in the kitchen doorway.

'Oh, Dominic, look. I think Tilly needs you,' I said.

He went to see her, and we heard them chatting in hushed tones. Finally, Dominic said, 'Okay, I'll come and get her.'

'Not another bloody dog!' warned Branwell.

'No, not a dog,' said Dominic. 'Excuse me for a moment.'

He returned quickly, with his arms full. Of a beautiful little girl, perhaps about two years old.

'You're on babysitting duty today, then?' said Branwell.

'Every day, actually.'

'Ah, that must be tough,' said Branwell.

'Well, my wife didn't make it through the birth, I'm afraid. Pre-eclampsia.'

'Very sorry to hear that!' said Branwell, and I mumbled similar condolences.

How absolutely awful.

The baby babbled cutely.

'So, this is Minty,' he said.

I went across to coo, and even Branwell was smitten. Minty had vast blue eyes, with long, dark lashes and blonde curls. She turned her perfect little doll's face towards us, breaking into a pearl-toothed smile.

We could have looked at her all day, and we had a thousand questions and commiserations we would have liked to offer, of course. But it was time to talk about the creative stuff. Tilly took Minty away to the playroom.

35

The Project

I hadn't said much, but the spotlight turned to me now. 'So, Daisy,' said Dominic. 'Love the book. What made you think of it?'

I blushed. 'Just one of those ideas that feels as if you've always had it. But, really, I have to thank Branwell for getting it in shape.'

Branwell stepped in. 'No, it arrived as a great proposition, if you'll pardon the unfortunate expression!'

It was that sort of book — made people giggle and blush.

We chatted over Dominic's vision for launching the 'series'.

Wow, he already sees it as a series!

'What marketing plans do you have?' asked Branwell in a manner which suggested he expected none.

Dominic produced three sheets of A3 paper from the kitchen table, printed with flow charts of his marketing ideas.

'We want to really hype up the mystery of Lucy Lovecake. I think she should remain unknown for about six months into publication. Get everyone talking about the book, and wondering who wrote it. THEN reveal the whole intriguing persona of Daisy Delaney — and I think it's a great backstory, you know, working in the lingerie store, helping your friend with the baking for the tea shop. It's really charming. That stuff Branwell put in the submission e-mail. People are going to love it. Makes ordinary people think they are sitting on their own solutions. We would do lots of publicity photography of Daisy before launch, but hold it all back until we want to explode!'

'Sounds great!' I said.

Branwell nodded.

Dominic continued. 'I thought we'd run a blog linked to three main beauty, baking and fashion blogs in the run-up to launch to create the right fan base,' he said. 'Then, we'll run cake-making demos at bookshops across the country in the week of launch, as well as — '

'Can I just stop you there,' Branwell interjected. 'What if I said to you that one of the bigger publishers is offering to do posters in all the tube stations — can you match that sort of campaign?'

'Well, that's straight advertising, normally associated with an established brand,' said Dominic. 'We'd be more enterprising. For example, we'd approach famous lingerie brands, like Victoria's Secret, and even department stores, such as Harrods, and get them to promote the book. We'd focus on daytime TV interviews, competitions . . . '

Branwell couldn't argue with Dominic's homework. He'd really thought it through.

'What we should do,' said Dominic, 'is to have a pretty cartoon drawing done of 'Lucy

Lovecake'. A bit like you, Daisy, but not so much as you'd know. We can start the branding early by using that image across social media. If I can offer you a decent enough advance, I'd like you to consider working almost full-time on this project before anyone even knows it exists.'

I'll have to see what's best for Clara, especially in her predicament.

'I'd need to consider that,' I said. 'My employer is so good to me. I couldn't leave her in the lurch. Nor could I demand my job back if this all flops.'

'Well, yes. Think it through. Maybe you could work in there three days instead of five?' Dominic suggested.

'That's a good idea,' I said.

'Well, a lot to think about,' said Branwell.

We could hear Minty becoming fractious in the playroom.

'Perhaps we should get going,' I suggested.

'Well, I hope you've heard enough to convince you about how badly we want to do this?' Dominic asked.

'It's been most enlightening,' admitted Branwell, as I nodded in agreement.

'I'm sure we'll be in touch soon,' I added.

Dominic was mortified about Branwell's suit, offering the part demolished trousers on a coat hanger as we left.

Dominic got out his chequebook too.

'That looks like a very expensive suit. How much do you think it would be to replace the trousers? Would £500 be fair?'

'I wouldn't dream of accepting it,' said

160

Branwell. 'All part of the wear and tear of the job!'

They shook hands firmly.

We didn't say much on the journey home. Branwell offered the odd thought, such as, 'Very nice little girl. Damn shame' and 'Talks a good game, that fellow, I'll give him that.'

I was lost in my thoughts. Dominic McGann was deliciously handsome and impossibly cool.

Some days, someone comes into your life. Someone who is going to play a big part in that life, and you could never have predicted it. Today is such a day.

36

The Offers

Within the next two weeks, two full letters of offer to publish *French Fancy* came through. They came to me via e-mail at once, from Branwell. I could see from the dates that the offer from Bluebells had arrived much sooner than the Lennox-Cooper offer, but he had waited for the latter before presenting me with Dominic's. The first to ping into my inbox as a forward was from Lennox-Cooper.

From: Branwell Thornton
To: Daisy Delaney
Subject: Fwd: French Fancy

Dear Branwell,
During a recent acquisitions meeting, the entire team here agreed that we would like to publish French Fancy in the spring of next year. In exchange for worldwide literary and all associated ancillary rights, we offer an advance of £10,500 on royalties at 8%, advance to be paid in equal amounts on signing of contract, on receipt of approved text, and on publication. Thereafter, royalties would be paid in March and September. We would reserve the right of first refusal to publish all associated books.
We look forward to hearing from you.

Yours sincerely,
Mary McCarthy
Publishing Director

I had no experience but I thought that was a lot to ask for in exchange for £10,500 and 8%. The offer from Bluebells was a scanned version of a proper, old-fashioned letter.

The Bluebell Press
Honeycomb
Oxfordshire
OX15PG
23rd March

Dear Branwell and Daisy,

It was my great pleasure to have your company the other day, and please allow me to apologise for the mayhem. It is impossible to express how much we would like to publish this book, and we can only hope that you give us that chance. We are prepared to dig deep, and the terms of my offer are outlined below.

We would plan to publish within four months of signing, and would pay an upfront advance of £18,000, payable in one tranche on signing. We would pay royalties at 9%, payable quarterly.

We would also offer unlimited resources for publicity and marketing campaigns, which, as suggested at the meeting, should begin with all haste, in establishing the online persona of Lucy Lovecake.

Please do not hesitate to get in touch with any questions, or indeed suggestions.

We would work closely with Daisy, seeing her as a key asset in the campaign to make this book widely known and loved.

Yours,
Dominic McGann

I knew that Branwell had ended up really liking Dominic, but that didn't mean he wanted me to be published by him.

'It's very high risk, Daisy,' he said when I called him.

'The whole thing is high risk, Branwell. Look at *The Hen Weekend*. It has outsold lots of contemporary fiction titles released by Lennox-Cooper. And I bet they turned it down.' I had done some research. '*White Wedding* only sold 130,000 copies, according to *The Times Bestseller List*. And that was hailed as the next big thing.'

'True. But . . . '

'But, what? He's offering more money. In one tranche. Higher royalties. What's to dispute?' I persisted.

'I've told you before. Bigger-picture things. Worldwide things. Publishing is not a short-termist occupation. What if Bluebells doesn't even exist next year? Have you thought of that? Your book might never even get to market.'

Good point. It had no heritage or security. I had thought of that.

'Yes, but if that happened, we'd be £18,000 up and could then look elsewhere again,' I said.

'Ha! In theory. But the moment will pass where other places are interested in your book. You can't turn them down and then go back six months later, cap in hand. They might have got hold of something similar by then. They can't

164

help themselves like that. If they lose out on something they wanted, they just create something samey in-house in their own time, claiming originality and trying to get it to the shelves before yours. They are scurrilous, I can assure you, but all with a nice Oxford graduate veneer of gentility.'

That did sound awful. Imagine if my idea is passed off as their own? *But surely we could prove they'd seen it on a certain date?*

No wonder Michel Amiel has more worries, not less, at the top of the tree.

'But there's another plus point to what Dominic is offering,' I continued. 'He wants to publish sooner than Lennox-Cooper. I think, in a way, he can give more to the project than the big house because he has fewer projects on the table, less to distract him. That's what he says on his website, about taking care of new authors. Having met him, I do believe that. And I don't think he looked as if he's about to go bankrupt, do you?'

'Well, no. But from where I was sitting, he already has far too much on his table, Daisy. Maybe not book projects, but other things.'

'I understand, Branwell. But you know, as my mother often says, there are times in life when you have to trust your inner voice, not just straight facts.'

'Well, I've given you my professional opinion. It's your choice, my dear. I beg you to at least sleep on it,' Branwell requested.

'Thank you. I will. I'll call you in a couple of days. Is that okay?'

'Yes, no rush.'

'Okay, bye for now.'

'Bye, Daisy. Speak soon. I'm off to get fitted for a new suit!'

I felt disrespectful for not automatically following Branwell's direction, but I badly wanted to work with Dominic McGann. I tossed and turned over the dilemma for the next two nights. Only Kitty knew, And she, bless her, didn't say, 'It's a nice problem to have,' which is what I knew a majority of people would have said to me.

37

The Decision

Bluebells and all things associated with it had made a huge impression on me, and I couldn't shift the feeling that they would do the best job with my book. I kept recalling a phrase from the meeting at Lennox-Cooper: 'Once we've knocked your text into shape in-house, we'll get a better idea of jacket looks,' they'd said. Well, obviously some editing would be required, I knew that. But 'knocking' sounded quite harsh, hammer-like.

I wasn't going to be persuaded, and I told Branwell as much.

'Ah well,' he sighed. 'I'll let Dominic know.'

'I know this is the right thing.'

Silence.

It bloody better be the right thing.

Dominic called me a day or two later.

'Daisy, thanks for this chance. I will make this book work, I promise. We'll create a Lucy Lovecake blog, Twitter account, Instagram feed, Pinterest board — the lot. We'll get the whole world talking about it from my kitchen table.'

'I can't wait. Just tell me when to get going with the Lucy Lovecake blogs. Do you think she should be very contemporary, or a bit of 1950s deb, or what?'

'I think quite modern, lady-like but a bit

naughty, obviously.'

'Yes, of course. Playful.'

'Yes, very playful. Let me strategise this and get back to you with a thought-out plan. But I have done one thing already since Branwell called me with the good news.'

'Oh?'

'Yes, I had been thinking. You have no real formal training in baking. And when your true identity is revealed after six months or so, people will wonder if you *are* trained, why you are such a voice of authority. So, with that in mind, I've booked you on a baking course, just to give you some confidence and to be sure you're using the correct terminology.'

'Good idea! Thank you. I was feeling a bit nervous about some of the recipes,' I confessed.

'Yes, I can imagine. I found a place in your postcode area. The French Cookery School? Gets good reviews. In fact, it's owned by Michel Amiel, no less! He's started ordering chickens and eggs from us, actually.'

A flutter of heartbeats, then: 'Wow, I've heard it's great. And I pass it every day. When do I start?'

'Next Saturday, if that's okay. I thought Saturdays would let you sort things out at the shop. We didn't quite establish if you'll be keeping on your day job full-time, but I know you don't want to let your boss down. Is that okay?'

'Yes, cool. Thank you so much. I know these courses don't come cheap,' I said.

'It's the least I can do. I want you to feel

confident that you've made the right choice.'

When I put the phone down, I realised the enormity of the situation. I, Daisy Delaney, of no particular significance in the universe, except to my mother and father (although Dad had started saying, 'Daisy Who?' when I called of late), was going to be a published author by Christmas. It was everything I had decided in the depths of New Year hell just a few months before. But it was hard to absorb, because I had decided all this every new year for the last five years. Why had it happened now?

Daisy, do not question the magic. Accept it.

38

Bakery (of) Course

The next few days passed in a blur of extreme excitement. When I told Branwell about the bakery course, he said, 'Well, credit where it's due. That's a bloody good idea.'

'Yes,' I said. 'It's at Michel's place.'

Laughter. 'You're destined to keep bumping into him. I take it you're in regular contact with him?'

I couldn't tell Branwell that Michel had been the inspiration for the book, or that I had been furious to see him out and about with Eve Berger.

'No, not exactly,' I said.

'Maybe that's just as well, because if your bakery book goes well, he's likely to be ungracious about that. You saw how jealous he was at the awards, the abuse he hurled at Rory B? He can't stand competition. He's very childish that way.'

'Branwell, it's so sweet of you to even imagine that I could be a threat to Michel Amiel. That is not even in my mind!'

'Aim high, Daisy,' advised Branwell.

I had to tell Clara I wanted to go down to three days.

'I knew you were going to be famous. You

won't forget me, will you?'

'Don't be so daft,' I said. 'If you'd like me to do more hours, just say.'

'Daisy, if I'm going to be completely honest, this has all turned out rather well. I'm not sure that I can afford a full-time salary for you, and I need to put in more hours myself. I've promised to pay back the bank loan in eighteen months, so reducing your hours is a blessing.'

I was so relieved.

I called home to get the reaction. 'A dating book, who will want to read that?' Mother had said.

To which I replied: 'Not everyone goes in for arranged marriages, Mummy.'

'Listen here, madam, your daddy and I fell in love, fair and square.' You caught her in other moods, and she would tell you that my two grandpas had offered their offspring to one another in wedlock as a bet at the races.

Kitty and I ate out at Benedict's on the high street on the Friday night before I started on the bakery course — and guess who was in there? The new James Bond! Our number six! Amazingly, I wasn't quite that star-struck. He was a lot less ripped than I expected. The problem was, he looked like a perfectly normal human being. And he looked so in love with his wife.

'Daisy, you are glowing. I've never seen you so happy,' said Kitty.

'Kitty, I think this might be the happiest I will ever be. Nothing could be as sweet as being lifted out of a relentless routine and given fresh hope. I very much doubt even the day of receiving the first book or the moment of publication will be as magnificent as this.'

'Does all of this sweetness have anything to do with Dominic McGann?'

'Not really. I don't know. Maybe.'

I realised that until the bakery course had come up, I'd hardly thought about Michel Amiel since the publishing capers had begun.

Hurrah, he means nothing to me.

39

Tosser

I was excited about the first Saturday baking class, and though still unimpressed with Michel for telling lies about his relationship with Eve, it didn't really affect me or my feelings about the course. He was a rat. I'd known that from the start. We'd never even kissed. He was insignificant.

If I see him, I will be casually aloof. 'Oh, hi. Of course, I forgot. This is your place, right? I'm just trying out one of your bakery courses . . . my new boyfriend loves cakes . . . '

I hoped he wouldn't get the idea that I wanted to get access to him. Nothing could be further from the truth, but how could I go to a different cookery school without alarming Dominic?

Daisy, how do you get in these pickles from such a boring start point?

I saw from the schedule that we'd be starting with choux pastry, which seemed an ambitious thing to kick off with. I'd made profiteroles a few times, but they'd been nothing special, so I was looking forward to perfecting my choux.

On the Saturday morning, fifteen of us — *God, he's raking it in!* — gathered in the reception area of the cookery school, filling out forms, then awaiting further instructions.

A lady by the name of Catherine arrived. According to her, she was the choux queen. 'And I don't mean Manolo Blahniks!' She guffawed at her own well-heeled joke. (We can all play at that game, Catherine).

This could be a long morning.

Catherine had a plummy voice, a horsey laugh, and an ego the size of Primrose Hill, but she turned out to be quite engaging, in a failed actress sort of way. I loved her dotty Fifties dress in red and white, shoulder-length blonde hair, flicking out as it did, and her cute ankle-strap shoes in cherry red patent leather.

The kitchen was, I must admit, totally fab. We all had a work-station fitted out in powder blue, complete with utensils (from the Chez Amiel range, *mais bien sur*), two fancy ovens, a hob, grill, lots of mixing bowls, saucepans and a double Belfast sink, as well as a dinky little fridge.

'Isn't this cool?' said Jessica, who was working next to me. She was a mother of two who had been, apparently, treated to this course by her husband, Ted, who was very senior at the BBC.

It *was* cool. 'It is a bit spoiling, though?' I commented. 'Not sure I'll get on well with the grotty kitchen back at the flat after this luxury!'

'Exactly!' she said. But I felt sure she had an even more stylish kitchen at home. She just looked that way. Very Prim Hill.

Catherine gave us each a tablet with the recipe instructions on it, complete with images of methodology and choux mixture consistency, then talked us through our prep. 'It's all about speed with adding the flour once the milk, the butter and water mixture has been taken off the boil,' she said.

She clearly knew her choux, and called us all down to the front for a performance of choux making. As she got started, Catherine heard a text and excused herself, saying it might be about an important delivery which had been delayed.

More like a man-friend issue.

Jessica was telling me all about her two children, Lily and Toby, who were both asthmatic, allergic, and maybe autistic, so I didn't notice when Michel slipped into the room. The pathetic simpering of the women was practically audible, though. I looked up to see what the fuss was about.

Oh. Him.

There he was, dishevelled, unshaven, chaotic. Deceitful.

He looks disgusting, unclean. Not even fit to work in a kitchen.

He didn't make eye contact with any of us. I remember thinking, *What a creep.* It was easy to loathe him. He invited it. *Everyone will be so disappointed with him because he is nothing to behold.* I assessed him from where I stood, with the luxury of knowing he had not spotted me yet. About six feet tall, I guessed, with a bit of a paunch. Pepper and salt hair, thinning a little, not so you'd notice at first glance. Dark eyes, full lips, a strong nose. Quite good bones, I supposed. Very French looking, and I had never liked Frenchmen, as a rule. Not that I'd given it a lot of thought in the past.

I definitely don't like his looks, so that's good. Nothing to stop thinking about because there's nothing to think about.

He took over, starting to demonstrate the making of a gateau St Honoré, with its choux base, covered in crème patissiere, decorated with caramel-coated choux buns.

I planned to retain a healthy disregard for him through the demonstration, barely looking up at first, fiddling with my tablet, zoning out his irritating voice. I glanced at the others round the island where we were gathered.

Look at these women, swooning! He's a cretin, that's all. It's all part of his own hype. But his devious ways are catching up with him. Soon, he will have annoyed the Brits as much as he's annoyed the French, then where will he go? The moon?

'You just melt the butter, very gently,' he was saying sensuously. 'Then pour in the milk. Like this!'

He was somehow, infuriatingly, mesmerising as he melted that butter, poured the milk from a height, tossed eggs in the air and caught them with one hand, cracking them expertly into his branded plum-coloured bowls. It was theatre, it was magic, it was fun. I tried not to be impressed.

He gave tips as he went, in that ludicrous French accent. 'Steer the butter with regard for it. We should not expect ingredients to blend together automatically, we should cajole them into harmonising, *oui?*'

I had managed to avoid him noticing me. Feeling that I may have succumbed to his mysterious charisma, I hoped he would leave without spotting me. Surely he would leave the rest of the lesson to Catherine now.

Please God, push off now.

We all went back to our workstations and started to get on with weighing flour and butter, cracking eggs into bowls, and setting ovens to heat. I was finding it a huge challenge, especially with him in the room. When I thought about it, I had been making the same three or four kinds of cakes week in, week out, for ages. It was nice to have to think about what I was doing.

Phew, there's so much to consider when not on autopilot. Don't make a mess of your profiteroles, Delaney!

My face felt a bit flushed as I referred to the tablet and found all the right implements in the drawer.

I got even more stressed because I could see that Michel was starting to wander around, making comments, making people giggle, scattering his seeds of charm carelessly.

Jessica and I were discussing how wet the mixture should be when he barged in on us. 'How are you, ladies?' he boomed.

I looked up, sensing blush upon flush. He paused, staring at me. Jessica clearly wondered why he was staring. It was easier for me than him; I had prepared myself to see him, but he was obviously confused. I couldn't think what to do, so I picked up an egg and tossed it towards him, lobbing it quite high.

He caught it, one-handed.

'Can't catch me out, Daisy Delaney,' he said.

He threw the egg back at me.

I felt colour rising in my cheeks as everyone stopped to stare.

Please catch it. Please.

I felt as if it was all happening in slow motion. It was like rounders in the third form. I never caught the ball. The egg was dropping towards me, my hands cupping to catch it. But would they be in the right place?

My hand-to-eye coordination was not the best, by any means. I used all my concentration. I reached out for it.

It fell into my hands. I clasped them round it, but not too firmly.

Yes!

'Not bad — for a girl,' said Michel, chuckling.

Giggles around the room.

That's what I hate about Frenchmen. So unreconstructed. So arrogant.

He came up close, checking all my ingredients, making a theatrical show of it.

Leaning in, he whispered, 'Lucky I recognised you with your clothes on.'

I busied myself in the little fridge at my workstation.

'What made you join my school?' he asked.

'My boyfriend likes cakes,' I responded, using the rehearsed line.

'Come to my office after class,' he said. 'It's behind the reception area.'

He says that like a command. As though I will not be able to resist.

'I'll think about it.'

He winked before carrying on with his tour of the room, and eventually he went away, although I was too immersed in oven temperatures to notice.

The choux buns turned out beautifully.

Catherine made an inspection.

'Very well done, Daisy!' she said.

'Thank you.'

'How did you find that?' she asked.

'Tricky, but I followed your instructions religiously.'

'That's all we ask. We've done it a few times, and we're all trained by Michel, on top of our other qualifications. No amateurs here!'

After the choux lesson, Jessica asked if I'd like to go for coffee in Prim & Proper.

'My friend works there!' I said.

'I love it there!' said Jessica. 'It would be nice to chat over a pot of tea.'

I thought about Michel waiting for me in his office, fully expecting me to waltz in. I thought about the photos in the *Sunday Times*.

He can wait.

* * *

Once inside Prim & Proper, Jessica and I found a table.

'What do you think of the classes?' I asked.

'I'm enjoying them,' she said. 'It's nice to get out of the house.'

'Does your husband look after the children on Saturday mornings?' I asked.

'Yes. Well, taxis them around. They go to swimming class, then pottery.'

'I see. I can't imagine how selfless you have to be, with kids,' I commented.

'It is hard. And it puts a big strain on your marriage,' she admitted.

'I can imagine! I'm not too good at relationships anyway, without the additional strain of children!' I revealed.

Jessica looked wistful. 'It's the way he doesn't seem to think of me as a woman any more. It's all contractual; 'You're supposed to do the laundry because I do the food shop.' Deals, rows, stress,' she said.

'I guess most couples must go through that?'

'Yes, but I really do feel that he doesn't even fancy me any more. He used to be crazy about me. Hard to think of that now. I'm invisible.' Jessica confessed all this in that detached way when it's sometimes easier to talk to a virtual stranger than a best friend.

I could see she was unhappy, but it seemed like she really loved him.

'Why not come round to Voluptas and buy something to surprise him?' I suggested. Adding, 'And offer him some little chocolate kiss-cakes while you're at it?'

Jessica blushed. 'I've never worn fancy underwear before. Isn't it just for hookers?'

'No! Some of our most faithful customers are the most lady-like. It's fun. We should be more French about all of this,' I said.

Jessica considered this. 'I'll think about it, Daisy. But that's enough about me. What inspired you to take the course?'

I liked Jessica a lot, and I wanted to tell her all about *French Fancy*. But I couldn't. Not yet, at least.

'I bake for this shop from time to time, and I wanted to make my skills a bit more official,' I explained.

'Makes sense,' said Jessica, deep in thought. 'Now, which days do you work in Voluptas?'

40

Introducing Lucy Lovecake

When the contract for *French Fancy* arrived, I read it ten times, in disbelief.

Contract to Publish

The content author agreement, hereinafter 'The Agreement', is entered into between Bluebells Ltd of Higgledy Piggledly Farm, Honeycomb near Chipping Norton, Oxfordshire, OX11 4CX, hereinafter 'The Publisher', and Daisy Delaney of 12B Rosehip Lane, Primrose Hill, London NW3 4TX, hereinafter 'The Author' represented by Branwell Thornton, hereinafter 'The Agent'.

Hereinafter 'The Author'.'

My proudest moment.

★　★　★

I started the Lucy Lovecake blog the weekend after I signed the contract.

What's she like, this Lucy Lovecake? Why does she have so much advice on dating and all these recipes? Has she had success in this area? What age is she? How does she know this stuff? She could sound oddly bossy if I don't get the tone just right.

I didn't want her to be a wiser, older lady

figure because she had to speak to girls the age of Kitty and I, as well as a little younger and a bit older than us. She couldn't be like one of those overly prim ladies who endeavours to turn 'ladettes to ladies', but at the same time she should have a feminine, genteel quality because this book was about turning away from casual sex and turning towards romance.

She had to have experience of dating — and how best to get that across? I concluded that she would be most effective as an 'agony niece' figure. I also thought it would make a nice little format for a blog, that it would open with a problem 'letter' and move onto her suggested solutions, and general tips on that theme.

In her blogs, she could be a little more daring than she was in the book.

Dating Dilemmas Solved by Lucy Lovecake

Dear Lucy Lovecake:
I'm fed up with drunken one-night stands. I'm looking for a proper boyfriend but it seems impossible. (Is it true that there are less men than women in big cities? My friends and I can't find any decent men in London who want to be monogamous.) Is the way to a man's heart really through his stomach? I'm not that interested in cooking, and I also think it sounds a bit old-fashioned. But I have to admit, all the men I've met are keen for me to make a meal or bake for them. How would I start? Also, how do I get a man I like to notice me in the first place?
Angelica, 24, London area

183

Dear Angelica:

I think it might be true that there are more girls looking for men than vice versa here in London. Same in New York. Nobody knows why for sure.

First off, you should only cook for them if they cook for you, or if you are happy to cook as a pleasure and it makes sense in the context of the rest of your relationship. One person shouldn't be doing all the work. If you do it under duress, you will soon tire of his demands. Both men and women like to be cooked for because the effort makes us feel loved, appreciated and cared for.

The fuss you make of a man in terms of cakes and dinners will only be effective if you are both enjoying the whole relationship. It's also a problem to do things in the early period which you don't want to do throughout the whole relationship. Generally speaking, girls make too much effort too soon, and men build up to effort as they fall more in love. It's worth holding out for a cool customer to warm up!

As for the sorts of treats and meals you might make at first, cake is always a good one, and the recipe for my First Date Chocolate Cake is at the bottom if this. If you are going to do a full meal, then ask about any allergies or dislikes to avoid disasters, practise your menu first and stick to something simple, like pasta with a sauce. Go for rigatoni or penne rather than spaghetti — long pasta can get messy, unless that's what you want!

Cake works every time, if served at the right moment. That golden or chocolatey mound of scrumptiousness sitting wantonly on your table, whether decorated ornately or naked save for a dusting of icing sugar on top and a smear of jam in the middle, will always tempt.

All of this is sensuous pleasure. This is not about bagging a man in the desperate style of a Jane Austen heroine who has no private income. But in the ways of romance, in terms of our array of love weapons, then food, cakes, deliciousness have their part to play.

We have developed an interesting relationship with food due to all the telly food shows we watch. Sometimes we prefer to watch rather than do. We can run to M&S and find a cracking cake, so why bake one?

In all matters of food, the *effort* is a sign of affection, that is why. Cake is love — for our children, our wider families, our lovers. Preparing food, serving food beautifully, communicating over food, these are the practical ways that we can show we care.

Good luck, Angelica. Let us know how you get on!
Best wishes,
Lucy Lovecake

I pressed 'send' to Dominic and waited for his response.

41

Rose

I almost skipped to work on the Monday, my head full of thoughts for Lucy Lovecake's Q&As. Just a few short months before, I had to trudge to work every day. I smiled to myself as I thought of the fun I was having now — and there was so much more to come.

'What's that naughty smile for?' said a voice I knew well.

Michel must have been skulking, waiting for me to pass. But, trying to act casual, he popped out from a doorway just before the turning for Voluptas.

I wasn't expecting to see him, or anyone, and the way he spoke, as if from nowhere, freaked me out. I screamed.

'I'm sorry!' he said, putting his hand on my shoulder. 'I didn't mean to scare you.'

I exhaled. 'You must have had a fair idea you might.' I sounded a bit fierce. 'Why did you do that?'

He looked conciliatory, as if regretting his tactics. 'Forgive me. I wanted to speak to you — without you running away. You never stay to talk after your baking class.'

'Because I don't want to talk.'

'I need to tell you something,' said Michel.

'What about?'

'About Eve,' he explained.

'What about her?'

'You probably saw us pictured together?'

'Maybe.'

'I thought so. I'm sorry about that. It was contractual, so to speak. She couldn't go to her premiere alone or everyone would start asking if we'd split, rather than talking about the film. I'd become the story, not her. It's not allowed. Her lawyers laid down the terms to my lawyers. I'm sorry. That's the world I live in. We were only together for twenty minutes that night. That's the last time I saw her.'

I considered this and it seemed plausible enough, but it wasn't really necessary for him to explain this to me. 'It's not as if we are dating. You have no need to justify the photograph,' I said.

'But it might have surprised you. I am sorry,' he apologised.

'I suppose it's not true to say that photographs never lie.'

'Exactly,' he concluded.

'Well, thanks for clearing that up! I have to go to work now, I'm afraid,' I said.

'Meet me at coffee time? Please? I will wait in my car, just over there. At eleven, okay? Please?' he pleaded.

This was all new. Michel Amiel begging to see me.

I hesitated.

'I don't bite,' he said.

'That's not what I've heard.'

187

'Please?'

'Okay. But I won't have very much time,' I said.

'That's okay. See you then.' He smiled broadly.

Very effective, ignoring him. Bear that in mind for the Lucy Lovecake blog.

*   *   *

As I pottered around the shop, music playing, somehow floating on gossamer wings, I heard the ping of an e-mail.

I rushed to check it. From Dominic! A response to the first Lucy Lovecake!

From: Dominic McGann
To: Daisy Delaney
Subject: Lucy Lovecake

Dear Daisy,
I read the blog this morning and absolutely LOVED it. You've nailed it, no question! Could you do twelve of these, with an overarching story arc, which we will release weekly before launch? Also, I am in the process of having some illustrations done to accompany the blog, so will send over as soon as! How are things with you?

From: Daisy Delaney
To: Dominic McGann
Re: Lucy Lovecake

Dear Dominic
Delighted to hear you like Lucy Lovecake, and

of course I can do twelve ... better for consistency if I just get on with them in one snap, I'm sure. How is Minty? She's a very beautiful child.

Really looking forward to viewing the illustrations you mentioned!
Best wishes
Daisy

A few minutes later, another message from Dominic:

Daisy, I've been thinking, and I hope you don't find this odd, but would you like to come to the village Starlight dance next week? It's going to be in the barn here. Obviously we can't mention your book (Mysterious Lucy Lovecake), but it would be very nice to have your company there. Well, no problem if you can't manage, it's on Saturday next. Minty and I could collect you at the train station. Tilly's babysitting. So long. D.

Ever since I'd seen Dominic standing on the steps of his beautiful house, I'd caught myself thinking about him in my daydreams. Heroic, yet human. Manly, but gentlemanly. I was feeling quite twirly and swoony when Clara came in.

'You seem to be up in the clouds,' said Clara. 'Next thing you'll be asking me to dance with you.'

'Yes, I might. It's all happening!'

'Do tell!'

'Do you mind if I go for coffee with Michel at 11 am? Would that be okay?' I asked.

189

'Yes, of course that's okay,' she said. 'So that's why you're glowing!'

'No, I'm glowing because Dominic has invited me to a dance in his barn!' I said.

'Right. So you prefer Dominic?'

'Of course.'

'Right. If you say so,' smirked Clara.

We worked solidly until a quarter to eleven, unpacking some new stock and cleaning the windows inside and out.

'Nearly coffee time,' she said.

I washed my hands, applied some lipstick, sprayed perfume and brushed my hair.

'See you very soon!' I said, grabbing my bag and coat.

'Lucky thing!' said Clara.

Michel was waiting at the corner.

I jumped into his fancy car, not completely sure what make it was.

'Thank you for coming. How long do you have?' he asked.

'An hour, maximum.'

'Okay, let's go to my place for coffee — that way people won't stare or talk about us.'

'You really think you're that famous?'

He laughed. 'That's what I love about you. You don't put me on a pedestool.'

'Pedes*tal*.'

'See? Nobody else corrects me all the time.'

'I'm not sure about going to your house . . . '

'I want you to know that Eve has moved out. I want you to be sure of that. Plus, my mother will be there. She follows me around the world. No wonder I've never married!'

190

'Yeah, well, okay then. That would be nice. So, I'm going to meet your mother?'

'Yes, Rose Amiel. A very fine Parisienne lady. She taught me to cook. She taught me to express myself.'

Hmmn, as you 'expressed' yourself at the literary awards.

I wonder if I'll like this lady, who clearly hero-worships this dangerous man.

We drove along to Elsworthy Road, and he went round the back and parked in a private bay in the Elsworthy Mews Lane.

The house he was renting was amazingly grand, but even so, there was still that country girl in me who couldn't believe the prices for renting and buying houses in London, when where I come from a castle would be on offer for a fraction of the cost.

It's obscene.

'Follow me,' said Michel.

As we went into a huge kitchen at the back of the house, he called out to his mother.

Rose Amiel promptly arrived on the scene, a picture of Parisienne elegance: cashmere wrap-sweater, black wool trousers, fabulous shoes, silver bob, very little make-up.

'*Bonjour!*' she said, addressing me directly.

'*Cela est Daisy Delaney, Maman,*' Michel told her.

'*Ah! Tu me dis au sujet de son avant!*'

Interesting. So, he's been talking about me!

We all sat round the big kitchen table, which was a bit like a massive butcher's block. The kitchen was quite rough in décor but very functional, and bright, with a vast glass cupola overhead.

Michel made some fresh coffee, while Rose chatted in fragmented English.

'Do remind me, are you a student at the cookery school?'

'Yes, that's right,' I replied.

'That is how you met?'

I looked to Michel.

'Maman, I told you. We first met when she bumped into me at the party, at the V&A, remember?'

'*Oui, oui*. It's all coming back to me now. He said he had danced the Village People with the cutest girl in London!'

I blushed, though I was secretly flattered.

Michel rolled his eyes. 'This is why I usually keep her locked up,' he said.

'I tell him, girls like to have compliments. Why he has to act like a bad boy, I will not never know!'

'There is no acting required,' said Michel.

'I'd agree with that,' I muttered under my breath.

'You want to improve your baking skills?' asked Madame Amiel, addressing me directly.

'Yes, I am an enthusiastic amateur at present. I need to polish up.'

'Why?' she asked, looking at me so intensely I almost flinched.

Oh dear. I am going to have to keep my secrets from them. That I am working on a cookery book, inspired by Michel.

'I bake for the Prim & Proper café chain

— you may have seen the local branch on the high street? I want to be able to do more elaborate cakes. And all the men in my life seem to love cakes too. So far, it's more or less a wing and a prayer. Do you know what I mean?'

'That you get by on luck alone?'

'Yes, more or less!'

'Thank goodness the cookery school is working well. This boy of mine, he needs some luck,' stated Madame, with her fingers crossed.

Oh, please don't confide in me, because I have no choice but to sit here and lie to you!

42

Kitty

But alas, Michel picked up the story. 'My book sales are plummeting — in every country except Denmark, for some reason. I don't know what to do about it. My whole lifestyle is geared to a certain level of earnings, it is really hard to take a hit. I need to stay on track with earnings. My manager is giving me hell. He hates my latest draft. I can't think of anything I want to write about. I've done it all.'

'Maybe you need a break, or a change?' I suggested. 'So much pressure. A new cookery school and a new restaurant. You will have burn-out. Why don't you travel and get new ideas for recipes from other countries? Relax, take a campervan round Italy?'

'I'm not Rory fucking Bridges,' he said fiercely.

Of course. His nemesis. Sore point.

'Clearly. But it must be tough, having to come up with fresh ideas for books all the time.'

His mother stepped in. 'He has been talking about getting a ghost writer to do the work on this book. But I have told him — that will be the death of your career. The book will not have his spirit. Am I right, Daisy?'

'Yes, I think the charm of your books is your

voice coming through,' I agreed.

'And the fact that he knows what he's talking about. He's a trained chef. Some of the new style cookbooks are terrible. Nonsense. So frivolous!' tutted Madame.

Oh, flip! This is awkward. Goodness knows what they'd think of my book.

I toyed with the idea of coming out with the news about *French Fancy* — just get it over and done with — but quickly decided to take things back to the topic of Michel's business woes. I felt emboldened by the cosiness of our chat. So, I said, 'Why don't you just adjust your lifestyle? Do you really need to rent such a big house for you and your mother? Surely a flat would do? The car, the trappings, do you need them, Michel?'

I thought of our humble little farm back in Cork, and my mother's voice ringing in my ears: *Always live within your means, and you'll sleep at night, Daisy. Are you listening? There are things we need and then things we desire. Our needs must be met, our desires controlled.*

'I don't even know what I need any more,' said Michel. 'I just try to keep doing what I'm doing because Auguste says I must. I've been doing these books for fifteen years. I always do a new one every two years. That's just what I must do. It's expected.'

I wondered about Auguste. So quick to palm Michel off onto me at the awards event . . .

'Does your manager move with the times? How much do you do on social media these days?' I queried.

'Social media? That's bollocks!'

'No, it isn't. It's the way to go. I mean it, Michel. You have to be on all platforms. People are spending more time online than with traditional books, or even TV.' I sounded like Dominic!

'Listen to you, you've taken in all that nonsense, haven't you?' said Michel. 'Anyway, I don't know why I'm confiding in you, it's not as if you have any experience of the book world. I'm sorry to burden you.'

Madame Amiel listened carefully, then chimed in with, 'Michel, you must listen to this girl. She is the new generation.'

'Mother, I am old-school. That's what works for me. You just said that the new stuff is nonsense!'

'But Daisy knows about these 'platforms'! Don't be left behind at the station!' Madame Amiel exclaimed.

'Pah! Tweeting and chattering on endlessly, self-importantly. That's for Rory Bridges! I am mysterious. A purist. And also such a lazy bastard.'

I looked at the clock. 'Oh my goodness. I should be getting back to work.'

'I will take you,' said Michel.

I said goodbye to Madame Amiel.

'It was a pleasure to meet you,' she said. 'Will you come back again soon?'

'If I'm invited,' I said.

Michel handed me a parcel as we were leaving.

'Can I open it now?' I asked.

'No, later.'

When we got back to the shop, I sat in the car for a moment and felt as if Michel was going to say something more. But I jumped out onto the pavement before he could.

Don't get in any deeper, Daisy. Because a whole web of lies is going to form. Secrets galore surrounding the new book. Easier not to see him than to deceive him.

'Bye, Michel. Lovely to meet your mother.'

'Will I see you again?'

'I'm not sure. See you around,' I said, casually.

He looked as if women didn't often play hard to get.

I opened the parcel in the shop. A perfect little china teapot. A card: 'From the klutz who adores you.'

Oh, don't do this to me. I don't want to like you.

The sweetest thing about Michel chasing me was that in his view I had, literally, nothing. I was not a potential big-author name. I was a shop worker and he liked me like that.

Clara was itching to hear about Michel, but my phone was ringing. Kitty. *Unusual at this time of day.*

'It's Kitty,' I told her. 'Mind if I take this?'

Clara must have been thinking I was more of a liability than an employee these days, but she smiled warmly and inclined her head towards the phone.

'I'm sorry, Clara,' I said before answering. 'I'll make the time up, I promise.'

I accepted the call.

'Hi. Are you okay, Kitty?' I asked.

Sobbing at the other end. 'No, not really.'
'What's happened? Is it Charlie?'
'Yeah.'
'Can you tell me? Do you want me to come round?'
'Could you?'
'I'll ask Clara.'
I laid the phone down.
'If you need to go to her, that's fine,' said Clara, waving me out the door. 'I'll let you off as one of your friends from your bakery class — Jessica? — just came in here and spent £500! As long as you're back for two o'clock. I have an appointment at the bank.'
Wow, Jessica going for it!
'Of course. I'll be as quick as I can,' I said. 'Kitty sounds really distraught.'

★ ★ ★

When I got to Prim & Proper, Kitty was serving, her eyeliner smudging her cheeks.
I took over for her, and when everyone was happy at all the tables, we spoke in the kitchen.
'Look at this!' she said, handing me a sheet of paper.
It was a letter.
'I found it on the desk. Read it.'

Prim & Proper Café
26 High Street,
Primrose Hill,
London NW1 6VC

Oscar's Tea Rooms
121 Bond Street
London
W1S 8HM

Dear Ms Valentine
Reference Request for Tea Room Manager:
Kitty Chang
With regard to your request for a reference for the above named employee, I regret to say that I am unable to recommend her.

We are trying to terminate her contract ourselves due to her erratic time-keeping and general unprofessional conduct.

I hope you find a suitable candidate for the role of manager of your tea room.
Yours sincerely
Charles Baxter, CEO Prim & Proper

'Kitty,' I said, disgusted by what I had read. 'We're going to get you out of here.'
'But how?'
I will find a way.

43

Back to Bluebells

Spring was bursting through the hedgerows when I travelled along the country roads to Bluebells, with scenes from *The Hen Weekend* playing in my head. It was time for the Starlight Dance. Dominic had offered to collect me at the station but I'd taken a cab to save him time. I sat in the front seat with the driver, Bill, taking in the view.

I was to arrive early in the afternoon to help set up. There was going to be a live band in the barn, and according to Dominic's to-do list, sent to me as an e-mail attachment, we had yards of bunting to pin up in there. There were strings of lanterns for the trees along the riverbank, and striped awnings for the food and bar areas. I couldn't wait to see it all and get started on the job of making it look pretty. And best of all, it was warm, still and sunny.

I'd brought three possible outfits. Two sundresses (I was wearing one) and one cute top and floral hot pants I'd got from Bygone Eros on the Prim Hill high street.

What a difference from the previous journey! Cheeky lambs played tig in the lush, green rolling fields, swallows swooped and wheeled in the pale-blue sky overhead, and the hedgerows were dotted with soft-yellow primroses and wild pink roses.

'So, you're off to Bluebells or Higgledy-Piggledy?' said Bill.

'Yes. I suppose I know more about Bluebells. A dance, apparently.'

'I heard about that. That rock band guy, isn't it? Does it every year. I've never been invited, though,' he complained good-naturedly.

'Oh, sorry to hear that, Bill! I have no idea how they decide who's going to be there.'

'Don't worry, love. I'm just glad of the extra work. Folks getting drunk means trade for me.'

'Of course. Well, that's good then,' I agreed.

'Does a lot for the community, that Dominic, I must say,' said Bill.

'Really? What sort of stuff?'

'Fundraising, fun days at the farm, you know. He's had a tragic time. Raising the little girl . . . knows what it is to suffer.'

'Very true. But not everyone turns that sort of thing into a positive. Says a lot for him,' I said.

'Oh yeah. And, of course, there's no problem getting local ladies over there. I don't know about these things myself, but they say he's the hottest thing since the summer of 1995.'

'Ha! Being a rock star does him no harm in the temperature test,' I admitted.

'Well, it's higher up the thermometer than taxi driver, I'm guessing,' said Bill.

It turned out he was a farmer's son, and that the farm didn't generate enough income for him to see it as a full-time job. We were chatting about the stress of living in a caravan on the hill during lambing season when the sign for Bluebells came into view.

We turned into the drive, much brighter this time, and I got out of the car near the house. As I paid Bill, Dominic and Minty came outside to greet me.

'Daisy! How nice to see you!' said Dominic. 'You look lovely!'

'Hi!' I said, adding, 'Hello, Minty!'

She smiled shyly, nestling her head on her father's shoulder.

'This little girl is looking forward to the party too,' said Dominic. 'That's why we're starting at four, so the kids can all have fun. There will be stalls and games — some of the locals are busy setting that up right now. Only the hardcore will be left after dark.'

'Sounds great. Just let me know what to do, and I'll get to work too.'

'Well, bring your stuff into the house and I'll show you to your room. Then, a cup of tea? I was thinking you might like to help with the fairy lights and the bunting. Maybe chop some of the salad things?'

'Sure, sounds great.'

As we walked up to the house, Minty asked to jump onto his shoulders. Agreeing, Dominic looked across at me, smiling broadly. I gave a smile in return, then focused my attention on the house.

As if on cue, Tilly appeared at an upper window, looking down on us.

44

The Starlight Dance

The first part of the event was like a sun-kissed scene from an idyllic 1950s fair day — little children and puppy dogs, toffee apples and three-legged races. A jazz band played under an awning in the last of the late afternoon sun. Sausages and burgers sizzled on the barbecue before being jammed into home-baked buns, dripping with sauces, relish and tangy pickles.

As dusk fell, the band arrived, and we switched on the fairy lights and lanterns, as well as doing a big tidy up, not that anyone had left much in the way of litter. Most people were recyclers by nature and custom.

I'd hardly seen Dominic in the afternoon, as I'd been so busy helping with the set-up, a stint on the tombola, then a dash indoors to my very comfortable en suite room to shower and change for the evening part. Any time I had seen him, Tilly had been in tow, helping with Minty, a casual hand on Dominic's arm.

Once ready, I reported to the kitchen where a local lady called Diane Medcalf was in charge, brandishing long lists of tasks and an inventory of items.

'Hi, I'm Daisy, a friend of Dominic's from London. What would you like me to do?' I asked.

She looked at me as if 'get out of the way' was on her lips, but eventually she said, 'You could start taking these salads out to the tables under the green-striped awning. Keep them covered, and be sure the labels of what they are stay with them!'

'No problem!'

I took vast bowls of exotic salads out to the food tables. Broadbean, barley and mint. Watermelon and feta with chickpeas and lemon dressing. Potato, broccoli and goat's cheese with sour cream and pine nuts. Sweet potato with crisp noodles and chili sauce. Courgette, brown rice, radish and balsamic dressing. Avocado, arugula, sweet peppers and chicken.

They all looked mouth-wateringly good, and Diane, although a tough leader, was certainly running a dream team. As I got to the food area, the sizzle of lamb steaks and the aroma of wild boar sausages filled the air. Under the neighbouring gazebo the bar team got to work, mixing vast bowls of summer punch and dumping bottles of beer in enormous buckets of ice.

I was returning to the kitchen when I heard my name being called.

'Daisy! Daisy Delaney!'

It was an unmistakable voice.

It took me a few moments to process.

What on earth is Michel Amiel doing here at Bluebells?

I swung round. Michel and his mother were approaching.

'Well, what a surprise!' I said.

How are you going to handle this? Why are they here? They can't find out about the book!

'Just as big a surprise for us,' said Michel, kissing my cheeks.

'You know Dominic?' I said.

'This farm supplies Brasserie Rose with chicken and eggs. They are *superbe!*' said Michel.

'Of course!'

'And what brings you here?' asked Michel.

'He's just a friend of mine.'

'From his rock days?' Michel pressed for more details.

'Erm, no, a bit more recent than that,' I said.

Michel winked. 'A customer in your shop?'

'No!' I protested.

'Ah, so discreet.'

Phew! I'll just go with the idea that I'm protecting customer confidentiality!

'Well, I have a couple of things to bring out from the kitchen,' I said. 'Why don't we meet up by the riverbank in a while?'

'Sure. We're going to have some of this delicious-looking food,' said Michel.

'So, you like British food now?'

'I'm starting to like a lot of British things,' said Michel.

I blushed. 'See you soon then.'

'Yes. And also, nice hot pants, Delaney,' said Michel.

I blushed again and ran up the path to the kitchen.

45

The Dance Move

By the time I'd finished all my tasks for Diane, the line dancing in the barn had apparently begun.

I'd had a nice chat with the Amiels, who were sitting on a bale of straw outside, enjoying the band, with cocktails in hand, but Dominic came to collect me for dancing.

'Dancing?' said Michel. 'I like the sound of that.'

'You are very welcome to join us,' said Dominic, adding, 'although, coffee and puddings are being served in the drawing room, if that appeals?'

Madame liked the sound of the latter, so Michel took her indoors, saying he'd be back soon for a line dancing lesson.

'Has to be easier than YMCA?' asked Michel.

'Don't think so!' I said, laughing.

As Dominic and I walked to the barn, he asked a bit about Michel.

'How funny that you two should come all the way out to Oxfordshire and know each other from Prim Hill!' he remarked.

'Yes. Ever since I met him at a party in January, I keep bumping into him.'

'He probably makes sure you keep meeting!' said Dominic.

'I doubt that,' I said.

Dominic didn't look convinced.

Pausing near the barn's entrance, Dominic then studied me. He seemed nervous, but determined. 'Daisy' he said, 'thanks for coming over today. I really appreciate it. It's lovely to have you here.' Before I knew it, he had put his arm around my shoulder.

'I've had a wonderful time,' I said, marvelling at the warmth of his body and not sure how to respond.

'Well, it's not over yet.'

At the doorway stood a supermodel in a silver dress and high heels, wearing lots of make-up.

'That girl is looking at you oddly,' I said.

'"That girl",' he responded, 'is Tilly by night.'

So, she's not babysitting then.

★ ★ ★

We all started on the summer punch, which was a deceptively innocent cocktail of vodka and raspberries on ice, with a splash of cloudy lemonade and a dash of brandy — this all according to the barman, occasional tractor driver Fred Gillies.

'Oh, this is lovely stuff, Dominic,' I said.

'I'm going to stick to the soft stuff, in case anything gets out of hand later,' he said. 'Has been known, and it is my gaff. Plus, I've got Minty to think of. She might not settle with this din.'

'Yes, good point. I won't go too crazy myself. Did Tilly put her to bed?'

'No, Tilly is very much off duty. I organised

207

another babysitter. Tilly refused.'

Maybe her main concern is not so much Minty.

He checked his phone for messages — all clear — but he decided to check on Minty anyway. She was in the care of Diane Medcalf's equally officious sister, Elaine Sanders.

'A great pair if you need to get anything done, not so great if you want to get a word in,' said Dominic, as he headed off for the main house.

'See you soon!' I called, thinking I might have some supper so that the punch didn't make me too idiotic.

Out in the food gazebo, I could see that Michel was holding court with some local women who recognised him. I nibbled on some salads and chatted to a nice couple, Ann and Dave, who apparently owned the neighbouring farm. But when the band struck up with Billy Joel's 'Uptown Girl', which they said was expressly for a jiving competition, Michel came over like a shot.

'I'm good at jiving!' he said.

'You totally sure about that?' I asked.

'I wouldn't need to be asked twice,' said Ann, nudging me towards Michel in such a way that I fell forward into his arms.

As we walked in the direction of the music, Michel confessed to some YouTube tuition in dancing. 'One must be convincing in matters of the feet. That is the first step to dance success.'

He's been learning to dance. That is cute.

We arrived at the dance floor. 'Okay, start with the footwork,' I said, 'then I'm going to twirl under your arm. Let's see how that goes.'

We bounced around quite well with some almost together moves. Okay, we weren't going to win the contest, but we weren't doing too badly. Towards the end, Michel decided I was going to jump up on his hips, as lots of the other couples were doing that.

'Okay, but I'll need a bigger run-up,' I said.

'Right, I'll move back,' Michel agreed.

He took several steps back, then a few more, as he got ready for me to lunge into his arms and straddle his hips.

'I'm ready!' he called.

As I started to propel towards him, he stepped back again, but there was a bale of straw behind him and he fell back over it, doing a dramatic backflip. He disappeared over the bale.

Oh no!

I ran towards the bale and dived onto it, finding him lying on his back on the other side, motionless and with his eyes closed.

'Michel! Michel! Are you okay?'

No response.

'Oh no! Help!'

I climbed off the bale to get closer to him, trying desperately to remember how to do first aid.

I wonder if he's breathing?

A crowd circled round us as I got closer to him, trying to see if his chest was rising and falling.

How do you give the kiss of life?

As my face hovered over his and I loosened his collar, he grabbed me and I fell on top of him and he folded his arms round me, laughing.

'You pig!' I yelled. 'You had me so worried. That's just not funny!'

He laughed wildly, tickling me as I tried to get away.

When I finally broke free, I jumped up and started to run, with Michel giving chase. It felt as if everyone was watching, so I ran out to the courtyard, where I finally ran out of puff.

I realised I was quite tipsy.

'Could you walk the line?' he asked.

'Yes, sure I could walk the line,' I insisted.

'Well, walk it.'

'What line?' I stepped forward by a few paces, trying to walk straight, but going hopelessly off course.

'Terrible!' he declared. 'Let's go back in for some more dancing. This time, try not to jump on top of me.'

I slapped his arm playfully.

When we went back in to dance, the band was playing a slow tune. Dominic and Tilly were dancing very intimately. It surprised me. Bothered me, even. Yet there I was, hand in hand with Michel Amiel.

As Michel and I began to dance, Dominic looked furtively across. I smiled, but he looked away.

46

On Writing a Book

Writing a book. The sweetest, hardest thing. My English teacher used to say that a good book is to be enjoyed like a good cake: 'You can either enjoy it as a whole and think not of how it was made, or make it your job to work out what the ingredients are. Once blended and bonded, it is hard to identify the individual parts. But I believe you will not understand its deliciousness until you understand what is in it.'

But even when I sat staring at a fresh white screen, reading the words 'Chapter Fourteen' (when twenty had been promised), I did not flinch from the task. Because this book was my destiny, my route to creative and financial freedom. I knew it. I could feel it. That knowledge was not in my imagination, it was in my bones, on my e-mails.

During the weeks which led us into late spring, I baked endlessly, making notes, taking advice from Kitty, asking Catherine for tips during Saturday morning lessons. I tried not to seem too academic about it all at the cookery school because I thought that might draw attention to myself. Jessica and I got to know one another better. One day soon after her purchases at Voluptas, she came into class, beaming and flushed.

'Well?' I said.

'Let's just say I'm back on his radar.' She grinned girlishly, blushing.

47

Arrested Development

For the next few weeks, Dominic and I exchanged lots of e-mails about the blogs and social media posts by Lucy Lovecake. He was also busy working with an artist for drawings for the books, and a designer to capture a look — somewhere between retro and racy. And we already had an image of Lucy Lovecake for badging on Twitter, Facebook, Pinterest and Instagram.

One Saturday in late spring I arrived at my Saturday class (mocha layer cake with vanilla cream) to find Jessica and a few of the others in a team huddle.

'Is this a private members' club?' I asked.

'No, come and hear this!' said Jessica, beckoning me over.

'Sounds like good gossip?' I said.

'Witnessed,' said Maura, a rather self-satisfied woman. 'So, technically not gossip. Fact.'

'Well, spill it,' I said, joining them, getting curious now.

'Wait for this. You will *never* believe it,' said Jessica.

I started to feel uneasy.

Maura leant forward. 'Michel Amiel left London by police escort yesterday evening!'

I took a breath.

'Really?' I said. 'Are you sure? Maybe there's an explanation?'

Maura fiddled on her phone. 'There's no doubt. The person who took this photograph — who was on the same flight out of Heathrow — heard everything.' She brandished her phone.

I looked at the image on the screen.

He was sandwiched between two British police officers, as though he were some risk to the wider community.

Oh, poor Michel! He looks so distressed. This is terrible!

There had to be a terrible mix-up.

How dare they treat him like this?

'Do you know what it's about?' I asked, working hard on my composure and impartiality.

'Yes, and no. The word is there is a court case in Paris — and that it involves Eve Berger! It's about money. What else?'

'Oh dear. Sounds really messy!' I said.

'Everyone is saying he's only in London because he's not welcome in Paris,' said Jessica.

I hadn't really liked the women drooling over him, but I liked them mauling him even less. I felt I needed some time to process this surprising news, but Catherine came bouncing in at that moment, obviously under instruction for 'business as usual'.

The lesson was under way within seconds, as she began to demonstrate how to make a deep, layered mocha sponge cake in the style of a gateau.

Once back at my station, cracking eggs

mindlessly, I kept thinking about how Michel must be feeling.

I wish I could do something to help.

'Why are you cracking all six eggs, Daisy?' I heard Jessica speak, but just smiled absently.

Was he being held in a cell? That was an unbearable thought. As I was beating together the eggs and sugar, I felt myself getting angry with him. *You are a fool, Michel. Why do you have this self-destruct button? All of your talent is going to be wasted.*

I was curious about how Eve fitted into the story. As soon as I got home (with a very wonky mocha gateau in my cake box) I googled the story. Maura had been right:

SCANDAL PRONE FRENCH CHEF IN THE SOUP AGAIN

Scandal has once again engulfed controversial French chef Michel Amiel. He has been ordered back to Paris by the French authorities amidst claims that he must pay $3 million to his former lover, Eve Berger, or face imprisonment. This payment, it is alleged, is due in respect of royalties for a cookery book which she wrote for him while he was suffering from depression. Lawyers acting for Ms Berger claim she has documented evidence of the work she completed and an informal letter of his intent to pay her 70% of his total earnings in respect of the book. Lawyers acting for M. Amiel say the book is his least successful and her estimation of earnings are 'over-egged'.

Michel Amiel was detained in police custody

last night following allegations of failure to make payments in accordance with a court order. It is believed that his former girlfriend alerted police to the non-payment, after the breakdown of their six-year relationship earlier this year.

Amiel's manager, Auguste Flaubert, said: 'The allegations are baseless. Ms Berger did no more than offer occasional suggestions on recipes. The book is his own work. We expect Michel to be released shortly without further enquiries.'

Monsieur Amiel's London house in Primrose Hill was in darkness this evening, although it is believed that his elderly mother, Rose Amiel, might still be residing there alone.

The troubled chef is no stranger to brushes with the law. He has been before a judge on several occasions, mainly regarding breaches of the peace and wild outbursts against photographers. Lawyers acting for the chef said: 'This is a matter of petty revenge, not a matter for the judicial system.'

Miss Berger was unavailable for comment.

I thought about Michel all day. I could see that Eve possibly *had* worked on the last book — because from what I could gather, it was different and not as passionate as the rest.

I don't know if it was ever since I'd 'rescued' him at the book awards, but I felt that he appealed to my superhero side. But that wasn't a side I was especially keen to develop.

★ ★ ★

Dominic called me on the Saturday evening to chat over some blog ideas I'd sent relating to types of baking for first dates. He recounted some stories of his dating disasters — such as being made to wear a plastic bib in a lobster bar — and he brought up the subject of Michel.

'Did you hear about our mutual friend?' he asked.

'Yes, at the cookery school this morning,' I said.

'Of course. Your baking course,' said Dominic. 'He'll bounce back.'

'Yes, but I feel like getting in touch. To offer some friendly support. He's always such a target, with him being so successful.'

'I wouldn't get in touch. No way, Daisy. Maybe Eve is quite right. He has something of a reputation. By all accounts, a very difficult man. Have you ever heard about his previous girlfriend? The one before Eve.'

'No, who was she?'

'Jennifer Lewes. She claims he caused her to have a nervous breakdown. He had to pay her off.'

'Really? Oh dear, there's a bit of a pattern to him, isn't there?' I conceded.

'Well, you can look at it in one of two ways. Either he is a soft target or he is a bit of a monster,' said Dominic.

'Or a third possibility is that women just can't stand it when he moves on?' I suggested. Silence at the other end.

I thought of Michel's honesty in the little kitchen in my flat. And in the café. Then in his own kitchen with his mother there.

'From what I know of him,' I continued, 'there is a sort of innocence to him.'

Dominic sighed. 'Oh, Daisy! You're too nice. Don't get close to him. You absolutely can't mention the book to him. You do realise that if your book sells well, you are going to become his number one enemy? He hates competition.'

'No!' I laughed. 'A book about dating with a few recipes is hardly going to be a threat to a world-renowned classically trained French cordon bleu chef.'

My fun little book is not even a micro threat to Michel! Dominic is crazy.

'You'd be surprised. Anything that sells well in the cookery realm bugs the life out of him.'

I had seen this at the awards. Even Branwell had said as much. But my book was never going to get on Michel's radar.

'Maybe you're right. But while he is Tolstoy, I'm more Mills & Boon. Let's not talk about him any more!'

'Agreed.'

'So, about the latest Lucy Lovecake. You think it's okay to extend the blog away from baking? Towards all meals and occasions, feasts and festivals?' I queried.

'Gradually. We need to consider seasonality as we're plotting these out through a whole year. And, of course, we can bring out other books on separate themes in due course,' said Dominic.

'More books? Cool. But we must get this one successfully launched first.'

'Sure. That's all in the planning. When do you

think you'll have the final copy to us?'

'Quite soon,' I explained. 'I'm just fiddling around with some recipes for picnics, then I think I'll be done.'

'Great. Once the text is edited, we'll show you the page layouts with the line drawings. It's going to be very pretty.'

'I can't wait. I suppose I'm a little bit sad that when the book first hits the shops, I can't tell anyone that I wrote it,' I admitted.

'Sure, that's really tough. But once we have 'outed' you — Daisy Deleany — as Lucy Lovecake, you will be in demand for interviews, literary festivals and parties galore. I do think the mystery is a clever marketing trick. We should stick with it. And it will give you some anonymity while we bed the book into the market. A more gentle route to stardom!'

Part of me wanted to suggest that my name went on the books from the start. I was getting so excited that it was nearly unbearable to keep it a secret. It was on the tip of my tongue to say, 'Please can we reconsider this?' But then I thought better of it.

'You're right. It's just that, you know, a girl wants to bring out a book, then she can't talk about it! It's hard.'

'Yes. Am I right in saying that you came up with the Lucy Lovecake sobriquet, though?' Dominic sounded just a tiny bit flinty.

'I did. I know, I know. I'm not being rational. It happens at times.'

'I understand. But you will be able to promote this glorious book soon enough. I promise! I

219

could book you in for some book festivals for next spring into summer as Lucy Lovecake, but if you are known as the author by then, that's fine, that's great. You can go to Hay-on-Wye as Daisy Delaney. I just want to make sure we have the slots — these book festivals fill up their schedules so damn quickly.'

'Okay, I trust you. You know what you're doing.'

'Kind of, yeah. From the band days and also from *The Hen Weekend*.'

I knew that Dominic was right in all he said. I hoped that Branwell would agree. I was due to update him soon.

'Thanks for everything, Dominic. I mean it.'

48

The Walk

When I got off the phone, Kitty still wasn't back from work. I ran a bath, pinned up my hair and soaked for an hour, thinking mostly about Michel.

Where is this concern springing from? He is nothing to you. An acquaintance. A rogue. A pain in the neck.

When I got out of the bath, I dried myself in a fluffy towel, rubbed rose body cream over my skin and applied some light make-up: a smidge of blusher, a slick of eyeliner, a smear of lip gloss. Back in my bedroom, I pulled on some black jeans and a T-shirt. Next, a champagne-coloured denim jacket (Kitty's) and a big sage-green scarf, tied close to my neck. A pair of beloved leather boots. Ready.

I took my key from the hook and let myself out into the evening darkness. It had been raining, the glistening streets of Primrose Hill somehow magical with reflected light.

There were so many pretty shops on the high street — that was why I'd fallen for this area after the crisis with Tom. I'd moved out of our flat in Pimlico in such a rush. Primrose Lane was the first place I'd looked at. Pippa had really sold it to me — especially the part that she was hardly there! — and Kitty had seemed so sweet when I was looking around. But the shops were as though from Camberwick Green. There was Unwins, the Purveyors of Finest Tea. Kent's Independent Book Shop. Lily's Flower Parlour. J&T Lennox, Antique Jewellery. Graham & Green's Home Accessories. Gorgeous Gallery 196 — I loved that place. Of course, Kitty's dainty café, Prim & Proper, caught the eye — still open!

As I approached, I could see her. Lovely Kitty, still smiling, serving sandwiches and cakes on a three-tiered stand to a mixed crowd of men and women.

Poor Kitty.

I skirted past, partly not wishing to disturb her, partly intent on my mission. Soon, I was passing the cookery school. All was dark in there, locked up for the night.

What will you do if the school closes down? If Michel never comes back to Primrose Hill? If he languishes for years in a Paris prison?

I shuddered, horrified at the thought of him in anguish.

I turned onto Gloucester Avenue, picking up speed.

I just hope this works out. Is it too late?

Nearly there. *Please be in.* I took a left onto Elsworthy Road.

Yes! Light at one window!

I'd only entered the house from the back before, but I was pretty sure I was at the right door. I rang the bell.

Nothing happened.

I tried again. I stood under the canopy. It was

possible that the lights were on a timer. I looked up to the lit window.

Did the curtain just twitch?

I waited a while longer.

I thought I heard a television.

One more ring.

I turned to leave, down the steps, back onto the shiny pavement.

But I heard the door opening and looked up at it.

'Daisy! Come in!'

Rose Amiel waved me through.

She took me into the kitchen. Poor Madame Amiel. She looked deathly.

'You heard?' she asked.

'I did. I'm so sorry to hear about this. Have you spoken to him?'

'Yes, once. He is very broken down. Back in the apartment now. My heart is aching,' she said.

'What can we do to help him?' I asked.

'I'd like to go to Paris, but I am afraid to travel alone. I've never done the trip without Michel,' she explained.

'I will come with you!' I said. 'Do you know where your passport is?'

'Of course. It is in my jewellery box. Would you really come with me, Daisy?' Her eyes sparkled with hope.

'Yes, of course. Let me organise some flights,' I suggested.

'I will give you my credit card. Really, it is too kind of you.'

We sat at Michel's computer and booked flights to Paris for the next morning.

49

A Brief Trip to Paris

We touched down in Charles de Gaulle late on the Sunday morning. Rose quivered with nerves.

'Do you think he'll still be under arrest? I could not bear it!'

Poor lady!

'I doubt it. He's back home already, you said. Let's find out what's happening when we get there. Try not to worry.'

'Thank you,' she said. 'It is too kind of you to travel with me. I appreciate it.'

'Don't mention it. I hope someone would do the same for my mother.' I was going to add, *if I were deported*, but thought better of it.

It was unthinkable that she should travel alone to Paris. We got in a cab outside the airport. Rose spoke to the driver in French, giving the details of Michel's apartment.

She turned to me. 'Pah! Eve Berger! I told him she was no good,' she said as we were whisked through the suburbs of Paris on the way to the cool sixth arrondissement.

I said nothing.

'Do you know that no one had heard of her before she met Michel?'

'I did not know that.'

'It's true. He took her to meet all the film

directors who come into his restaurants. He funded her very first film, a short, about a girl puppet, I think it was based on *Coppelia*. Went down well at Cannes. That's how she got started! He looked after her, bought her things, spoke up for her in the press. And now she does this to him!'

'People are surprising,' I said.

'They are disappointing. Spiteful. Greedy. And of course, Michel, he does not see it coming. I do. But what can I say? What can a mother do but stand in the wings and watch the performance, with tears in her eyes.'

Although Madame Amiel often veered towards the melodramatic, there seemed to be a smack of truth in her words. I paused. I wanted to ask if it was true that Eve had written his last cookbook.

'You poor thing,' I said instead. 'This will all pass over, try not to fret.'

'Can you stay with us for a few days?' she asked.

'No, I'm afraid not. I must get back to London this evening. But I can come back another time if you need me.'

'Ah! You are so sweet. Once we find out what's happening with Michel, I will decide whether to return to London with you or stay here.'

The cab drew up at Michel's apartment block on the Place des L'Etoiles. It looked like a palatial stately home. There were a lot of police around — not because of Michel, but because the French president had a residence nearby, according to Madame! Michel had positioned himself in the very heart of elite Parisian society, for sure.

Madame Amiel paid the driver, while I jumped out and grabbed both cases from the boot. The doorman of the block immediately recognised Madame and approached us warmly.

'Madame Amiel! It's wonderful to see you back!'

'*Bonjour*, Christophe!' she said. 'This is my friend, Daisy Delaney.'

'*Bonjour, Madamemoiselle. Comment-allez vous?*'

'*Ca va bien, merci.*'

Christophe helped us with our cases. Inside, we went towards the lift and, with the press of a button, launched towards the fourth floor.

Out on the landing, daylight flooded in from an overhead cupola, and fancy paintings hung on the aqua walls.

Rose marched towards their apartment, preparing herself for the reunion.

'Did you tell him I'm with you?' I asked.

'No, of course not. Let's surprise him.'

Oh great, this could go either way.

I couldn't quite work out how I'd ended up in the middle of affluent Paris inside the apartment of one of France's most famous sons, who was in massive trouble with the authorities, who I found deeply offensive, who I definitely didn't even fancy. *All because I steamed open an invitation at New Year.*

The door was opened by a cool butler guy, very handsome, relaxed. This was Paul.

How ridiculous — a butler?

Paul took our cases and we went inside. I found myself in a vast hallway, with a great

Versailles mirror, slightly tarnished, forming the centrepiece of many antique pieces and paintings. This foyer was larger than our entire flat at Rosehip Lane.

'Michel! I'm here!' called his mother.

No reply.

Paul came back from wherever he'd put the cases.

'He's miserable. Won't say a word,' said Paul. (I gathered this from my basic French.)

Oh no. I suddenly felt this was a very private, painful situation, and that it was going to be a terrible shock that his mother had brought some girl from a little backstreet shop in Primrose Hill to visit.

What if he pretends he doesn't know me? He's capable of anything.

I followed Madame towards a vast drawing room ahead, but while she lunged in there to embrace her son, I hung back, waiting to see how she was going to handle things.

'*Maman!*' he said, and I could hear sobs from both.

May the ground eat me up.

I thought about leaving. I looked at Paul, who seemed to be silently asking, in a nice way, who are you?

'I'm a friend from London,' I said. 'I've only come to make sure Madame Amiel got here safely. This is very embarrassing. I feel I should go now . . . '

But then I heard Madame, in French. 'I've brought someone with me, someone to see you!'

She came to the door and pulled me into the

stately room, verging on palatial in its grandeur. I entered shyly.

'Hi!' I said.

Michel sat on a velvet sofa, but stood up as soon as he saw me.

'Daisy Delaney!' he said, lips curving into a smile.

'I came to make sure your mother got here okay,' I explained. 'I'll be leaving very soon. Sorry to intrude.'

'Don't leave!' he pleaded. 'Come in, sit down. It was so kind of you to bring my mother! Have you heard what happened?'

'Not exactly, just gossip,' I said.

I remained standing.

'Sit, please.' He turned to Paul 'Could you bring some coffee, sandwiches or cake, please?'

'Yes, sure. Give me a few minutes,' said Paul. He disappeared shortly after.

'I want to tell you exactly what's happened,' said Michel, focusing back to me.

'Really, it's not my business, Michel. I went to visit your mother, and she asked if I'd come on the flight with her. That's it.'

He insisted on telling me the whole story of how Eve had indeed helped with his last book, under his direction when he couldn't make deadlines, and she'd said it was in exchange for his help with her career. But when they'd split acrimoniously, which was, by his account, his decision, Eve had revised the writing agreement and sought legal intervention to claim her share of royalty earnings.

'It's clearly a very tricky situation, and I don't

228

want to interfere. I guess love and business should never be mixed or whatever,' I commented.

Paul brought some delicious club sandwiches and a pot of coffee, as well as a mound of madeleines on a fluted plate. I tried to change the topic as we ate our way through the whole lot, chattering on about how great the cookery classes were at Michel's school. Anything to make him feel less abject.

'Everything he does is splendid,' said Madame, 'but then he goes too far and messes it up. Been like that since he was a schoolboy. And how do you think it makes an old mother feel, to watch it happen time after time? Eh? And to wonder how he'll cope when I'm no longer here.'

'Oh, Mother!' he said.

'Are you going to stay on here for a while, Rose?' I asked. 'Make sure he eats and washes and stays off the booze?'

'Yes, I think I had better do that. Don't you, Daisy?'

'Yes, definitely. I'll go back later tonight. I'll look at Air France now and check in on the evening flight. Do you think Paul would arrange for a cab to get me from here?'

'Sure,' said Michel. 'We have an account.'

'Do you two mind if I go off to bed for a lie down now?' said Madame. 'I've hardly slept all weekend.'

'You must sleep!' I said. 'Of course.'

Once she had left, Michel and I went out onto a leafy balcony off the dining room. Paris spanned spectacularly from this viewpoint. I felt aware of the gulf between Michel's physical

229

world and his emotional one. His life looked so pretty, but it was a horrible mess.

'Would you walk with me?' he asked then.

'Yes, of course.'

'Bring a jacket, don't get cold.'

We walked side by side, along the river, not touching, passing the National Opera House. I felt as if my feet were not quite touching the ground.

'I suppose my life could recover from all this,' he said, as if this thought had just dawned on him.

'Of course it could! It will. Definitely.'

'When I'm hung over, I see no point in fixing things, then I have another bottle to make the pain go away,' he explained.

'Well, you shouldn't. That's ridiculous. Actually, pathetic.'

'Who are you? Head of school?' He smiled.

'Maybe. It's nothing to do with me. It's just a pity, that's all. To see your hard-earned success being squandered now.'

'So, what do you think I should do? How can I sort out my finances?'

I hesitated. 'Well, what's it to do with me?'

'I'm asking for your advice,' he said.

'Well, do you think you ought to pay Eve the money she's asking for?' I asked bluntly.

He walked on, silently.

I said nothing.

Finally, he spoke.

'I do.'

'And is it a lot of money?'

'Three million euros.'

Inwardly I gasped, but outwardly I tried to maintain a cool composure. 'I see.'

'It's a lot,' he admitted. 'I've got it, but it would leave me very short of working cash, you know?'

'Sell your apartment then.' I didn't mean to say it out loud, and I felt very impertinent. But it was ludicrously large for the two of them, and more of a museum than a home. A bit like the Givenchy House, overly grand and opulent. A bit obscene.

He looked slightly stunned by the notion. 'But that's my home,' he said.

'Yes, I'm sorry. It's none of my business. Do forgive me.'

'There is nothing to forgive. I had not thought of it before. Sounds crazy, but it has never occurred to me. Maybe I should get a smaller place. Do it differently. De-clutter?'

'I don't know, that might be helpful. Oh, look at the Louvre. It's so magnificent!'

We walked across Pont de l'Archeveche and paused in the middle, watching the play of light on the water below.

'Daisy?'

'Yes?'

'You relax me, and you excite me. How do you do that at once?' he asked.

'I'm an enchantress.'

He looked at me searchingly.

I was unnerved. I almost leant into him, but instead set off again. We carried on walking, saying nothing.

When we returned to the apartment, I asked

him when he'd be back in London.

'I'm not allowed to leave Paris until this lawsuit is resolved — a type of house arrest, if you like. I can go around Paris, but I have to let them know if I intend to go further.'

'So I won't see you for a while.' I knew I sounded wistful.

'No,' he confirmed.

'Who will look after your London businesses?' I asked.

'I have some good managers there. They will report to me every day.'

'That's good. Let me know if there's anything I can do,' I offered.

'Thank you. What will you do back in London? Sew ribbons onto bras on your velvet chair?'

'Mostly,' I lied.

'Do you never want to do more than that?'

'Yes, of course.'

Don't mention the book, Daisy. You mustn't.

'What sorts of things?' It was as if he knew I had a secret life.

'Designing my own range of lingerie, perhaps,' I ventured.

'Ah, good idea. Good luck with that!'

'Thank you. I must freshen up,' I said. 'The cab to the airport . . . '

'Your visit has meant a lot to me. Let me pay for your flight.'

'Your mother did that already,' I said.

'Ah, good.'

When the cab arrived, I kissed his cheek gently.

'Could you leave me your e-mail address?' he asked.

'Yes, of course.' I scribbled it down and handed it to him.

★ ★ ★

As I flew out of Charles de Gaulle, I thought about the conversation on the Pont de l'Archeveche.

However troubled he is, I will always remember that look of unchecked tenderness.

★ ★ ★

Back at the flat, there was no sign of Kitty.

Surely not still working?

I sent a text to track her, then logged into social media to see what was going on there with Lucy Lovecake's various Dating Tips accounts. It was time for another blog to be released, shared on all platforms.

When I went to the Lucy Lovecake home page on Twitter, I did a double take as my eye caught sight of this: FOLLOWERS 3254.

Last count, Lucy Lovecake had about 350 followers. Could there be some mistake?

But it was right. And what's more, as I stared dumbly at the figure, it went up in front of my eyes.

3255. 3256. 3257.

How did this happen?

I went into the FOLLOWERS list to see who was there.

Lots of young girls, mature ladies, dating sites, men of all ages, beauty bloggers, singles holiday companies, celebrities from reality shows. A staggering diversity of followers. Fluttering inside, I lifted my mobile phone to find Dominic's number.

Ah, a message from Kitty: *Hope Paris all okay. Still working, can't get away as Millie didn't turn up. Been here since 7am! X*

I looked at the time on my phone. 8pm! Sunday night.

Right, that's it!

50

Empowered

I put on my coat and stormed round to Prim & Proper. When I looked in on her, Kitty was mopping the floor. She was pale and exhausted.

And we think Cinderella is a notional, outmoded folktale?

I didn't have much money, but what I had from Dominic would do us both for a while, if we were careful. Anyway, I could do with someone to manage the social media accounts while I got on with writing the book.

I went inside.

'Daisy!' she said, eyes lighting up. 'You're back! It's great to see you. How was it?'

'Hi, Kitty! I'll tell you all about it. Where's Charlie?'

'He's doing accounts in the office,' she said. 'Why?'

'I've got something to tell him,' I told her.

'Oh, Daisy! Don't go and say something crazy. He's going to make sure I never get employed anywhere else. We know that.'

'Kitty, this is the twenty-first century, not Victorian Britain,' I said.

'What are you going to say?' she asked anxiously.

'Well, if this is acceptable to you, I want you to

work with me on the Lucy Lovecake blogs, and you can look for something else after you've had a bit of a rest. I can afford to pay you for a couple of months.'

Kitty looked stunned.

'You do want out of here, don't you, Kitty?'

'Of course I do! But I can't take money from you. You will need that. You've earned it. It wouldn't be right of me . . . '

A voice from the office: 'You finished yet, Kitty, or still swanning about with that mop?'

She ignored him.

'I still have my income from some days at the boutique,' I said. 'We will manage. Go and get your coat. Go home, leave him to me.'

Kitty breathed out a long sigh and grabbed her jacket before slipping out of Prim & Proper forever.

I found Charlie at his laptop, not doing accounts but messaging about six people (female) on Facebook. He looked up, flashing his charming smile.

'Ah, it's the delicious Daisy Delaney. How are you, babes?'

'I am very well indeed. But Kitty looks exhausted, don't you agree?'

'Well, if she will burn the candle at both ends.'

'No, she doesn't do that. She has no energy for going out. But that's all going to change.'

'Why's that, love?'

'Because, as from now, she no longer works here.'

He got up, his face changing from charming to threatening in a nanosecond.

236

'What do you mean?' he asked, getting closer.

'She's left,' I told him.

'But she's got to give notice,' he insisted.

'No, she will forfeit any rights associated with notice-giving and by morning will be medically signed off anyway. So, there's nothing you can do.'

He was dumbfounded. Next, he rushed out to the shop floor, calling her name.

I followed him out. 'She's gone.'

'I'll get her for this. I'll never give her a reference!' he ranted.

'No change there, then. You've been giving bad references to keep her trapped, haven't you?'

'Says who?' he demanded.

I took out my phone, showing him an image I'd snapped of his vile slurs on her character.

'Fucking little sneak!'

I walked away feeling triumphant, and just a little nervous.

What have you done, Daisy? It's not as if you're a millionaire!

I forgot to call Dominic.

51

Tilly

Dominic was delighted with the way that Lucy Lovecake was picking up new followers on all platforms. He called during the week to congratulate me.

'This is exceeding expectations, Daisy. I'm thrilled. It's given me a new lease of life. I tried to call you on Sunday, late evening?'

'Ah, I was probably asleep after a flight back from Paris.'

'Paris?'

'Yes. I went over there with Madame Amiel. She was in such a flap about Michel. Poor old thing!'

'So, did you see Michel?'

'Yes,' I admitted.

'Right,' he said. 'I see.'

I changed the topic. 'When do you think we should tease the Lucy Lovecake followers about the fact that a book is on the way?'

'That's a good question,' Dominic replied. 'I think the best thing would be to imply that we've only just thought of bringing a book out due to popular demand on social networks. What do you think?'

'I think you're a genius at all this. I am so grateful to you. I wanted to mention something else,' I told him.

'Yes?'

'It's about my best friend, Kitty. My flatmate.'

'Yes, works in a tea shop, taught you some baking skills?' he confirmed.

'That's right. Well, I've recruited her to help with the Lucy Lovecake online presence and blogging. She's between jobs, and she's completely trustworthy. I hope that's okay. I want to be straight with you,' I explained.

'That's fine,' said Dominic, sounding relaxed. 'Makes sense. You're finishing off the manuscript, that's the main thing. Kitty can reply to tweets and add bits that you've approved. Sure.'

'Exactly. Thanks, Dominic. Just wanted to let you know. I think she can help build the following prior to launch.'

'Sure.' He paused. 'So, did you have a nice time in Paris?'

'Paris? Oh, well, not as such.'

'Ah.'

'How is Tilly?' I asked.

'Tilly left Bluebells. We have a manny, Felix. He's amazing.'

Interesting.

'Great. I look forward to meeting him.'

52

Blogging

The sun grew stronger as spring turned to summer, and Kitty and I were blissfully happy working together on the Lucy Lovecake sites. There was no need to invent fake problem letters! Every day, there were new followers and new ideas spawned from messages and questions left for Lucy Lovecake. *So many people having dating disasters! And I thought it was just me.*

Dear Lucy Lovecake,
I really fancy a man at work but he never notices me. What should I do?

Dear Lucy Lovecake
Is first date décolletage a good thing?

Dear Lucy Lovecake
We're going away for our first weekend to a fancy hotel, what sort of underwear should I be packing?

Dear Lucy Lovecake
It's his birthday and I've only known him for a few weeks. I want to bake a cake. Is that too keen and what sort might I bake?

Kitty and I had such fun working out what Lucy Lovecake would have to say on such matters.

'Is she a feminist?' she asked.

'Of course.'

'So, all this stuff about baking for men and dressing up in lace is okay, as a feminist?' she questioned.

'Yes, definitely,' I asserted.

'Are you sure?'

'Yes. It doesn't mean women are objects, nor does it mean we are controlling men. It's just a nice thing to do, for both parties. It's about caring enough to make an effort. As for baking, that's just what you do when you love someone, isn't it?' I said.

'True. I do think you're going to get some stick from intellectual second-wave feminists, though,' said Kitty.

'Well, I'm ready for that!' I replied.

'So long as we stick to a line. Powerful femininity. Empowered,' said Kitty.

'Agreed. It's funny how we love all the retro 1950s stuff — the styles, the curves, the lady-like ways — but in reality, those were terrible times for women, weren't they?' I said.

'Yes, but look at me. If you hadn't got this book deal, I would have still been working for a monster who was blocking me from moving on.' Kitty was starting to wonder how she'd ever lived like that.

'Don't think about it now. You're well out of that, Kitty.'

★ ★ ★

I received occasional messages from Michel in Paris via e-mail. I didn't reply too hastily. Sometimes he messaged twice before I replied. I felt for him and I wanted to help him, but I wasn't sure if he was going to help himself. I asked how long he was going to be there.

Could be back in London within a month, he wrote. *Why do you ask? Are you missing me?*

I took my time in replying to that.

No, I just wondered when I'd have to start hiding from you on the streets of Primrose Hill again.

He came back swiftly. *A nice double-bluff, you are obviously dying to see me, Delaney. And I can assure you, that's mutual.*

I left it there for a few days.

One day soon after, I received this message from Michel:

Dear Daisy
I've been thinking a lot about our walk through Paris, and your idea about my grand apartment. I've decided to move to a smaller place, and pay Eve the money. Why fight this in court? There is the legal law, and there is the moral law, and I will never find peace until I sort out the values in my life. Since you bumped into me in the V&A, I have thought about you every day. Perhaps you did put a spell on me. I am looking forward to seeing you soon.
Mx

53

Meringue Surprise

The fifth of August came and went. I did not even consider going to Tom Percy's fancy launch in Liberty's. He was part of my past and I was looking ahead.

I still worked two days a week with Clara, and the business was booming. We had a new customer: Gary Hopper, secret agent, from the book awards had found his way there and was always great fun.

Clara now did all her own beauty treatments and cooked several meals on a Sunday, which she froze for the week ahead for the family. 'We are moving house and Phil is going to invest the surplus in a sailing school on the south coast — it's something he's always wanted to try,' she said. She glowed with happiness, and said Phil was happier than ever too.

Kitty had been for an audition at a modelling agency. They loved her and had taken some shots. She was waiting to see if any jobs came in.

I was madly finishing the book — there were some rewrites — plus, working on blogs and articles, and I was halfway through another batch of advanced baking classes, again paid for by Dominic, as he wanted my credentials to be just so.

'Imagine if you are invited to talk on a daytime chat show, for example, and you don't know what goes in a Bakewell tart?' he had said.

'What *does* go in a Bakewell tart?' I asked.

'I rest my case.'

As Kitty and I lay on the grass in the park one glorious Saturday just before my baking class, chattering under a big cherry tree, I pinched myself at how much my world had changed since Christmas.

'We've come a long way in a matter of months,' I said.

'Yes,' Kitty agreed. 'I'll never be able to repay your kindness.'

'We've done this together, Kitty,' I said. 'You have supported me, inspired me, guided me.'

'Don't exaggerate!' said Kitty.

'Well, you've made scrambled eggs when I would have eaten Doritos,' I explained.

'I'll agree with that.'

'Time for me to go to class. See you later on. Don't get burnt,' I said, jumping up.

'Bye, Daisy. I'm going to log on here and check the Lovecake sites. I'm having so much fun!'

★ ★ ★

There was a whole different group in this baking class now, and it wasn't taken by Catherine. This time, we were taught by an elderly lady, very like Miss Tiggywinkle, called Marguerite. She gave a wonderful meringue-making demonstration that Saturday, and I immediately started to think about how I could incorporate meringues into the book. Dominic said I only had a window of two more weeks to add new material. I was forever changing bits, and adding sections as they came to me, but I knew this couldn't go on forever. After all, it was going to print in early October!

'Make-love Meringues' . . . *dainty, chewy meringues, filled with sweetened chestnut cream, the perfect treat for sensuous Sunday afternoons . . .*

I really focused on the meringues that day, intent on creating glossy, soft peaks, baked to chewy perfection. As for the crème de marrons filling, I blended chestnuts with sugar and vanilla, then added this to gently whipped cream. Once assembled in a pile of little clusters of creamy perfection on a cut-glass plate, Marguerite came to inspect.

'Well,' she said, studying my plate. 'They look wonderful, but now to taste.'

My heartbeat quickened. The standard of my work mattered a lot to me.

Marguerite lifted a tiny, silver dessert fork and broke a dainty amount off one of the meringues, making sure she had some cream too.

She closed her eyes as it melted in her mouth. *Well?*

'This is . . . quite perfect!' she declared.

I broke into a schoolgirl smile. 'Really?' I said. 'Thank you!'

'Everyone, gather round,' said Marguerite. 'Daisy's meringues and 'marrons' cream are simply scrumptious.'

Everyone tucked in, showering me with praise.

I was so proud. I immediately photographed the pile of meringues and sent the image to Kitty for the blogs.

Within minutes, she messaged back: *65 responses already!*

Dominic was so right about going on these baking courses. And so right about everything. He has turned around my life!

After my baking class, I bounced out into sunshine, trying to decide how to spend the day. To my complete surprise, I found Dominic and Minty waiting for me on the pavement, beaming broadly.

I was thrilled to see them.

'Hi, you two!' I said, hugging them, and ruffling Minty's blonde curls, caught at the back of her head with a pale blue ribbon.

'Fancy bumping into you here!' said Dominic.

'Yes, how could you possibly know I'd be in baking class?! Checking up on me?' I laughed.

'We thought we'd come to the big city to see you,' Dominic explained. 'And Minty here has been asking about you — lots.'

'Well, you must come to the flat, see where I live. Maybe we could go to lunch?'

'We're one step ahead of you on that,' said Dominic. 'Minty wanted to try some proper French French fries, so I've booked a table at Brasserie Rose, seeing as we supply them with chicken and eggs as well.'

I wasn't sure about the reminders of Michel that would be there, but didn't want to make a fuss. 'That sounds lovely,' I replied. 'I'm starving, come to think of it.'

Minty walked between us and we each took a hand. Every so often she jumped off the pavement as we took her weight. We all giggled as we made our way to Michel's restaurant, which was just around the corner.

54

Brasserie Rose

The Brasserie was very traditional, with checked tablecloths, lots of shiny silver cutlery and sparkling little wineglasses. We were shown to a table and ordered heaps of fries, as well as steaks, omelette and salad. Minty climbed onto my knee and we did some colouring in. I was immersed in a decision between turquoise and deep pink felt-tip for the Cinderella gown when I noticed Michel.

'Daisy Delaney. Welcome to Brasserie Rose!' he cried.

He hadn't messaged to say he was back in town, though it had been a week or more since his last e-mail, and I had not replied, when I thought about it.

Minty went back into her own chair and I stood up to embrace him. He looked confused by my company.

'Dominic and his daughter came to meet me from cookery school today,' I said. 'Minty has been longing to try proper French fries.'

'I hope they don't disappoint,' he said, turning to Minty. 'Nice colouring in!'

'Good to see you, Michel,' said Dominic, shaking his hand. 'You've had a rough ride, mate.'

'Yes, but I'm back,' replied Michel.

'Great news,' I said. 'It's nice to see you back in Prim Hill!'

'I was going to come round to see you later. I just got back last night,' he explained.

'Is your mother back too?' I asked.

'Of course. No show without Judy.'

'Ha! Everything okay?'

'Yes. I managed to sell my apartment, so that has helped in a lot of ways.'

I gasped. 'You sold your apartment!' He'd said he might in an e-mail, but to have done it — already. I was shocked.

'Don't sound so surprised. You told me to sell it!' said Michel.

'It was a suggestion! Did you buy somewhere else?'

'Yes, close by, quite a bit smaller. I think I prefer it, actually. I will use all of it, all of the rooms.'

At that, the food arrived, looking wonderful, and Michel excused himself as we feasted on mouth-watering sirloin steaks, crispy little fries, delicious cheese omelette and a simple salad smothered in dressing. Not content with demolishing that, we ordered chocolate mousse and coffees.

As we rose to leave, Dominic put his arm around me. 'Thanks for joining us,' he said.

'I've had a lovely time!' I told him and, without thinking, looked up to him, kissing him on the lips.

It was then that I realised Michel was standing watching us from behind the bar.

55

French Fancy!

Dominic and I exchanged lots of messages over the next weeks — little ideas, jokes — and then one day in early autumn, an attachment arrived by e-mail entitled SURPRISE! I couldn't wait to open it.

My heartbeat quickened. It was the fully designed layout of *French Fancy*.

I opened the document nervously.

My heart almost stopped when I saw the front jacket. It was sublime. A gorgeous girl in a pretty bustier brandishing a luscious assortment of French fancies with slightly imperfect icing. It read, *French Fancy: Dating Tips from Lucy Lovecake*.

The inner pages were all decorated with lovely little line drawings, some coloured and others in black and white, all done with exquisite attention to detail. The recipes were presented clearly, the images of the cakes quite scrumptious, as were the pictures of the girl in lacy little teddies and cute camisoles. It was sweetly sexy, not sleazy at all. Every so often a 'top tip' appeared in a heart-shaped bubble. The whole effect was delectable.

I called Dominic straight away.

'Well?' he said.

'Perfect. I adore it!' I exclaimed.

'Take your time to read it through. You have a few days before it goes to print. This is the last chance to make any changes. This is it, Lucy Lovecake!'

'Okay. Once I've come back down to earth, I will study it hard and get back to you. But I wanted to say thank you. I'm delighted.'

★　★　★

Not long after Michel arrived back from Paris, Clara sent a text on one of the days I didn't work in Voluptas: *Michel just came here looking for you! I said you don't work so many days now. He asked if you had another job. I said no. He looked quizzical. I changed the subject. He might come over to the flat . . . best get your story together, sweetie. CXX*

I jumped into the shower.

What will I say if he shows up? That I'm part-time as I'm taking an Open University course? But what course? That I'm burnt out? How so, on a little job in a bra shop — I'd sound so flaky! Exhausted selling three bras a week?

I resolved to see what passed my lips if he turned up. Never a great strategy, I've found.

As I was blow-drying my hair, I heard the doorbell ring.

Damn, no make-up, but at least I'm dressed this time.

It was Michel.

'Come in!' I said. 'I'll put the kettle on.'

'I forgot how nice this place is,' he said.

'Remember to protect all teapots and other china objects too!'

'Will do. It was a lovely surprise to see you in the restaurant the other day,' I said.

'I got a surprise too. Do you get together often with Dominic?'

I was about to say, 'only on book matters,' but I stopped myself. It was getting so awkward, this whole Lucy Lovecake thing, the secrecy of it all.

Maybe I should just tell Michel everything about the book. What harm would it do? It's going to be so hard when he finds out that I've kept all these secrets from him.

'I see him occasionally. He's a very good friend,' I said.

'I can see that,' retorted Michel, his tone loaded with disapproval.

'His daughter is adorable. It was very sad about his wife.'

'Tragic. Makes you think . . . At least money worries are not terminal,' said Michel.

'Exactly,' I said.

'So, you're not working so much these days?' he asked.

'Erm, no. That's right.'

'Ah. Well, lucky you!'

Just leave it. Don't tell any more lies. Drop it.

But of course, I had to dig myself in deeper, with the Open University option playing on my mind.

'I'm studying,' I ventured.

'Are you? That's great. What's the course?'

Oh dear goodness, what are you doing, Delaney?

'Oh, it's a MOOC, a massive open online course, in . . . .'

I saw that an e-mail had popped in from Horse Rugs 4 You — and for that reason, I said, 'Equine Studies.'

He looked shocked. 'My goodness. You are full of surprises.'

'I'm a little bundle of them'.

Surprise myself half the time, too.

I made a pot of tea and toasted some fruit bread, spreading it with butter Mum had sent from the farm.

We sat at the table.

'I can talk to you with complete honesty, Daisy,' he said.

I felt awful. *I wish I could do the same back. I want to, I really do.*

'I don't think we ever tell anyone the whole truth,' I said, turning amateur philosopher. 'But all that matters is that we're honest in spirit.'

Such shit. You're drawing attention to your deceit now, Daisy, you muppet.

'What are you getting up to, now that you're back?' I asked.

'I wish I could write a new book, but I've just lost the discipline of all that,' he said.

'Perhaps you need to come at it from a new angle? Write it differently from before? Maybe as a diary?'

He shook his head. 'Sorry, I shouldn't bore you with this — writing a book is the sort of thing you can't explain until you've done it for yourself.'

'A bit like childbirth,' I suggested.

'Have you done that?'

'No,' I said. At last, an honest answer.

He looked around the room, seeing a copy of *Empire* magazine on the table.

'Would you like to come to a movie with me?' said Michel.

'Sure, I'd love to,' I replied. 'What? Right now?'

'Yes, right now!' he said, checking on his phone to see what was showing.

I tidied up the dishes and applied some lipstick at the mirror in the hallway.

You are going to regret keeping secrets.

56

The Text

When I was ready, he turned to me and said, 'I rather hoped you were going to say you were expanding on your lingerie side of things, but, ah well, I guess you've had enough of all that.'

'Yes, I suppose I have, really. What film shall we see?' I said, swiftly changing the subject.

'There's a new one. It's playing at that cute little private cinema near the station. It's called *Parabolas*. A thriller.'

'Can't wait, let's go.'

We walked arm in arm, with Michel telling me terrible jokes all the way. They were not cruel jokes or bad taste jokes — they were just very silly. At the counter, he bought two tickets and a packet of strawberry bonbons.

Once seated, we were reminded to switch off our phones.

I reached into my bag and went to turn it off. There was a text in — from Dominic.

I opened it quickly, and noticed Michel looking over at my screen.

'It's nothing important,' I said.

The message read:

'*Daisy, this is the best fun I've ever had, been thinking about lingerie all day today!*'

'Nothing important, *oui*,' he said rather

tetchily. So tetchily that I was convinced he saw that it was from Dominic and that he read it, and that my assertion that I'd had enough of lingerie and replaced it with horse matters didn't quite ring true.

A few months ago, lying to Michel Amiel would have been simple. He had no right to know my business. But I know him now and he trusts me, and I am betraying that trust. I have to tell him.

Next time, I'll tell him about Lucy Lovecake. Absolutely.

★   ★   ★

An intriguing box was delivered to 12B Rosehip Lane some weeks later. A pale blue box, a bit larger than a shoebox, bound with matching satin ribbon, delivered by courier, addressed to me.

A pretty box for me! What can it be?

'I wonder what this is,' I said as I carried it to the table. It was late October, and Kitty and I were in lazy mode after some manic last-minute recipe changes to the book. Cookery classes had ended and the blogs were written up to the following June. Kitty now had some modelling jobs and worked part-time as a nanny to the family who lived above us, which fitted in perfectly.

'I can't wait to see what that is!' said Kitty. 'Please open it! Quick!'

I took off the ribbon and removed the lid.

My heart soared.

'Ah! Copies of the finished book!' I exclaimed.

It was such a satisfying moment I almost collapsed with relief.

I fell back onto the sofa, excited, overcome, almost too afraid to open a book, handle it, see the finished entity after all those months of redrafting, inventing, and creating. And all the years of hoping before that.

What if there is some major, glaring flaw that we have not noticed?

Kitty, bolder than I, looked through one — there were about ten in the box, with a card from Dominic.

'Well?' I said, forgetting to breathe.

'Perfect, no problems at all that I can see. Looks just lovely!'

Gingerly, I took a book and sat with it on the sofa, flicking through the pages. I became immersed in it.

After looking right through, I burst into tears.

'I could not be happier with it!' I sobbed.

Kitty started as well. 'I know. You did it!'

'*We* did it!'

57

Publication Day

French Fancy was published on the first day of November. By coincidence, Michel had invited me to afternoon tea at The Wolseley. I didn't care that I wouldn't be able to boast about my book. I was happy that it had reached the shops — and happy to be seeing Michel as well.

That morning, Dominic sent a bunch of pale pink cabbage roses, mingled with mint and lavender.

Daisy, Daisy! You are lovely to work with, hope there are many more projects to come! Dominic. X

I called him.

'Hi, Dominic. Thank you for the flowers. Thank you for *everything!*'

'Daisy, this is just the start. You have to keep blogging, and we'll decide when the unveiling of Lucy Lovecake is appropriate! That's our trump card — trust me. Once you're out there, your life will change forever.'

'I just hope someone somewhere buys it!' I said, feeling the enormity of it now being in bookshops. The hypothetical stage was over.

'Pre-sales on Amazon were up to eight thousand the other day — don't worry. Signs are good.'

Eight thousand? I struggled to take this in.

'Really? Are you sure? Wow, I had no idea. Eight thousand people want to read my words?'

'Yes. And there will be many more. With the social media sites promoting the book at a special price, sales are guaranteed. But we must never take our eyes off it. Strategy all the way. That's what I did with *The Hen Weekend*.'

'Just keep telling me what to do, and I'll keep doing it!' I promised.

'What plans do you have for today?' Dominic asked.

For some reason, I didn't like to mention that I was spending my launch day with Michel Amiel.

Dominic will give me a lecture about discretion if I tell him my real plans.

'Kitty and I are just going to hang out,' I told Dominic. More lies. 'We might go out for tea.'

'Sounds nice. Wish I lived a bit closer.'

'Yes, it would be nice to see you again soon!' I replied.

'We must make sure that happens. I'll monitor sales for a couple of weeks and decide if we need a Christmas push or not.' He sounded like he knew what he was doing, which filled me with confidence.

'What would a push consist of?' I asked.

'Wait and see. We have ways and means of pushing.'

58

Dates & Deceits

Over the next couple of weeks, Michel and I went on a few dates, and I don't know if it was because I was feeling elated about my book or he was more relaxed about his business affairs, but we had the most delicious times. We went to the little Curzon cinema again, and he put his arm around me as we watched a 1970 French film, *Le Genou de Claire*.

'I like your knees,' he whispered.

'Oh. Just my knees?'

'And your thighs.'

'You have not seen my thighs!' I said.

'I believe I have . . . '

'Oh yes. THAT day.' I blushed.

'That marvellous day, when I became enchanted by you.'

An old lady behind us *tssked*, so we giggled and stopped whispering.

On another occasion, we walked through the park in a snow flurry, and he insisted on taking off his overcoat and wrapping me up in it. He blew a snowflake off my hair. I couldn't bear to wash my sweater after that walk. His scent was on it, and there was something about that which drove me a little bit wild.

The closer we became, the more he confided in me.

'I have never told anyone half of these things,' he said over dinner one evening in a little bistro in Knightsbridge, after revealing all about his first love. 'Whereas you remain mysterious. Tell me about you. Your family. Your hopes and dreams, love affairs. I want to know everything.'

'I don't like talking about myself,' I said, feeling convulsed by guilt, fiddling with my mobile phone, which lay on the table.

I should just tell him. He will get over it. How can we develop this friendship if I don't tell him about Lucy Lovecake? I am going to ruin everything.

'Actually, there's something I need to tell you,' I said.

'That sounds ominous. Something bad?' he said, sounding alarmed.

'No, just something I've been meaning to tell you for a while, and I've been putting it off.'

'Well, fire away!'

I swallowed hard.

A text pinged into my phone at that moment, flashing the name 'Dominic'.

We both looked at the phone.

'You don't have to tell me your secret,' he said. 'He is your secret, isn't he?'

In a way, that was the truth. 'Yes, I'm sorry. We are close,' I said, by way of explaining the text and wriggling out of my ill-judged near-confession.

That word: Dominic. I could hear him telling me I must not tell Michel about Lucy Lovecake.

That Michel would hate me if my books sold well. That he might sabotage my sales somehow. And there was also some kind of loyalty to Dominic.

It's not that he saved my life, because there were other publishers that wanted the book. It's something else. But what? I'm not in love with Dominic McGann. But there is something. We work so well together. He is reliable and sincere.

Michel looked hurt. 'Why have you been going out with me these past weeks if you are in a relationship with Dominic? I saw you in the Brasserie with him, and of course I saw that he loves you . . . '

'No, it's not like that. We get on well, we have some shared interests, that's all. But I need you to know that he is a big part of my life.' I fudged around the truth.

This wasn't turning out well.

'So, what are you saying?' asked Michel. 'You don't want to see me again? I don't go out with the girls of other men. That is not my style. It is your choice — be honest with us both.'

Oh no! Why does he go on about honesty? I am a deceiver in every department.

'If I am being as honest as I can be, I don't want a boyfriend right now, but I enjoy the company of both of you,' I said. That was somewhere near the truth.

'Well, if you are not deceiving either of us, what harm are you doing?' said Michel.

Oh, please stop it.

'None, I suppose.'

59

The Deceit Deepens

I thought it would be rude to read the text after that, though I was dying to see if it was concerning some news about sales, or the 'push for Christmas' that Dominic was always talking about, somewhat mysteriously.

When I went to the Ladies, I checked.

Daisy, first fortnight sales are great, topping 15,000 units. That's great. I spoke to Branwell earlier today, and we agreed that we should turn up the heat a bit for Christmas. Could you call me asap as I have an idea I want to run by you? Thanks, Dx.

I freshened my lipstick, considering whether or not I should call Dominic right then. I had already been away for what seemed like an age and, as Michel knew about the text, I didn't want him to think I was conducting a text chat.

I'll call him later or in the morning.

As I walked back to the table, I thought that Michel looked distracted.

'Everything okay?' I asked.

'Just been thinking. There's something about you. Something deeper, something I don't know yet. You're holding something back,' he concluded.

'There are lots of things you don't know,' I said. 'My father is a farmer and Ireland's horse whisperer. Did you know that?'

'I did not. What else?'

'I have a brother called Conor who is the greatest man who ever lived — according to him,' I added.

'And your mother? You know all about my mother . . . '

'Yes, my mother is Diana Delaney. She's an artist — paints horses mostly, so you can see how Ma and Pa got together. She's a free spirit. A wonderful mother, but often quite detached, dream-like.'

'She sounds intriguing. Maybe that's where you get your mysterious edge?'

'Perhaps. It's not something I'm conscious of, and I don't like the idea of keeping secrets from you.'

'You are private, discreet. That's good. I don't know why I keep telling you things about my life. I usually lie to everyone. But you listen so well, and you don't judge.'

★ ★ ★

Later that night, when I was alone in my room, I felt a knot inside about the way I was ruining my friendship with Michel.

Should I write to him? No, never put anything sensitive in writing, even I know that.

I tried to push the deception out of my mind. *I mean, it's not as if we're married or even a couple,* I reasoned. *And my book comes before everything — this is what Dominic has told me to do, so I must.*

264

60

Elle

I called Dominic first thing in the morning.

'Sorry I didn't get back to you last night. I was out for dinner with a friend,' I said.

'Ah, do I know him?' he laughed.

'Not this one,' I lied. (*Tripping off your tongue now, Delaney!*)

'Once your identity is out there, as the author of this sweet, sexy little book, you're going to have more offers of dinner than you could ever eat!'

'Well, I'm on a diet, so that's going to be a problem,' I said.

'Don't lose weight! You're lovely as you are,' he assured.

'And that's why I love you!'

'Ha, if only. Well, let's get serious. I mentioned in the text that we could do with some subtle tricks now.' He said, turning to business.

'Yes, what were you thinking of?' I asked.

'Well, a magazine article would be great. In a glossy, with some lingerie on show, and cakes on fabulous stands, rich and Christmassy. A great headline, maybe something like: *Stocking Fillers! Stollen Kisses! Classic Tarts! Or your Cream Tease!* We'll need a model, the cakes — and, of course, the magazine. Any ideas? Any connections?'

I considered this. It all sounded great, and just right for the sorts of readers we had in mind. But it was all a bit last minute, as I explained.

'Dominic, one concern is that they usually work very far in advance with these glossy magazines. Do you really think we'd get in the Christmas special now? It's mid-November already!'

'Yes, it's all a bit of a long shot, but seriously, sales always do plummet from Christmas to spring, so we really need to act now or never.'

I didn't like the idea of this all fizzling away to nothing in the new year.

'The only person I can think of who MIGHT be able to help is Clara's sister, Annabel. She is editor of *Elle*. And as for a model . . . '

'Daisy, you would look gorgeous, I know, but we're still keeping you under wraps until we have a bigger following,' said Dominic.

'Oh, Dominic, you're so sweet, but I'm hardly right for that. Not me. Never. But I'm thinking of Kitty. She's a perfectly proportioned size 8. She'd look amazing, I'm sure.'

'Great idea!'

'We have to find out if the magazine would consider this. I'll call Clara and get back to you.'

'Okay, if anyone can sort this, Daisy, it's you!'

'I'll do my best. Bye for now.'

I called Clara straight away and explained what was required.

'Oh, fuck. Annabel. She's such a bitch. But anything for you. We could try. This could be great for Voluptas too. Let's see if we can persuade her. But I must say, Daisy, I think it'll have gone to print already,' she said, echoing my own thoughts.

'I know. I think so too,' I agreed.

'I'll try everything, darling, I promise! I'll mention the ball dress I lent her in '92 for the Oxford Ball. She can have the French villa every August! Whatever it takes! I will be charming,' Clara vowed, clearly getting fired up now with the idea.

Clara was, in general, a changed woman. She'd found this energy inside her since she'd had to provide for her family, and she looked and acted ten years younger.

★ ★ ★

I paced around the flat, waiting to hear. I threw together the ingredients for Stollen, and Christmas pies, as well as a lavish chocolate roulade.

An hour or so later, Clara called.

'Okay, Daisy. We have to be at these studios tomorrow morning. Some place in Shoreditch. A photographer will be there. We have to take the lingerie, the cakes, the model — is that Kitty? Annabel can get hold of a great stylist for hair and make-up, Mandy Hinchcliffe. 'Lucy Love-cake' has to give an interview. I said you'd have to remain mysterious ... so you won't be photographed.'

'Tomorrow! Wow! How are we going to do that?'

'We are going to use superhuman powers. Annabel is holding back the second print run for us. Some of the Christmas editions are already in the market, but she's going to run this as a bannered De Luxe December edition with Lucy Lovecake in it. How about that?'

I did a twirl.

'I'm spinning. Clara, that is too brilliant. I owe you one! Dominic's going to be ecstatic!'

'We'll all benefit from this. Can you guarantee Kitty is going to be up for posing in underwear? She's very shy and sweet.'

'I'll ask her. Persuade her, if need be.'

'Okay, so if you could both come here this afternoon, we could sort out what to take, what looks you want, everything.'

'Okay, let's say two o'clock. And I'd better get baking!'

★ ★ ★

Kitty was still in bed. When in doubt, be direct, I decided, so I came straight out with it.

'Want to be a lingerie model in *Elle* magazine — shooting tomorrow?' I said.

'Me? Model lingerie?' said Kitty, rubbing her eyes.

'Yes! You have a beautiful figure! Please say you will?'

'I'm not sure. For *Elle* magazine? Are you sure they're going to accept me? They have really high standards.' Typical Kitty, putting herself down.

'Kitty, *please* say you'll do it. It will lift sales of *French Fancy* by thousands. Come on, please? You've helped me so much. We're in this together,' I implored.

'Oh, why not? If I had more than a day to worry about it, I'd probably be ill with nerves, but, hey, let's get on with it.' She sounded decisive.

I hugged her. 'Thank you!'

She examined her thighs. 'Reckon you can get rid of cellulite in a day?'

★ ★ ★

Dominic was delighted when I told him what we'd put together.

'Well done, Daisy! This is going to be the making of it, I promise,' he said.

'We are all working flat out — it's really exciting. I think the shots will be gorgeous!' I told him.

'Daisy, I love working with you. I can't imagine life without you now.'

That's a bit strong.

'I mean work life,' he clarified. 'We're a good team.'

'I agree,' I said. 'But I must go for now. Will be in touch.'

Later that morning, I missed a call from Michel. *Too busy with my magazine shoot to return calls from famous French chefs!*

61

Lingerie Again

We spent the afternoon in the boutique. Clara had persuaded her sister Annabel to come over.

She was very beautiful and not quite as monstrous as Clara had indicated.

'Thank you so much for this!' I said. 'It really is appreciated.'

'Well, it's got the blood pumping round the office, that's for sure. We're all so set in our ways, but I thought, well, if I can't pull strings for my sister . . . '

'It's too kind of you. This is Kitty. She's going to be modelling for us.'

'Great to meet you, Kitty. You'll look great. I'll brief the hair and make-up people. Yes, I can just see this! Very opulent, cute, sexy. How perfect for Christmas!'

We started looking through the silks.

'Absolutely the red,' said Clara, deciding on items we would take.

'And the rosebud bustier for sure,' voiced Annabel.

'Some ivory would be nice,' I said. 'What will the backdrop be?'

'I've organised for some crimson velvet falls and a bit of gold chiffon, plus lots of gold candlesticks, as well as a very traditional tree.

Hopefully it will look fab — not much we can do if it doesn't, actually!'

★ ★ ★

That night, I rushed around the kitchen.

Buzz! Another missed call from Michel. I'd have to ignore it. I couldn't bear to lie to him any more.

Stollen kisses done! In the box.

Christmas pies dusted with icing sugar! In the box.

Chocolate roulade! In the box.

Fresh cream chocolate truffles — finished. In a little gold box.

I fell into bed at midnight. I didn't even glance at my phone. The next morning I saw that there were missed calls from Michel and Dominic.

Too busy for men. Shoreditch, here we come.

Clara drove us over to the studios. I was a total mess, hair scraped back off my face, no make-up, wearing jeans, a polo and a parka. Boxes of cakes were piled on my lap. Kitty, for her part, was sitting in the front in a Tigger onesy with the hood up. Clara, behind the wheel, was joyful.

'A name check in *Elle*! This could be a changer for our little silk store!' she said.

I loved the way we were all benefitting from one another while helping one another.

Once inside the building, which seemed like a disused biscuit factory, we met up with Annabel, who was in professional mode, a bit less fluffy than the day before.

'She's so Headmistressy,' mumbled Clara.

271

'Consider your son's school fees, think not of your dignity,' I said.

The stylists started working on Kitty, while the 'set' was constructed by the photographer's assistants, brandishing bales of red velvet and gold chiffon. Nearby was the photographer herself, a feisty woman called Babsy, who peered into a laptop screen with glasses perched on the end of her nose.

I set out the cakes, and an assistant produced lots of gold cake stands and platters from Fenwick's. People were diving and dashing around in every direction. Corners were not cut as such — there were so many people, everything was given due attention and co-ordinated by Annabel, who was in full flight.

We had fun arranging the set. Before long, some coffee, pastries and sandwiches arrived, though most of the magazine types floating around notably ate nothing at all.

When Kitty emerged in the pretty rosebud bustier, her black hair piled high, her gorgeous face made up to perfection, we all knew this was going to work.

62

The Shoot

'Left a bit!' Annabel screamed to Kitty.

'Go easy,' said Babsy. 'She's not a professional model.'

'Every pantomime needs a bitch,' said Clara.

'Sorry,' called Annabel. 'Kitty, you're actually better than many a professional. I'm being so particular because you are so great. I don't want to miss a trick. Forgive me, I'm going to be like this all day!'

Kitty just smiled serenely. I guessed that nothing could be as terrible as her days in Prim & Proper.

'You look gorgeous, Kitty!' I called.

'Wish I could return the compliment!' she said.

'Ha! I know. I'm the ugly best friend today!' I told her as I pulled an even uglier face.

Lunch arrived. Sticky mango chicken with a massive green salad and mounds of rice. Nobody seemed to be 'allowed' to eat rice. Except Clara and I. More for us!

Only eight hours later, it was a wrap. Kitty was totally exhausted, but we viewed the images on Babsy's laptop and, even before the edit, they were utterly spectacular.

'Sis,' said Clara, 'you might be a bitch, but you

are a professional bitch, and I salute you.'

As I was tidying up, I put the little rosebud bustier in my bag. I'll pay for that next time I'm at work. I might want to wear it one day.

63

Daisy's Secrets

Within two days, a full double-page spread was e-mailed over to us. Kitty and I pored over it, incredulous.

'Is that really me?' gasped Kitty.

The whole piece was stunning, and it struck me that my book wasn't a random collection of ingredients. It all blended together perfectly; the silk, the cakes, the love tips. The Lucy Lovecake interview sounded excellent, and at the very end of the article, there was the little bit of blurb which mattered: *French Fancy by Lucy Lovecake is priced at £9.99 and is available at all good bookstores or by order from Amazon, or at www.bluebells.com.*

Kitty and I were out Christmas shopping on the high street when we bumped into Michel.

'Hello, stranger!' he said.

'Hi, I'm sorry I didn't get back to you. I've been really busy!'

'You always say you're busy — but busy doing what? Your horse course?'

'What? Oh, yeah, mostly that and some top-secret missions,' I said.

'Yes, you are obviously an agent. That would explain it,' he said. Leaning forward, he whispered, 'I'm quite excited by that idea.'

I smiled enigmatically.

This is so easy, turning men on when you don't have time for them.

'Why don't you come into the city with me to help me do some Christmas shopping?' he suggested. 'Say, tomorrow?'

'Yeah, I could do that,' I said. 'Sounds nice. Do you have a big list?'

He reached into his pocket. 'Yes, here it is.'

Maman.

That was it.

'We should manage to find something nice for her,' I said.

'I'll come round to your place about ten. Is that okay?'

'Sure, I'll be ready.'

★   ★   ★

Kitty and I spent the evening tidying the flat and checking that all copies of *French Fancy* in all its forms (drafts, sections, finished copies) were well hidden.

I was ready when he arrived — eager to get away as soon as possible. Michel was insistent on driving to Knightsbridge, where he knew of a great place to park.

'Let's go to Harrods' — which he pronounced Arrods — 'I'd like to buy something nice for you for Christmas.'

'That's very kind, but I'm not sure that I really need anything,' I said.

'This is not about needs. It's about desires.'

I laughed at his corniness, but was unclear if

he was being ironic or not.

Inside Harrods, we wheeled around, through cosmetics, perfumes, handbags.

'Anything you want, it is yours,' he said, though he hardly stopped long enough for me to look at any one thing.

I saw a little purse, beaded, a bit like one I'd had as a girl.

'That's nice,' I said.

'It is £12!' he said.

'I like it.'

He bought it. 'Lunch?' he suggested afterwards.

'That would be lovely.'

'I like the restaurant near the book department,' he said.

'Whatever you say. I'm not familiar with any of the eating places in here,' I confessed.

We went up to the second floor.

'Let's look at the books,' he said. 'Maybe something will take your eye in there. And we'll see if my lumps of forest are shifting.'

'Okay, great idea,' I said.

There was a display table with suggested Christmas titles in the middle of the department, positioned by a red-velvet armchair, faux fireplace with felt stockings, and a magnificent Christmas tree.

'Ah! Gift ideas,' I said. 'Shall we take a look?'

My heart stopped, I'm sure it did, momentarily. In pride of place in the middle of the table with a label stating *OUR CHOICE* was a whole pile of *French Fancy!* The label further stated: *The perfect stocking filler for him or her! Buy early to avoid disappointment. It's the book everyone's talking about — as featured in the new edition of ELLE magazine!*

'Nothing much here. Let's look in the cookery section,' I said.

'Hold on a minute.' Michel paused. 'What is this cake book in the middle of the table?'

I said nothing. *He'll gloss over this. His eye will go elsewhere. Please may he not examine a copy. He'll see Bluebells and might think of Dominic. Then he'll wonder about my texts with Dominic . . . me being at the barn dance . . .*

He picked one up. There were only the line drawings and nothing that especially linked it to me.

Stay cool, Daisy. The real risk is if he sees the Elle piece! He knows Kitty, he knows the rosebud bustier.

'You see this piece of tat?' he said. 'This is the sort of facile nonsense that has ruined sales for me. Gimmicks. Probably 'written' by someone who has no baking credentials at all.' He examined the jacket more closely.

'Lucy Lovecake?' He chuckled dryly. 'Probably someone who is embarrassed to be associated with it. Maybe even a committee of people in a publishing house. What a joke.'

I feigned disinterest, heading over to the cookery section.

Inside, my mind was buzzing. In fact, I thought I might collapse due to the colliding thoughts going through my head. There were thoughts along the lines of: *So, Dominic was dead right. It does bug Michel when rival books* come out, no matter how different and how trivial. There were other thoughts: *I should feel so proud. This is a wonderful moment — my books are prominent in Harrods. I'd like to call Dominic, and Kitty and Mum and Dad.* And yet more thoughts. *Just tell him you wrote it, because you are getting deeper into this deceit, Daisy. There will be no way back.*

Michel followed me to the cookbooks. We struggled to find his books, but eventually located two from the Classic Cuisine collection.

'Look at the state of these!' he hissed. 'Dusty old things been here since dinosaur gangs controlled Knightsbridge!'

'Ask your manager to speak to someone about this. You should be on a Christmas promotion!' I said.

'You are so right. This is disgraceful. No wonder I have problems,' he complained.

I didn't like to say that since his dramatic departure from Britain by police escort a few months before, he was perhaps not the man of the moment any longer.

'Michel, I wish you'd let me set you up on Twitter. You'd enjoy it. I'm sure you'd get millions of followers overnight. And you could reconnect with your readership that way? Very directly.'

He seemed to be considering this.

'I'll think about it,' he said eventually. 'Now, let's get lunch.'

64

The Guessing Game

The *Elle* magazine piece was one of those break-through features. Other publications noticed it and began to ask: so, who is this Lucy Lovecake? There were spin-off articles in the *Daily Mail*, *The Telegraph*, *The Sun*, *The Guardian*, *The Evening Standard*, and *The Times*.

Dominic called. 'This is really working, Daisy, we're being bombarded with questions about the identity of Lucy Lovecake. Just say when you want me to spill and I will. Any time now. We have really got them guessing.'

'Wow, I didn't think it would be this fast. It's amazing. I even saw the book on promotion in Harrods the other day,' I told him.

'Great! What took you up to Harrods?'

'Christmas shopping,' I said.

'What are you doing for Christmas, Daisy?' he asked.

'Not sure yet. Mum and Dad are going to my brother's in New York. I might fly over there. How about you?'

'Nothing much planned. Just Minty and I, and the dogs and hens, round the tree.'

'That sounds very nice,' I said wistfully.

'If you decided against going to New York, you know you'd be very welcome here,' he said.

'That's very kind. Thank you. I'll get back to you on that shortly.'

'Great, so what do you say about revealing, the face behind Lucy Lovecake now, just to lap up the Christmas spirit some more?'

This threw me.

I desperately wanted to be able to shout from the rooftops about *French Fancy*. I was so proud, and I did think that the anonymity thing was possibly a mistake. Unsustainable, and extremely frustrating.

But what about Michel? I will never see him again.

I had been hoping that I'd start to dislike Michel intensely and not care what he thought about my double life. But that was not the case. If anything, I liked him a little more than before.

'Let's wait and we can use the revealing of my identity to pep things up a bit in the new year,' I said. 'You said it would be flat in the early part of the year. Let's not do all of our tricks in the one show!'

'Sure, I just thought it might be a bit tough for you to hold it in! Have you seen the attention Kitty is getting online since the shoot?'

'Yes, and I'm delighted for her,' I said. Everyone was asking, *Who's the model?* I was so proud of Kitty.

'I love that you love your friends. Daisy, you are the sweetest girl.'

I'm really not.

65

Sunday Times

Christmas in New York had been a welcome relief from the complexities of London. New Year, without a sense of impending doom, had been a novelty, for sure, though I missed Kitty. Now, it was a Friday in mid-January, a year since it all began. Bleak, colourless, virtually without light. I was working on the second Lucy Lovecake book, tentatively called *Noodles and Canoodles*. Less patisserie, more main mealsy in tone. Kitty was away at a shoot with her modelling agency.

My phone rang. I pounced, keen for distractions.

Ah, Dominic! I can truthfully tell him I'm busy on the second book.

'Hey, Dominic. How are you?'

'Great, thanks. You?'

'Yeah, all good here.'

'Brace yourself, Daisy!' he said, his familiar voice bristling with excitement.

'Good or bad?' (I knew it was good. The games we play.)

'Good. Very good. Maybe the goodest thing ever.'

'Well, spill it!' I said impatiently.

'Ready? *French Fancy* is going to be at

number six in the *Sunday Times* bestseller list this weekend!'

People talk of collapsing with shock, and I always thought it was a metaphor for despair, but I really did fall over. My legs became like two matchsticks, unable to support the vast combined weight of my torso and my suddenly heavy head.

I think Dominic heard the THUD as I fell. The phone was temporarily out of my reach, but I could hear him calling my name. I reached across for it.

'I'm here,' I said in a pathetic little voice.

'Oh God, I didn't mean to cause you injury!' he said.

'I'm fine, really.' I composed myself.

'You know what this means, don't you, Daisy?' he asked.

'It's time?' I replied.

'Yes.'

'What's the plan?'

'I've decided to reveal you at a signing at Harrods!' he said.

'Oh. When?'

'Three weeks from now. Valentine's Day! What could be better?' he declared, expecting me to be delighted.

'That sounds like a great idea,' I said flatly.

'Well, say it like you mean it!' said Dominic, laughing.

'I'm sorry. I'm thrilled. It will just be the end of a stage, you know. The anonymous stage. It's quite nice to go out quietly for potatoes and leeks without anyone caring that you're making potato and leek soup.'

'Yes, but this will be so much fun from now on, Daisy. You can still have the Lucy Lovecake persona, but you will also have the real you out there, so your friends and family can celebrate this wonderful book with you.'

'Where are you going to advertise the book signing?' I asked. 'We want lots of people there, don't we?'

'Absolutely. We will send out a press release, as well as private invites. We can also do a 'Meet Lucy Lovecake' banner on the social media pages. I think it will be rammed,' said Dominic.

'Just tell me what to do, what to wear, how to be. I am so excited. It's time to come clean.'

★ ★ ★

The following week, Michel called, inviting me over to his house for supper the next evening.

'Let me cook for you. Mother is back in Paris, seeing her sister, Martine. I want to take care of you. Secret agents need to be pampered,' he said.

'That would be nice,' I said. 'Let me bring a pudding?'

'No, I'm doing cherry clafoutis for you. See you at seven tomorrow then?' he said.

'Yes, bye for now.'

The next day, I thought a lot about the consequences of 'coming out' as the author of *French Fancy*. On the one hand, I wanted to sing from the rooftops that it was my book. On the other, I would lose my freedom — and even worse, my friendship with Michel.

Face it, Delaney. You're in love with him.

I spent a while getting ready for dinner at his place, fluttering around my room, trying to decide between French chic, English Rose and Pippa Cavanaugh numbers. I decided on jeans and a little blouse. I was ready to leave, and at the last minute, I ran to my room and put on the rosebud bustier, the one he'd loved when browsing in the shop, under my top.

Just for luck.

I was shaking as I rang the doorbell.

He must have been standing behind the door, waiting, as it opened immediately.

'Yes, m'lady,' he said in a British accent, giving a little bow.

'I was invited to supper by the gentleman of the house,' I said.

'Gentleman, you say?'

I laughed. 'Yeah, that is a stretch.'

He kissed me on both cheeks, then on the lips, just a bit longer than a gentleman would.

'Well, this is cosy,' I said, as he took my coat.

'Yes, just the two of us. Me and my enchantress, sans chaperone.'

He stepped closer and encircled me in his arms.

'You must know that secret agents are trained to always get away,' I said.

'Unless they meet their match,' he said.

I ducked out of his hold. 'Let's see if you can really cook. I'm starving.'

I watched, transfixed, as he diced chicken and chopped asparagus and mushrooms in that masterful way. He then made a batter for crepes, cracking the eggs expertly with one hand, chatting all the time about the things he'd like to do before he died. Fly over the Grand Canyon, see the Northern Lights, go to Amish country. I realised that I was imagining myself at his side.

'So much still to do,' he said. 'And according to my doctor, only a couple of years to do it in, if I carry on this way.'

'Why don't you look after yourself?' I said.

'I don't know. I've gone too far into debauchery,' he replied.

He was so adorable when he was being himself like this. Unrecognisable from his boorish, public persona.

'Do you have children?' I asked.

'Not that I know of,' he said. 'I don't think all that's for me. What kind of example am I?'

He cooked off the chicken and vegetables with some white wine and cream.

'You're an inspiration when you're not being an idiot,' I told him.

'Why thank you for your lavish praise!' he said, coming across to look right into my eyes. He touched my hair and kissed the top of my head in a very loving way.

I couldn't help but smile.

⋆ ⋆ ⋆

The crepes were so retro, so French. Seriously delicious.

'Thank you. That was lovely,' I said after the last bite. 'And the cherry clafoutis?'

286

'Yes, then maybe we should go upstairs after that?'

I wanted to. More than anything. But I didn't want to go to bed with Michel without telling him the truth.

'Yes, if the pudding gets my approval, we should do that.'

The clafoutis was perfect. It melted in the mouth, effortless to eat yet deeply satisfying.

'I am happy to say, that was superbe,' I announced.

Michel winked. 'Glad to hear that.' He grabbed my hand. 'Follow me.'

I was mesmerised by him and the lovely meal he had made for us. So entranced, in fact, that I forgot all about coming clean.

Instead, I let him lead me silently up the grand staircase and into his bedroom. He closed the door, and we melted together, his cherry kisses firm but tender.

'The rosebuds,' he said. 'I've wanted to see you in it from that day in the shop.'

66

The Guilt

We slept blissfully together until noon the next day.

'Happy?' he said.

'Very.'

Except for the fact that I now have a LOVER I have lied to again and again, not just a friend. A man I adore, who trusts me and confides in me. I am hateful and despicable and wicked. And what would Dominic think?

I shuddered.

'Daisy?' he said, as I rested my head on his chest.

'Yes?'

'Teach me about the Twitters,' he said. 'Please.'

'So there really is no such thing as a free supper!' I said.

'You don't think I treated you to all this just for fun, do you?' he laughed.

A pillow fight resulted.

We decided to spend the rest of the day setting him up with various social media accounts.

'Keep it easy. Start with Facebook and Twitter, possibly Instagram,' I advised, then we can introduce more. 'Most of your fan base will be on those.'

'Whatever you say,' he said.

'We'll start with Twitter,' I said, making him an account, with a photograph and cover shot of one of his books.

'This is easier than websites,' he commented. 'How will people find me?'

'Easily,' I said. 'See, you have followers already!'

'Do I? Who are they?'

'Fans, just people,' I explained, as his followers increased before our eyes.

'Weird. Amazing. Are they nutcases? Why aren't they busy doing real life?'

'This is the new real life. Now, let's make a post and see what reaction you get,' I said. 'You have to be brief on Twitter. What would you like to say?'

'That I'm in love!'

I blushed, then laughed. 'No. About food. About your books. About your professional life. Come on, we are re-branding here.'

'Okay, how about I post the recipe for my crepes? The ones we ate last night?'

'Great, lovely. A nice supper recipe, add some banter about how quick and easy they are. How the ladies love them. Look, click on this tweet box and write whatever you like.'

He took charge of his page. I watched him type (well, thump at the keys).

I am in love. My girlfriend liked these crepes, so I'm going to share the recipe with you. Enjoy!

Oh God, I thought, reading the screen. *This is so much worse! His girlfriend? What kind of cruel person am I? Tell him now, Delaney, before it's too late!*

But I couldn't. I just kept watching.

He then pasted the link to the recipe on his website.

'How's that?'

'Very cute. Now, give it a few minutes,' I said.

'Why?'

'To see how many people have liked your recipe,' I told him.

'Okay, boss.'

I checked the screen. 'Wow, seventy-eight already!'

'Seriously? That soon? This is fun.'

'Yes, it is. See, there are comments coming through. You can reply to those. But just be careful what you say, and never log on here when drunk, okay?' I looked at the clock. 'I have to go. Let me just explain about re-tweets, and also, you can follow people.'

'Oh! Why do you have to go? Secret Service calling, huh?'

'Yeah. I have things to do. I have a busy life.'

'But Clara says you hardly work in the shop now. You must have another job, right? Seriously. Are you building a business or something? I don't buy that horse studies thing. You can tell me anything, darling.'

'I don't want to talk about that right now. I can't. I'm not allowed,' I explained, groaning inside.

Daisy, this is the moment. You have never been closer, he won't be mad for long. He'll come round. You've been loving and helpful towards him. Just tell him, blurt it out, go on.

But I just couldn't. Our first time in bed

together, and it had been so blissful. I just wanted to feel the magic for a little while longer. I hated myself for the ongoing deception.

'I want to see you again soon,' said Michel. 'I have a dental procedure going on tomorrow, and a TV appearance soon — but in a few days?'

'That would be nice. I'll get in touch.'

I'll have him round for supper next week and tell him everything, then beg for his forgiveness, and we'll go to bed and everything will be fine.

67

L'Internet et TV

It only took two days for the chaos to begin. A follower of Lucy Lovecake made an indignant post on the Lucy Lovecake Facebook page: *Michel Amiel is an ignorant, fucked-up French has-been. In fact, I thought he was locked up in some danky French prison right now! Just ignore him, Lucy!*

What's all this about?

I followed the thread back to its source.

Earlier that day, Michel had been on *This Morning* with Georgie and Simon. I played the clip of the interview with him, which someone had posted. It seemed to be the tail end of a chat they'd been having with Michel. I stared at it intently, thinking how handsome he looked.

'So, Michel, it's been great to talk to you, and lovely to hear that you're back in Britain for the foreseeable future after all those, erm, uncertain times!' said Georgie, all fluttery eyelashes.

Michel stood to leave.

Georgie continued, 'But it's not time to go yet. We've actually got some questions via Twitter from our viewers. Would you mind answering those?'

'Sure, it would be my pleasure,' said Michel, clearly on his best behaviour.

This is torture. He clearly says something rude about Lucy Lovecake, but what?

A few questions in, someone called Anna wanted to know if Michel had read Lucy Lovecake's *French Fancy?*

He recognised the reference, that was for sure. 'I've just joined Tweeter at the suggestion of a very dear friend of mine — and I keep hearing about that blooming book!' he said, more than a note of frustration in his voice. 'I saw it in Arrods. It's not a serious cookery book. It's a joke, a silly book, by some silly person who is so ashamed of it he or she cannot admit who he or she is!'

Simon stepped in. 'But it *is* good fun,' he said. 'Surely there's a place for all kinds of books about food, and would you not agree that linking food tips with dating tips makes a lot of sense? Food is a sensuous experience and eating is somehow wrapped up in romance.'

Thank you, Simon!

'I was asked for my opinion, and I say, please don't buy it!' said Michel. 'Buy quality cookery books you can learn from, by someone who is besotted by food, not romance.'

Georgie picked up from there. 'Well, unequivocal words there from Michel Amiel on the popular new book *French Fancy*. The next question is about your cookery school. Is it true, asks Harriet, that you are planning to open new branches across the UK in the spring?'

'Yes, that is quite true,' he said proudly.

I paused the clip. My mobile phone was buzzing.

Probably Branwell or Dominic.

I was reeling. Michel was so vitriolic about my book. *How dare he? But he doesn't know it's my book. How can he be loyal when he doesn't know it's your book?*

In a way, it made the guilt of deceiving him diffuse a little, the fact that he was so mean-spirited about someone else's work. It could have been anyone's book. How was he to know who he was offending?

In particular, I hated the way he banged on about classic cookery, as if everyone wanted to learn to cook in a serious way.

Books about food are about titillating and teasing as much as instructing, are they not?

I looked at my phone. As I thought, missed calls from my agent and publisher. Dominic was hyper: *Hey, can't get a hold of you? Did you see the clips from This Morning? And the furore on Twitter. Now 780 posts of support on Lucy Lovecake's page. This is FANTASTIC. We could not afford PR like this! The man is a twit, good and proper. And what a rat. I'm going to consider ending my business dealings with him on the chicken front. He's a liability! No wonder he's going down the tubes! Daisy, as I thought, everyone's asking, Who is Lucy Lovecake? Not long until Valentine's Day! Also, I think it would be in order for Lucy Lovecake to give a genteel but firm retort to the obnoxious French swine — see what you can do!*

A call came through as I was reading that. It was Michel. I wanted to speak to him.

'Hi, Michel,' I chirped.

'Daisy, you are going to be so proud of me!'

'Why so?' I asked.

'I am fixing my career. I've been on TV slamming my rivals, and I've got thousands of new followers today, even if some of them are shouting and swearing at me! I love it, the tweeting. It's cool,' he said.

'Right, well, as long as you are controlling your temper and not going on there drunk, then that's all good,' I said, trying to sound encouraging as, after all, I'd suggested the new approach.

'Can you meet? I want to see you again,' he said. 'I want to tell you about the new recipes I'm working on.'

It was lovely to hear him so enthused. 'Sure, when were you thinking of?'

'In a few hours?' he suggested.

I thought of Dominic's directions to get online and start bashing Michel Amiel in the voice of Lucy Lovecake.

Oh dear. What a mess.

'I'm sorry, I'm going to be busy tonight. Can I call you when I've got some time?' I said.

'Oh, okay.' A disappointed Michel. 'It's up to you. Make sure it's not too long.'

'Yes, okay. Bye for now,' I said breezily, my mind aching with colliding thoughts.

'Bye, beautiful.'

I knew I couldn't look him in the eye with all this going on. I had to make a decision before Valentine's Day. He had to be told. But a weak little part of me thought it might be better just to withdraw from him, end our affair, and then it wouldn't matter when he found out.

295

I lay on my bed, reflecting that I should feel so happy, but instead I was tied in knots. I would have to reply to Michel Amiel as Lucy Lovecake soon.

Then I started that thing we sometimes do. I began to tell myself that I didn't have feelings for Michel anyway, and that he was a horribly mean, jealous, and self-obsessed man, that I could do much better. Sometimes if you say such things to yourself often enough, you actually start to believe them.

As if reading my mind, Michel sent a text late on: *Daisy, you should know that I love you. Please do not withdraw from me. I need you. Mx*

At first it touched my heart and I longed to call him and tell him everything. But then I used that whole narrative about him being a loser, and I started to think, *Well, he needs me, does he? What of my needs — does he ever wonder what I might need?*

A tiny voice inside me was saying: *How can he know what you need when you don't share your true self with him? Be fair to him.* But I ignored that inner voice and ploughed on with my withdrawal from the man who excited and inspired me. There were many of his texts left unanswered, calls rejected by me. He was nonplussed. Gradually, I learned to live without the buzz of meeting him. I used up my energy on Lucy Lovecake matters.

68

Valentine's Day

Valentine's Day. A bouquet of flowers arrived in the morning. I was curious to see what the card said. Branwell perhaps, thinking of my signing that evening? Dominic, in the same mode? Or Michel, still trying to reach me? It had been almost two weeks since I'd last seen him, and considering how delicious our first night together had been, it must have seemed very strange indeed to him that I had retreated so quickly. I must have seemed like a lunatic.

Ah, from Dominic.

I was delighted, of course, but I also felt troubled that Dominic's note had a slightly personal tone to it: *Daisy, love working with you, and everything about you. Can't wait for the world to know how brilliant you are, Much love, Dom. x.*

I like Dominic and maybe if Michel Amiel would completely vanish once and for all, then who knows, maybe something would bubble up . . .

It had been a week since the last text from Michel. I kept thinking, or maybe even hoping, that he'd come round to the flat. But he didn't. *I think I've really hurt him, and confused him. No wonder. He was feeling so good, about tweeting and his new book. I've been so cruel.*

I had started to do that mad thing of looking at his Facebook and Twitter posts. How batty that sort of thing can make you feel. There was nothing of any great surprise — disagreements with other well-known chefs, abundant opinions and some photos of fresh fish, beef and cheeses he spotted in markets and shops as he went around London. It was all quite captivating — he was on-song about food, but I stopped looking and began to feel that our one night together was a moment in time, locked up in my heart.

And now it was the day of my public outing as the author of *French Fancy: Dating Tips from Lucy Lovecake.*

I was nervous about the big night ahead. I knew my parents would be there (they were staying in a small hotel round the corner from Harrods), and Kitty would be there, and of course Clara and Philip, plus her sister, Annabel, and one or two old friends from art school who now lived in London. I suppose I wanted all of this to get back to Tom Percy. Not that he really bothered me any more. I hardly gave him a thought.

I had agonised over what to wear. Lucy Lovecake on Valentine's Day. I had wondered about something red, enlisting Kitty's help.

'What about a warm pink?' she suggested. 'A little softer than red, less tarty and more sensuous?'

'Good thinking!'

I'd gone to John Lewis and bought a pattern for a dress — very Fifties — fitted at the waist and bust, very curve-enhancing, and had it made up in ZIPPIT on the high street.

'Wow,' said Kitty when she saw it during a try-on. 'Could not be more flattering.'

I was in the bath about three in the afternoon, trying to get in the spirit of the evening but feeling very shy and overwhelmed, when a text flashed up.

I grabbed my phone from the chair by the bath and gulped. From Michel.

Dear Daisy, please say you'll meet me tonight. I've booked a table at the Ivy for 8pm. There is no one else I'd rather spend the evening with. Please say you will be there. I love you.

I started to feel uncomfortable. *Damn, why does this have to come through now? What shall I say?*

I started to shake. The last lie? Or time to come clean? *There's no time to come clean now.*

I wrote a short text, hands shaking: *Michel, it's lovely to hear from you, and I would love nothing more than to meet you for dinner, but unfortunately I am unwell! Could we try later in the week? Please say yes!*

69

Anonymous No More

No reply came back. I got ready with a heavy heart. *He obviously thinks I've got another boyfriend.*

The dress fitted like a dream. Elegant kitten heels, cute box bag, hair up, soft make-up. *Not too bad.* I went to see what Kitty thought.

'Daisy, you look lovely,' said Kitty. 'Try smiling though.'

'I'm nervous!' I said. 'You look magnificent!' She was a picture in a black cocktail dress, not attention grabbing, just very, very classic and serene.

The car arrived for us at 5.45pm; the signing was advertised to begin at 7pm, along with cakes, champagne and a talk from the real Lucy Lovecake.

I checked my notes on the way over in the car. My mouth was dry, my heart raced.

'This is a book for both women and men who want dating to be fun, and at all times delicious.'

I felt panicky. 'It sounds rubbish!'

'Relax,' said Kitty. 'This is going to be fine.'

'But I had to turn Michel down, and he'll never get in touch again now. Especially when he hears about the outing of Lucy Lovecake on social media.'

'It's inevitable that he will hear, Daisy. If only you'd told him early on!' said Kitty.

I shot her a look.

She seemed contrite about stirring emotion on the way to my big moment. 'Sorry! But a few days ago you said you'd gone off him?'

'I know, I've been convincing myself of that, but I'm just not sure. I keep thinking about him, but that's probably just the guilt I'm feeling,' I said. 'I'm sure I can forget him.'

'Try not to let it spoil your night. I'd imagine you'll not be short of male fans after tonight, especially when you appear in the press in THAT dress!'

'I'm just starting to realise how scary it is, that it won't be a secret any more. Oh, Kitty! Should I stay a secret?' I asked.

'No. We're here now,' she said. 'Let's get on with it.'

Dominic and Branwell had done a great job of planning the signing event. As soon as we stepped out onto the pavement, someone from Harrods, a pleasant woman called Bridget, whisked us inside, into an elevator, and up to a beautiful lounge where we were offered an array of refreshments.

'How many people are going to be at the event?' I asked.

'Several hundred, but we are going to have an organised queuing system,' said Bridget.

'Several hundred? Really? Gosh, how long will it all take?' I queried.

'Probably until around ten. We thought you could make your speech first because everyone is going to be curious as we've billed this as the 'outing' event.'

'Sure. May as well get it over with,' I mumbled.

'Are you dreading it?' asked Bridget.

'Yes, very much so. I think I've been living with the perfect scenario these past few months — a successful book and complete anonymity,' I admitted.

'It's going to be so much fun, though,' said Bridget. 'You'll be invited here, there and everywhere after tonight! I wish it was me! And by the way, I love the book. We all do in the store!' Bridget was so kind and soothing.

'Thank you! You know, you're right, it will be fun! I'm going to have a glass of champagne, relax, and enjoy myself.'

Bridget dotted in and out between the lounge and the book department, telling me that my parents had arrived, my agent, publisher and quite a few others. But that I must stay 'backstage' until given the wink.

'No problem, I'm quite happily enjoying my last minutes of freedom here,' I said.

Someone came to put a discreet microphone on me.

'Sorry, this dress is rather tight!' I admitted.

A wire was discreetly draped through the neckline.

Finally, it was time to go through to the event. My legs felt like rubber as I approached the event space. Branwell and Dominic were waiting for me by a seat covered in a cupcake fabric. Mum and Dad waved, looking so proud. I'm not sure they understood the fuss on social media about this Lucy Lovecake, but they were delighted to be part of the occasion.

70

Unveiled

One thing that surprised me was that there were more men than women in the audience.

'Lots of men liking Lucy!' I whispered to Kitty, who was at my side.

She nodded emphatically.

Dominic handled the press, and after a few short words from him, setting out my credentials, I was propelled forward, hailed as the true author of *French Fancy*, and it was time for me to give my speech.

There were gasps, mutters, giggles and some reassuring cheers as I took my place. I cleared my throat and composed myself.

I delivered it slowly, surely, with as much grace as I could muster, apologising for the charade, thanking everyone for their interest, and expressing my disbelief at the popularity of the book.

'I only hope that Daisy Delaney is as acceptable to readers as is Lucy Lovecake!' I concluded. 'Otherwise, we're in trouble.'

Dominic winked at me when it was over and came to my side. 'That was tremendous. Very well done!' he said.

He turned to face the crowd again, which was so dense it was impossible for me to pick out individuals. I could see that there were lots of security men dotted around, and more and more people were arriving all the time, trying to push through the edges of the party.

'Time for questions now, then Daisy Delaney will be signing and meeting fans,' Dominic explained.

A whole sea of hands went up. Dominic selected a questioner and the microphone was passed to her.

'Miss Delaney, have you not been tempted to shout your identity from the rooftops before now, with the book being such a huge hit?'

I considered this carefully. 'Not really,' I began. 'Dominic — my publisher, as you know — always said that it was best to make people wonder. And I must say, it seems he was right!'

'Lady at the back,' said Dominic.

'My question for Daisy is: How did she research the book? I mean, what made you think of lingerie and cakes combined?'

'Yes, ask her that!' said a voice I knew too well.

Oh. My. God. Help. Me.

71

Accusations

It was, of course, Michel. He came barging up the middle of the crowd, his face contorted with rage.

'I've been listening to you from the back, Daisy Delaney!' he called. 'Or do I mean 'Lucy Lovecake'?'

A hush fell over the throng.

Michel made his way to the front, pushing people aside aggressively, and he stood in front of me, eyes glaring, mouth set in a twist of vitriol, a strong aroma of alcohol around him.

'Deceiver!' he cried.

I was frozen to the spot. From the corner of my eye, I could see Dominic move towards him, but the crowd was densely packed.

My heart had either stopped or was beating so fast it was off the scale. Either way, I struggled for breath and clutched my throat fearfully.

Michel continued, turning to face the stunned audience.

Can't someone help?

'This woman has been encouraging me to spill my heart out to her. She has taken a baking course at my cookery school. She has lied to me time and time again. And there I was, at my dentist the other week, flicking through a magazine I found in the waiting room, when I saw an article in *Elle* magazine . . . '

Security guards approached, two burly skinheads. One said, 'Come this way, sir.'

'I'm not finished,' growled Michel, being half-jostled now by the guards. 'I asked her to dinner tonight — giving her one last chance to come clean — but she LIED again! Said she was ill. Do not trust her! She pretends to be Lucy Lovecake. She pretends *everything*. She has forgotten how to tell the truth.'

Dominic reached me as Michel was whisked away, arms flailing, knocking over a pile of *French Fancy* books as he went.

I still couldn't move, but I was aware of flashes going off — press photographers snapping gleefully — and mobile phones in the air, capturing footage of a madman on the rampage.

Branwell was at a loss for words. Meanwhile, Dominic tried to calm things by taking command at the microphone.

'Well, that was a vintage performance from Monsieur Amiel. Let's be rather more British about things and pretend that didn't happen! I think the best thing is that we start the signing, and you can meet Daisy in person. Please observe the queuing system, and continue to enjoy the refreshments. Many thanks for coming here this evening, and here's to many delicious offerings from Lucy Lovecake!'

He raised his glass, confirming: 'To Lucy Lovecake!'

There was a resounding echo: 'To Lucy Lovecake!'

Dominic ushered me across to the signing table.

'Are you okay?' he whispered.

'Not really, but I must do this,' I replied.

'Yes, I think you have to. But you can come out of this well. He's presenting as a bitter and twisted nutcase — it's perfect PR for you, if only he knew it.'

'But I betrayed him,' I said with half a sob.

'Does he deserve your loyalty? Are you in a relationship with him? You *had* to keep Lucy Lovecake a secret. You did what you had to do for your career,' said Dominic firmly.

But there was no more time to talk. The queue snaked all around the second floor of the store, and I had to get on with being a professional author, getting the books signed as efficiently — and charmingly — as possible.

'Thank you for coming!' I said to the first in line, beaming.

'Love the book, Daisy. It really cheered me up!' replied a rosy-faced lady of about thirty.

'Thank you. I'm so thrilled to hear that,' I said, giving a grateful smile.

I tried to ignore the sound of raised voices and scuffles — clearly Michel was still acting up. But here I was at my book launch, a moment of my life that had been a long time coming, and I had no choice but to carry on as if I was unfazed. The truth was that I wanted to run after Michel, apologise, console him, and make things right.

Deep inside, I knew that was going to be an impossible task.

'When's the next book coming out, Daisy?'

asked a man in his early forties. 'I loved it!'

'I'm working on a sequel,' I said.

'Oh, don't say there will only be two of them!'

I smiled until my cheeks ached and spoke until my throat was dry and sore. The line of Lucy Lovecake fans seemed to go on forever.

Towards the end of the signing session, I looked up to find a man before me. A man I knew well but barely recognised.

'Daisy,' he said in a voice full of tenderness.

Tom Percy.

'Tom, how nice to see you.'

'I just got here. I'm sorry I missed your speech. Someone here tipped me off — just about an hour ago!'

'It's all been very silly, the pseudonym thing,' I replied, suddenly feeling exhausted.

Dominic stepped in. 'Daisy, sorry to rush you, but there's still a bit of a queue — '

'Yes, sorry. This is an old friend of mine.'

'Can I call you?' asked Tom, stepping aside.

'It's too late, Tom. I'm in love.'

72

Press Dishes up Michel

At ten o'clock, I was still signing and looked up to find my parents standing with their copy of the book.

'Daisy!' said Dad. 'What a night for you! You've done so well, what a trouper.'

Mum looked misty-eyed with pride. 'What a dreadful man. Was that the maniac French chef who is always making a fool of himself?' she said.

'Yes, that's him. But he was right. This whole secret thing around Lucy Lovecake meant that I've been fibbing to him. I hated being dishonest. And now look what's happened!'

'How could you ever confide in a right eejit like that?' said Dad, which made me laugh, briefly, through some tears.

Dominic came to join us. 'Daisy, what a star you are. I was going to say 'in the making', but you are already. Thank you for carrying on after that astonishing disruption. That man has gone too far now. He will not be welcome at any functions across all of London. I hope he is sent back to Paris for good.'

'Hear, hear,' said Branwell, who had extricated himself from a conversation with a would-be author looking for representation.

'Where do you think he is now?' I asked.

'Most probably in a police cell, if he didn't calm down by the time they arrived,' said Dominic.

'What? They called the police?' I sighed.

'Yes. He was out of control.'

I thought back to the book awards. It had been so easy to calm him down with some coffee and gentle words on that occasion. Then, when he'd come round with the taxi money, he'd inspired the book. And we'd had such fun together. But I could never recover his trust now. It was over, as I had always known it would be when my identity was revealed.

Maybe I was a coward about telling him, but I would never have had some of those special times if I'd told him sooner. I wouldn't want to have missed any of those lovely moments.

'Shall we all go to dinner to celebrate this amazing evening, and the performance of a lifetime by Daisy Delaney?' said Dominic.

The consensus was yes. Dominic put his arm around me as we left the store. I couldn't help glancing around for Michel, half out of fear, the other half hope.

'Don't worry,' Dominic reassured. 'He's far away now. That's the end of him.'

I felt a tear trickle down my left cheek.

★ ★ ★

I hardly dared to log in to my tablet the next morning. I just knew that the signing was going to get lots of coverage, but for all the wrong reasons.

311

Kitty knocked on my bedroom door.

'Come in, Kitty!' I called.

'Hi, Daisy. I brought you some tea,' she said.

'Tea and sympathy, huh?'

'Yes, exactly. Well, I say let's just face up to all the reports. They'll blow over soon enough.'

I braced myself. 'Go for it.'

Kitty went to fetch her laptop.

'Shall I read the headlines and you can let me know if you want any expansion on those?' she suggested.

'Perfect.'

'Okay, here goes: 'Violent-ine's Day Disaster for Debut Author Daisy Delaney!' 'Fancy French chef flips his lid!' '(Very) Hot Cross Buns at Book Event!' 'Lovecake not to everyone's taste, as chef goes wild.' 'Bitter chef spoils tasty dish with too many sour grapes!' 'Chef Boils Over!'' Kitty paused. 'Some of the photos are quite racy.'

'Really? From the magazine shoot?' I asked.

'Well, yeah, but they seem to have photographed you looking a bit Nell Gwynn last night as well! You are leaning over the signing table.'

'Oh no. Let me see!'

I shrieked. 'That looks awful. This CANNOT get worse.'

I reached for my phone. Seventeen missed calls. I rang Dominic at his hotel.

'Good morning, Daisy!' he said, sounding jolly.

'What's good? I'm totally mortified!'

'Don't be. We have eight requests for appearances on TV for you already, six for radio interviews, and all the major papers and magazines looking for times to meet you. This is a perfect scenario! Monsieur Amiel has given us oodles of press on a platter!'

I knew I should be happy about that, but how could I feel happy when I felt so deceitful?

'Will it ever calm down?' I asked.

'Hopefully not,' he said, chuckling.

'I suppose I just have to get used to this, selling my soul for silver pennies,' I said.

'You have not sold your soul. Michel Amiel is a despicable person. You did exactly the right thing in keeping your identity as Lucy Lovecake from him. I am very proud of you.'

73

Where the Sympathy Lies

Kitty was now looking at Lucy Lovecake's pages for feedback on those.

'I have to go and check out what the fans of Lucy Lovecake are saying about this,' I told Dominic.

'So, can I take it that you are willing to appear anywhere and everywhere? We can probably get this story spinning way out of the UK now, into Europe, the US, Asia. That's what we need next, Daisy — foreign language deals, a TV show. I've got it all planned and so far that plan is unfolding pretty much perfectly.'

Good for you.

Why had I not noticed this very calculating side in Dominic before?

There was a note of glee in his voice and I wasn't sure that it was ALL to do with the fresh batch of publicity.

'You must be exhausted, Daisy,' he said. 'Why don't you come out to Bluebells for a few days, relax here? We could do some walking, eat in the village pub, switch off from the whole hulla-balloo?'

'I'll think about it. Thanks. I've got a few things to catch up with here, but yeah, that does sound very nice.'

I needed some quiet time. But with Dominic?

I bathed, dressed and had some breakfast with Kitty.

'I need to get out, go walking, clear my head,' I told her.

'Sure. That'll do you good,' she said. 'I'll do some replies to messages.'

'Thanks. I really don't want to look at all that stuff for a while,' I admitted.

I wrapped up in a big coat and set off towards the park.

I was on the corner of West Street when I first noticed it. People nudging each other, giggling, staring at me.

Is my hair sticking up or something?

I carried on, but even in the park, dog walkers tittered and looked sideways as they went by. And as I took refuge under a big chestnut tree, it dawned on me.

I am 'out'. Lucy Lovecake, Daisy Delaney, whoever I am. People are recognising me from the newspapers this morning.

It was a horrible feeling because I couldn't feel joyful about the growing success of Lucy Lovecake's dating tips until Michel forgave me. And, of course, that was never going to happen. I had joined the ranks of women who had betrayed him. *And I hope that Madame doesn't hate me!*

It was when I was walking that I realised how much his friendship meant to me. The thought of never sitting in the cinema with him again, or dining with him, or chatting through life problems. My eyes began to well up.

Don't be silly, Delaney. It's not as if you were in some big relationship. Don't be a fool.

I didn't plan to end up at Elsworthy Road, but that's where I went.

I climbed the steps and pressed the buzzer. No reply. Of course, Madame Amiel was back in Paris, I knew that. But I was hoping that Michel would be back in residence. Surely he wasn't still in a police cell? It's not as if he actually hurt anyone.

I looked up and saw a curtain twitch at an upstairs window.

Someone is in there. It could be him!

I tried again. I heard movement inside. I peeped through the letterbox.

'Michel?' I called. 'Are you in there?'

Nothing, yet I could tell he was there. A trace of his scent.

I couldn't leave without saying how sorry I was.

'Michel, please forgive me,' I called. 'I was sworn to secrecy, and by the time I wanted to tell you, I was in so deep it seemed impossible. I should have told you! I'm so sorry, I really am. I miss you!'

More footsteps inside.

My phone buzzed in my pocket. I checked it. From Michel!

Fuck off, liar.

I walked away, feeling desolate. He was not the forgiving type, I could see that from the way he spoke about his previous girlfriends and the way he went all the way with Eve before relenting and paying her off.

His disappointment in me was tangible, and understandable too.

When I got back to the flat, Kitty told me that she'd had a message from Dominic to say that I was to appear on a daytime show for the BBC — the next day.

'This is just the start of it, Daisy,' said Kitty. 'You're going to be so famous.'

'All I wanted was to have enough money for my rent,' I said.

'Daisy, Michel will come to his senses, you'll see. I'm sure of it.'

'What makes you think that? I certainly don't think so, Kitty.'

'He makes a huge fuss and calms right down, that's his style. Just wait, be patient, leave him alone for a while.'

I hoped she was right.

'I don't think he'll ever forgive me.'

'He will forget why he's so annoyed. He's had a shock, there's more to you than meets the eye, but he likes you, Daisy, and he's going to reflect on that.'

I envied Kitty the way she had been raised to reflect on problems calmly, never taking the impulsive route. Whereas, at that very moment, I was all for chaining myself to the railings at the front of Michel's house.

74

Cashing Up

Over the next weeks, I saw nothing of Michel. I had messages from Tom Percy on Twitter and calls galore from Dominic McGann, but not the call I so badly wanted. I would rush to see what a ping on my phone heralded, always to be disappointed.

Life was changing for me in so many ways. I was due for a royalty payment at the end of March. Dominic e-mailed to let me see the calculation. I'd never had such a big payment in my life.

'This only takes into account a few weeks of market trading, because this royalty period ended at the end of December,' he explained. 'In other words, your next one will be very much greater, as it will include the period of soaring sales, after *Elle*. However, all that said, you will be receiving your share of royalties via your agent for the sum of £28,546.86! That means you have cleared your advance, and it was a big advance already! Congratulations. We at Bluebells are delighted with this!'

I was thrilled as well. So many people had scared me by saying that you never make any more than your advance, and there I was after only a few months in the market, with fresh earnings and the advance paid off! Considering I knew how to live like a country church mouse, this new payment would suffice very nicely. As long as I didn't have to buy too many new outfits for all my appearances.

75

Bound for Hay-on-Wye

Dominic had booked me into one festival after another. I'd had a few frocks made with tight bodices and swing skirts — and that was the start of the phase I call Lovecake on Tour. More like Tart on Tour. I would turn up anywhere I was asked — well, apart from a working-man's club in Bradford, but that was just because the dates clashed. Dominic kept saying that there might only be one year of interest in Lucy Lovecake and that we had to roll with it, and that I could make my whole life's fortune in this one year, so I may as well go for it. There was no disputing that Dominic knew what he was talking about when it came to contemporary marketing trends, so I didn't argue, and with Michel no longer a part of my life, I was happy to be the hard-working singleton. Everyone knows that's how to build a fortune, isn't it? Avoid wasting time on the opposite sex.

But Dominic and I were getting very close. We were on the phone most days, discussing stuff like percentages for deals for Lucy Lovecake in Mandarin, and sometimes he came up to London for meetings or just to have lunch. He always stayed at his friend's house in Notting Hill, but sometimes when we were out, we would slip into walking arm and arm, very comfortable and companionable. There had been a few times it seemed we might roll in the hay, but I was terrified of ruining our perfect working relationship. And as he kept saying I would only have a year of fame, I thought, well if we still like each other after a year, maybe we can develop things from there.

In late May, Dominic collected me in his open top Aston Martin and we travelled to the Hay-on-Wye literary festival together. The sun was shining, with not a cloud in sight, and the forecast said this was to last for days. It was the stuff of idyllic childhood summers — glorious, contented days when you thought it would never rain again.

I was wearing one of my sprig pattern sundresses for the journey and some 1950s white-framed shades I'd found at Portobello Market.

'You look lovely,' said Dominic as I got into the car, and he popped my little suitcase into the boot. I was so good at packing now I could practically fit everything into a clutch bag.

He played some lovely Louis Armstrong songs — 'We Have All the Time in the World' and 'My One and Only Love' — as we barrelled along the A40 to Hertfordshire in style. His mother was looking after Minty.

'I have you to thank for all this,' I said.

'I'm not feeling completely sure that's a compliment?' He smiled.

'Ha, yes it is, actually. Of course, it's all been rather overwhelming, and not being able to go to the corner shop incognito on a bad hair day is seriously annoying, but honestly, Dominic, I was looking at going back to Ireland before all this happened, getting a little job, giving up on my dreams.'

'Well, I'm so glad that didn't happen. But Daisy, if I hadn't published that book, a dozen others would have. I am the lucky one. You picked me! You changed your own luck with your talent and ingenuity.'

'You silver-tongued charmer that you are.'

We travelled in sweet silence after that, smiling occasionally across to one another, Dominic touching my knee lightly on occasion, while sometimes I touched his shoulder and told him how great his driving was. The early summer wildflowers decorated the fields and hedgerows with yellow, blue and pink polka dots. Chubby lambs frolicked in the fields, while whitethroats and willow warblers sang contentedly.

Could this be the weekend where things change between us?

Without saying as much, I had the feeling he was thinking the same way.

76

Lovecake on Tour

The main street in Hay was strung from side to side with coloured bunting, and the cutesy curiosity shops hid beneath striped canopies, shielding their small-paned windows from the heat of the sun. The little Kilverts Hotel was picture-book pretty, with tables and chairs to the front of it. People sat there happily, enjoying the warmth of the sun and the coldness of their beer, or sipping on refreshing pots of tea poured into china cups on saucers.

'This is just as pretty as I expected,' I said.

'It's a bit cute, but I think it's really special. I think you're going to shine here. It's the perfect place for you,' Dominic replied.

'Oh yeah. I forgot. I'm here to work.'

'I'm relying on you, Delaney, for that Caribbean island I'm hoping to buy.'

'Well, I'm going to get a helicopter first,' I jested. 'Or maybe one of those yachts that you see moored at Cannes. That reminds me, why don't we go to Cannes?'

So far, I'd earned £60,000, but I could dream.

Dominic knew only too well that none of that really mattered to me. All I wanted was enough in the bank for me to assess my life without fear of imminent insolvency.

'We're looking for the Swan,' he said.

'There it is!' I said, pointing across the street to a little whitewashed hotel on a corner.

★ ★ ★

'There's your key, Mr McGann,' said the sweet-faced lady, possibly the owner, who had introduced herself as Mrs Burton.

'Ah, I booked two rooms,' said Dominic.

'No, sir. Just the one. A double.'

'Oh, I'm sorry, there must have been a misunderstanding. We will need a room each,' he said, looking at me with rolling eyes, as if to say, 'Country folks, country ways'.

'We're crammed for the next few nights, I'm afraid,' said Mrs Burton. 'That's the only room free, but it does have a sofa bed as well as the double.'

Dominic scratched his head, turning to me for ideas.

'What shall we do — we're unlikely to find anything other than a Travelodge at Leominster,' he said.

'Why don't we take a look at the room? The location is fantastic. We can get by for a night or two, I'm sure.'

And that was how Dominic and I came to be shoe-horned into the world's teeniest double room.

'Well, this is dinky!' I said as we got ready for dinner.

'Which side do you like?' asked Dominic, ever the gentleman.

'I'll sleep on that sofa bed,' I said from the bathroom as I freshened up.

'Oh, right then,' he said, sounding very disappointed. 'Or I'll take that. You need to sleep well for your big event in the morning.'

'Well, we can argue about that after dinner. Are we booked for dinner here?' I asked.

'Yes. Do you think that will be okay? Might we be expected to share a plate?'

'Ha, I'm sure it will be lovely.'

Dominic decided that he would freshen up quickly and go down to the bar, giving me space and time to get ready and sort my things for the morning. I was grateful, as I was nervous about the event. Not just an interview about my book. I was to take part in some kind of cake-off contest, in a specially rigged kitchen in one of the big sponsored tents. Against Myles Munroe from *Bake It!*

I decided to make an effort for dinner and tried peach bloom no-make-up make-up, and put my hair up. I wore a pink and white polka-dot sun dress, and espadrilles with a bit of a heel. Not too bad, I thought as I bent double to look in the half mirror below the coombed ceiling. Almost banging my head on the way up, I decided it was time to make my way to the dining room.

Dominic was waiting for me on the sofa in the reception area.

'You look gorgeous, Daisy,' he said, kissing me.

'Thanks. I'm starving.'

We decided to check at the reception desk that

our table was ready, where we found, of course, there had been a mix-up with tables and we were not in fact booked in for dinner at all. Mrs Burton was adamant that no table had been reserved. Dominic was frustrated that he had no evidence, as everything had been settled on the phone. It was all most unlike him.

We were trying to decide whether we should wait for a table or take our chances elsewhere when Dominic spotted a copy of *French Fancy* behind the reception area.

'Ah, Mrs Burton, I see you're reading Lucy Lovecake's book there?' he said.

'Yes, I am indeed. I love it. I'm going to see the author tomorrow — it's a cake-off with Myles Munroe, and I must admit, I don't like him one bit. Those creepy eyes, like a wolf. A chancer. You can always tell.'

Dominic leant in towards her. 'Don't broadcast this, but this lady right here is Daisy Delaney, the author of that book! The real Lucy Lovecake. And I am the publisher of it.'

Mrs Burton's face was a picture. 'You can't be serious!' she said, wreathed in smiles. 'This is like having royalty to stay. Well, better than royalty. Everyone's talking about that book. All my friends are reading it! My friend Gina bagged herself a man with the red-velvet raspberry cake — and some red lace, I might add, just like Lucy Lovecake recommended! Let me see if I can find you a nice quiet table in the corner, even if I have to add an extra one.'

I was stunned. It was the first time the book had empowered me in a public space. I wasn't sure if I liked it. I was also rather surprised that Mrs Burton was part of the demographic market for the book.

When Dominic and I were settled in the dining room, I asked him what sort of people were reading the book.

'Everyone!' he said. 'All sorts.'

'I thought it was mainly young professional women who had found out about Lucy Lovecake on social media. And there are lots of male fans. But this is really exciting — to be spicing up the love lives of the middle-aged Middle Englanders as well!'

'Like all great books, it's not for one niche,' said Dominic. 'But this has really surprised me too. After a few months in the market, you can command a table at the Swan in Hay! You have arrived!'

'Yes, I suppose I have,' I giggled.

We didn't overdo the wine due to my early start, but a couple of glasses of cold Chablis had helped to ease my nerves a little. We went up to our room just after ten o'clock.

I got ready for bed, changing into my little white nightie.

'Sorry if you were expecting something of Lucy Lovecake standards,' I said. 'I was planning to sleep alone.'

'Daisy, I think you know there's no need for embellishment where you are concerned.'

I made up the sofa bed with the spare sheets, duvet and fat white pillows, and climbed into it.

'Oh, springy,' I said.

'Are you sure you won't let me sleep on that

thing?' said Dominic.

'Well, I suppose I ought to get a really good sleep,' I said.

Something went wrong during the exchange of beds though, and we both ended up in the snug double.

★ ★ ★

We woke up to more mellow sunshine streaming through our window, and birds chirping. *6am. This is it. The cake-off!*

'So, I'm appearing at eleven o'clock. Time for breakfast and a nice stroll through the town?' I said, lying in the crook of his arm.

'And time for more kisses,' said Dominic. I was powerless to refuse, although I did wonder if we'd crossed some kind of author-publisher line of decent conduct.

'Does it say anything in my contract about this sort of thing?' I said.

'As you know, I've thought of absolutely everything when it comes to your career, darling.'

That was indisputably true.

77

The Request

I had a wardrobe malfunction when getting ready for the event. The zip broke on my cupcake print dress.

'Oh God, what will I do now?'

'What else do you have?' said Dominic.

'Just this little sundress which I planned for later. A bit revealing.' I held it up.

'That'll do nicely,' he said.

We arrived in good time at the reception area of the festival. Early though it was, it was already buzzing with people setting up picnics; the cafés were bulging and the bookshops teeming with punters. Delivery vans were coming and going, depositing vast amounts of food and drinks.

'Looks like it's going to be a busy day,' said Dominic.

'Do you think there will be many people at my event?' I asked, feeling nervous. How embarrassing it would be if just Mrs Burton turned up, and I wasn't at all sure how popular Myles Munroe was these days.

'I meant to tell you, I checked on the website — it's a sell-out!' he said.

'What?!'

'Yes, there will be around two hundred in the audience.'

329

'Bloody hell.'

Focus on this, Daisy. Run through your recipe.

Dominic stroked my hair gently. 'Relax. You're wonderful,' he said.

The trip had taken a romantic turn and it was hard to cut back into work mode so quickly after all that love.

We were met at reception by Tara, who seemed to be in charge of this event and pretty much everything else, judging by the number of times she was stopped on the way to the Green Room.

'I'm the 'fixer', in charge of non-literary literary events,' she explained.

'Non-literary?' I asked.

'Political memoirs, accounts of life as a rock star, comedians, cookery, Bear Grylls-y things — you know the sort? The types of books most bookshops are rammed with these days.'

Tara took us to a table surrounded by lime green tub chairs and invited us to relax. One whole wall was covered by an enormous panoramic photograph of the Welsh countryside, which *was* relaxing. There were free newspapers everywhere, a table set up with hot drinks and pastries, a fridge filled with cold drinks, and piles of fruit in silver bowls.

We saw some comedians in there. According to the programme, they were doing a three-player event, each promoting a new book, asserting their views on the link between stand-up comedy and manic depression.

I noticed some heavyweight politicians too, and, incredibly, some real authors. David Hurd was there, and, jaw-droppingly, Mary Lennox, as well as Dr Sarah Hove. I loved her programmes on the Tudors.

Oh, how embarrassing to be such a silly tart amongst these Oxford heavyweights. Daisy Delaney with no literary credentials. A degree in fashion, if you please! I am not worthy of book festivals, I am just a girl who got lucky with an idea because of social media. Why would anyone want to see me bake a cake? It's like the new version of watching people being hanged. The entertaining disasters of other people.

As if he'd read my mind, Dominic whispered, 'You can hold your own with any of these. They've been hogging the show for far too long.'

I longed to be back in the tiny lingerie store on that cobbled lane, dreaming of moments such as this rather than living them.

We sat on the tub seats and Tara gave me a run-down of what was expected of me.

'So, we have Victoria Darling compering this contest,' she said, beaming.

'Wow, make me more nervous, why don't you?'

'Sorry, just bringing you up to speed. We never quite know who's doing what for sure until everyone turns up on time. This is not the easiest location to get to. Middle Earth, practically! Anyway, we're still waiting for Myles Munroe, but he sent a text to Caroline — that's Caroline Bateman — to say they're not too far off. Caroline is one of the judges who will be tasting your cake.'

'Caroline. Bateman. Judging. My. Cake?'

I had admired Caroline Bateman since I was a little girl.

Dominic put his arm round my shoulder. 'There's nothing to fear. Your cakes are awesome.'

'It's all a bit of fun,' said Tara. 'We've had some right disasters in our celebrity kitchens this festival. The electricity went off during the cooking of a *tarte tatin* just the other day.'

She really needs some training. Her comments are not helping!

'You'll be in the Glenfiddich tent — that's our biggest, for our crowd-pullers. There are about forty complimentary seats for bloggers and journalists. We find they really do help to spread the fun far and wide, so it's worth losing the ticket price on those seats.'

At that, three people swished into the Green Room in a great rush of heightened energy. Tara became distracted by them and went off to find out what was up.

'That's the director of the whole shebang,' said Dominic. 'Stephen Murray, and his sidekicks, Will Adams and Jonny Cavaye.'

'They look like they just got chased by a lion,' I said. 'Or they've been sent a ransom note.'

'You're right,' he agreed. 'Something's troubling them.'

Tara joined them and another official woman, and they formed a huddle in a corner. We could hear odd, leaked phrases, such as, 'That'll never work!' and 'What a fuck-up' and 'But will she go for it?'

There was a hum of ideas after that, some nodding.

'A solution, it would seem,' said Dominic, looking up from *The Guardian* on his iPad with amusement.

Tara came buzzing back over, all pink cheeks and fake chipper.

'Daisy, I'll come straight to the point. We need to ask you a HUGE favour, and I know it's going to be controversial. I'm so, so sorry about this. Why do I get all the shit jobs round here?'

'What is it?' I said, wondering what could possibly be this bad.

'Myles Munroe isn't going to make it on time. We can't have a contest with one celeb.'

Please don't call me that!

'The thing is — and stuff like this happens every day — someone due to appear next Saturday has turned up today in error, and we have decided to run with him today as your opponent because if he goes away, he most likely won't come back. As I said, it's not that straightforward to get here.'

'Right . . . '

'Well, the organisers think you could do a great joint event with this other author, and we want to ask you, pretty please, would you agree to such a thing?' said Tara, clearly cringing at the whole business.

Dominic stepped in. 'Tara, just get to the point, please. Who do you want her to work with? I'm not sure about all this.'

'I don't really mind,' I said, trying to sound as undiva-ish as possible.

Tara swallowed hard.

'Well, come on, who is this other author?' urged Dominic.

She looked sheepish. 'This is such a fuck-up, totes sorry, hope you're okay with going against Michel Amiel? You're a lifesaver, Daise.'

78

Just Cake Off

I gulped. 'But we don't get on,' I said. 'He hates me. He ruined my first ever event in Harrods on Valentine's Day and he hasn't spoken a word to me since. He was taken away by the police that time.'

Tara looked sympathetic enough, but it seemed as though an exit by police escort wasn't the worst thing she'd ever had to deal with.

Dominic was thunderous. 'This is really too much to ask,' he said. 'You'll just have to ply him with booze and send him on the next train out of town. It's his own fault that he turned up on the wrong date. She can't work with that car crash. He's been so rude to Daisy — how can you ask this of her? And do you even imagine he would agree?'

Dominic was getting really annoyed now and everyone in the Green Room was watching salaciously.

Tara went back to the boss people, who came over and asked us to step into their offices to the rear of the Green Room.

Dominic was still livid. 'Daisy's new to this. How dare you set her up like this?' he stormed.

'I can assure you,' said Johnny Cavaye, 'it's not planned. He turned up out of the blue and is insisting that we use him today or not at all. Meanwhile, Myles has been delayed.'

'Couldn't Caroline Bateman go against her and Michel could be a judge?' Dominic queried.

'We've suggested that, but he's not up for it,' said Johnny, beginning to sound despondent for the first time.

Stephen and Will kept out of it. Tara kept smiling inanely, that lipsticky gash irritating. Whitened big teeth, maybe veneers, blood-red lips; the insincerity of it.

This is so silly. Here I am, due to appear at Hay-on-Wye, something I would not have thought possible a year ago, and 'my people' are arguing about my rights already. What I will and will not do. I'm not even famous. I've only been around for five minutes — an internet sensation. This is the route to ruin. Let's all grow up.

'I'll do it,' I said. 'Just don't expect me to be best mates with him because that's never going to happen.'

I thought Tara was going to hug me. And I surprised myself by backing away, a little bit aloof. I was being accommodating, but I wasn't being cuddly.

Branwell turned up at that moment. On hearing of the situation, he said, 'Daisy, you're a trouper.'

I was happy with that. I wasn't a star or a darling, an angel or a sweetheart. I was a trouper.

It was time to go to the big tent and get wired for sound.

'Good luck, Daisy,' said Dominic, kissing me

on both cheeks. 'I'll be right there in the front row.'

'Thank you.'

I summoned all my dignity, as one always should before a cake-off with an arch enemy.

79

Frenzy

After Hay-on-Wye

I couldn't wait to get home after Hay. I felt as
though I'd been assaulted. Every part of me
ached, most of all my heart.

Dominic was alarmed at my mood after the
disastrous cake-off with Michel. Our homeward
journey was less jolly.

'I'm sorry — that was all very difficult,' he said
when he dropped me off after a very silent car
ride. 'Trust Michel Amiel to spoil our first
romantic time together.'

It was true that Michel always upset things,
wherever he went.

'I just feel traumatised by the machine — the
whole process, close up like that. It's as if we're
not people. Commodities, or caricatures, for
manipulation. It scared me. I just need a couple
of quiet days then I'll be good as new,' I
explained.

'I hope so. I know you're upset about Michel.
And if you want to track him, that's nothing to
do with me. But be careful. He repeats patterns.
It's a self-destructive trait — I've seen it in other
guys before. You want to help them break out of
it because you're very sweet, but you can't,
Daisy.'

'You're right. I was just afraid for him, seeing him so close to the edge. It's not as if I'm obsessed with him. I'm just obsessed with making people happy.'

Dominic smiled. 'And that's what's lovely about you. But you need to toughen up. We've had a request to go to New York, to meet with Upper East Publishers — we need a big player like that to handle the US rights. Bluebells can't do that part. We need to be strong, negotiate hard, get what we want from the deal. They are nothing without bestselling books. We hold the power. You do.'

'Yes, I'm ready for the fight. I just need a rest, that's all,' I said. 'Thank you for bringing me back. You need to get back to Minty now.'

'Yes, let's talk in a day or two. We'll get our travel plans firmed up once you're feeling up to it.'

I waved him out of the lane, and when I opened the front door of that little flat, I felt as though it wrapped its arms around me. I slammed the door on the outside world.

For two days, I lay in my bed in the foetal position, considering what had happened in my life. At one stage, Kitty went out to the corner shop for supplies.

'Don't want to alarm you, Daisy,' she said on her return, 'but there are some photographers on the lane.'

'Why?' I mumbled, still dozing. It seemed no amount of sleep was enough.

'They've found out you live here. They want to photograph you,' she replied softly.

I sat up. 'Really? What would they do with a photograph of me?'

'Sell it. To a newspaper or an online publication,' she said. 'Daisy, you're trending — since Hay.'

'Oh no. I haven't been online lately. What's been happening?'

'Let me make you some tea, toast and scrambled eggs, and I'll bring you up to date with all that. Okay?' said Kitty, tidying up my bedclothes and fussing around my room.

'Kitty, that would be lovely, thank you,' I told her. 'I suppose I should check messages and what not.'

'Well, check your phone, but don't go on any social media until I speak to you about it, okay?' she said.

'Sure, okay. I'm getting worried now, though. Should I be?'

'Nothing to worry about as such. Just that your book, your brand, you — it's all gone to a whole new level. It was something about that appearance with Michel. Your cake was so fabulous. You were so composed. His behaviour was so bizarre. There were so many tweets about it. Let me bring this tea to you,' she said.

Kitty went off to the kitchen.

I reached out for my phone. Text messages from Mum, Dad, Clara, Dominic, Branwell. Nothing from Michel. I had so many messages. When I went back two days, I noticed that there was one from Madame Amiel. She hated texting. I guessed it would be all upper case.

DAISY PLEASE CALL ME URGENT

I jumped out of bed.

'Kitty!' I called. 'There's a message from Michel's mother! It's dated two days ago. Do you know if there's anything up?'

She came through with a tray laden with tea, buttered toast and mounds of softly scrambled eggs.

'Not heard anything. He hasn't posted anything for a day or two now,' she said.

I felt ravenous, and as I ate, Kitty began to fill me in.

'After you won the cake-off, the hits on the Lucy Lovecake pages went sky high, almost one hundred per cent supportive, save for one or two die-hard Amielites,' she explained. 'Michel took to Twitter and he tweeted: 'She's a lovely woman but she deceived me'. This got everyone asking — how and why did Daisy Delaney deceive Michel Amiel? They don't want to believe it's just that you didn't tell him you were writing a book. Conspiracy theorists put forward explanations for your spat.'

'No! This is getting out of hand. Maybe we'll have to come off Twitter.'

'Well, that's up to you, of course. But just as things were cooling a bit and nobody had any hard facts, step forward a Mrs Burton who runs the Swan Hotel in Hay.'

'Oh God! We met her! We stayed there. Dominic and I. She didn't — '

'She did,' said Daisy. 'She spoke to the *Mail*, saying that you and Dominic were an item, as you'd insisted on a 'compact' double room at her hotel.'

I held my head in my hands. 'But it was a mix-up and anyway this is not anyone's *business*!'

Am I more concerned about my privacy or about Michel's feelings? Hard to know.

Kitty nodded sympathetically. 'But there are those who think when you blog and tweet and Instagram like crazy, when you become famous because of social media, that you have to take the rough with the smooth,' she said.

'And do you think that, Kitty? Do you honestly think that?'

'No, of course not, Daisy. It's outrageous, but it's what goes on. The invisible wall that people can hide behind online makes them so much ruder than they would be in person.'

'So, did Michel tweet anything else after Mrs Burton waded into the mire?' I asked.

Kitty looked down at her hands. 'No, that's when he went quiet.'

★   ★   ★

I sent a message to Rose: *On my way, Daisy.*

She replied: *THIS IS NOT DAISY, IT'S ROSE.*

I replied: *I KNOW, I AM DAISY.*

I showered and dressed as fast as I could. Kitty called a cab. When the call came to say they were outside, Kitty went to check if the coast was clear.

'No photographers that I can see,' she said. 'Think I put them off earlier — said you were in Ireland. It was all I could think of.'

342

'Well done, Kitty,' I said. 'I'll make a dash for it.'

Within ten minutes, I was at Elsworthy Road. Rose let me in.

'Madame, I'm so sorry I couldn't tell you! I wasn't allowed.'

'Daisy, he trusted you. He loved you,' she said simply.

'I am distraught. I am, really!' I told her.

'I can see this is so. Poor girl.'

'Can I see him?' I asked.

'I told him you were coming, and he says he doesn't want to see you. That you are a double traitor, that he will never see you again,' she said.

I sighed. 'Can I just say something to him, through the door even? I must.'

'I'll ask him.'

Rose went upstairs while I sat in the sitting room, wringing my hands. *Bloody Mrs Burton, nasty old cow.*

I started to wonder if Dominic had ever booked two rooms, but my thoughts were interrupted as Rose returned.

'He has said some terrible things, that he doesn't want to hear your pathetic, self-pitying excuses. He says: 'Ask her why she didn't stay loyal to me if she loved me so much?''

Madame looked at me, not judging so much as despairing.

'Tell him I am sorry. I can't live with histrionics, but I love him.'

'Wait here,' she said. 'I'll tell him that.'

When she returned, her head hung low, she sighed. 'He says, 'I'll never change, forget me.

You deserve better.' He has turned his head to the wall.'

'Madame, tell him to find me when he wants to talk. But I will not put my life on hold.'

'Okay. I will tell him. You two are driving me crazy. Acting like teenagers. I've never seen him in love before. He adores you. So dramatic — what's wrong with young people nowadays, eh? Making private thoughts public on the internet, sending messages and tweets which everyone can see — it's undignified, appalling.'

'You are right, Madame. I'm sorry you're involved in this,' I said, embracing her. 'Stay in touch.'

I decided to walk home in the afternoon sun. On my way, I stopped in the park and sat on a bench. *I just don't believe that Mrs Burton would have spoken out. She's of the same generation as Rose Amiel. She loved my book and we'd had some nice exchanges. But I suppose everyone has their price . . .*

Kitty and I ate quietly together that evening, dining on asparagus, poached eggs and toasted rye bread, neither of us daring to pick up the tablet and look at Lucy Lovecake's accounts.

'None of it is real,' I said.

'Yes, but is this real? Sitting here in this little space in a corner of London. It seems real to us, but in the wide world, it is not validated, is it? How do we define reality?'

'Something you can respond to with the senses?' I offered.

'Maybe. But I don't think cyberspace *is* fantasy. It's just a new reality.'

344

'True. It connects with the physical world, doesn't it? All those people at Hay in the audience had first heard of the book on the internet. They're not bots.'

'Exactly.'

'I am so weary. Might have to get drunk.'

'Let's.'

'Yes, why not? And I really must call Dominic. I haven't spoken to him since he dropped me off after Hay.'

'How did it go, spending all that time with him?' asked Kitty.

'You mean, spending the night?'

'Yeah.'

'It was lovely. I mean, I was preoccupied about the event, but it was beautiful. He's . . . velvet, whereas Michel is . . . '

'Broken glass?'

'Ha! No, I was going to say leather!'

'Don't you think you need to put Michel out of your mind? Give this a chance with Dominic? You seem so right together. You have loads in common. Neither of you attracts police escorts with any regularity, for one thing.'

'True.' I went to make coffee.

Kitty's right. Michel makes me scared, uneasy, depressed. He will never change. Yes, I regret having to deceive him, but he is not a part of my life. I couldn't have trusted him with a secret book, knowing how wild he becomes. Let go of the guilt. Let go of Michel Amiel. Enjoy your success without suffering.

80

Goodbye, Rosehip Lane

Eventually the Hay-on-Wye fuss died down a little, and Kitty and I took to tweeting again. Michel recovered and went back to Paris, giving up his house in Elsworthy Road. This I heard from Madame. He never did seek me out, and I came to the conclusion that any explanations I could offer were flimsy. He was someone who had passed through my life, unsettling and inspiring me in equal measure. I had a farewell lunch with his mother. I asked how he was.

'Depressed,' she said. 'He loves you but will not back down.'

I told her I was happy, that it had been a moment in time. 'He should focus on his health,' I said.

She said he was the most stubborn, infuriating and truthful man in the world. I agreed. The future of the cookery school seemed uncertain, but it remained there for now. Saying goodbye to her was awful, knowing that she'd probably never be a part of my life again.

However, business was blossoming for *French Fancy*. It was proving to be a popular summer beach read, with high airport sales, and bookshops — both chains and indies — were ordering in big numbers for the run-up to

Christmas. Dominic told me that we were on the fourth print run.

'How many books in total have now been printed?' I asked.

'About 250,000, including eBooks.'

'What? That's crazy!'

'I know, and we're going to Frankfurt in October, where we expect to sell this into twenty foreign languages,' said Dominic.

'What happens in Frankfurt?'

'It's one of the biggest international book fairs in the world. All the rights teams sit in booths and have ten-minute slots to sell rights to foreign publishers. It's a three-day event which feels like two weeks of work. But it gets results. It changes the game, opens things out to the international market. We've already had calls from European publishing houses about Lucy Lovecake, and the diary is filling up. I'm going to employ a new member of staff to look after your rights. I've been interviewing for that role.'

'So I don't have to come to Frankfurt?'

'You can come to keep me company, but an author wouldn't normally get involved in selling rights. You should be scribbling away on book two. We need fresh material. When something's as popular as this, the next phase is that people want more.'

I learned so much from Dominic, and Branwell was brilliant too, always advising me and nurturing my writing. I liked to send all drafts to my agent because I respected his industry knowledge and he would always have a clear view on what was and was not in the 'voice'. Dominic and I saw more and more of each other, with business matters mixed up with our personal affairs, and vice versa.

I was growing fed up of life in Primrose Hill. It made me feel hemmed in, and I spent more and more time at Bluebells. I loved the peacefulness, the country air, the privacy and the realism of the people there. It didn't seem to matter that Dominic and I were tied together twice over: one minute we were talking about a literary event, next we were cooking dinner together, sleeping together, or caring for Minty.

I spent the month of July very quietly at Bluebells. We picked fruit and made jam, went to the swing park with Minty, sunbathed on the terrace, sipping mojitos made by Dominic.

'Are you happy?' he said as we lay side by side on sunbeds one Saturday afternoon in late July.

'Very. Perhaps city living isn't for me. Could've saved myself a fortune on rent over the years if I'd just moved out to a country cottage!'

'But none of this would have happened, would it?' he said.

'No, that's true. And I'm so glad it did.'

'Me too,' he agreed.

I wondered where this was all heading.

Suddenly, my phone rang, breaking the spell.

'It's Branwell,' I said, glancing at the screen. 'I'd better take it.'

Dominic nodded.

'Hey, Branwell. How are you?'

'Daisy,' his god-like voice boomed, 'I wonder if you'd like to come to lunch in London soon. There's someone who would like to meet you.'

'Sure, when were you thinking of?' I asked.

'Friday sound okay? He's in town for a week and suggests lunch any day this week. I'll book Joe Allen's.'

'Yes, Friday sounds great. I'll get the train into Paddington. See you around noon?'

'Perfect. See you then.'

I hung up.

Dominic was curious. 'Did you say you're going up to London?'

'Yes, on Friday. There's someone Branwell wants me to have lunch with.'

'What's it about?'

'I have no idea,' I admitted.

'Did he say that I should come?'

'No. Maybe it's to do with the agency.'

81

London

I had mixed feelings about my day trip to London. I was so used to open farmland now — just like in my childhood — that I was almost panicked by the whole idea of negotiating the city. First thing on the Friday morning, I soaked in a bubble bath, looking out onto the rolling Oxfordshire fields. I tried to think about very little. I was learning to let go of fears, and worry less. Minty and I went to the village hairdresser's, Tasha's, where they did a very smooth, bouncy blow dry for me while Minty read one of her picture books.

Once back at Bluebells, I decided on a pale blue shift dress, simple, cool, elegant.

'I'll just leave the car in the train station car park, shall I?' I said to Dominic.

'No, no. We'll take you down there,' he insisted.

'But what if I'm back late?'

'Are you planning to be late? Why would you be late?' he quizzed.

'I don't know. I don't even know what the meeting is about. I don't want to trouble you if it's near Minty's bedtime, that's all.'

'Okay. Text me, though,' he said.

★　★　★

I enjoyed the train journey, the patchwork of farmland gradually giving way to the grids of the city.

When I got to Joe Allen's, Branwell was already at a table with a silver fox, an American silver fox, I felt. Perfect teeth!

They stood up. I kissed Branwell on both cheeks and shook hands with his guest, introduced as Tony from NBC.

'Good to meet you!' I said, taking a seat. 'Did you have a good journey?'

'Very pleasant, thank you. It's all worth it, to meet you.'

Now don't go all schmaltzy on me or I'm going to take an instant dislike to you.

'Ah, well you won't be saying that by the end of lunch, isn't that right, Branwell?' I joked.

'He'll be even more enchanted.'

'Stop it!'

'She doesn't like compliments — until she does like them,' explained Branwell.

Tony laughed.

Branwell picked up the story of Tony's visit.

'Daisy, Tony has approached me about creating a TV show based on Lucy Lovecake's Dating Tips,' said Branwell. 'This would be based in Boston, a slightly Anglo version of *Sex and the City.*'

'I see,' I said. 'Fictionalised?'

'Ish,' said Tony. 'We're envisaging a blend of fact and fiction.'

'Scripted reality?' I said.

'Not exactly. Viewers are tired of that. But the new wave from there is for programmes that

351

educate as well as entertain. Our research shows there is a dating crisis. People want to know about ways to be successful in dating. We would present a show that does that. We've been looking for a vehicle for a long time, then we heard about your book. It was trending on Twitter after Hay, right?'

'Yes, that's right,' I confirmed. 'Hay was a bit of a riot!'

'Sure was — fantastic! We love all that stuff you have going with the chef guy,' Tony chimed.

I was about to say that was at an end, but Branwell shot me a look.

'It all sounds great, and I'm sure we'd love to see what you propose in more detail,' I said. 'I'll have to see what my publisher thinks, of course.'

Branwell leant forward, hands clasped together. 'Why?'

'Because. He makes the books, and — '

'Exactly,' Branwell cut in. 'He makes the *books*. We didn't sell him TV or film rights. This has nothing to do with Dominic, outside of the fact that it will boost book sales.'

'Oh, okay. One of these days you'll have to give me a lesson on rights,' I said.

'It's easy. Any book has ancillary rights outwith publishing. Such as TV, radio, theatre, games, serialisation in magazines. These all have a value. Your publisher agrees to make your story into a book. That does not mean they have the right to make money from these other forms of your story. That's your right. Unless you sell these extra rights to them or others for a good price.'

'I get it.'

'Always remember that Dominic knows he has no right to ask about ancillary matters. Refer him to me if he does, okay?' said Branwell.

'Yeah. I will.' *But will I?*

We chatted to Tony for a while — he had lots of tales to tell about life inside American TV — mostly the terrifying blurring of make-believe and reality, which was becoming a preoccupation of mine. He excused himself after coffee, heading to another meeting, after which Branwell and I ordered a dessert to share and chatted some more.

'Daisy?'

'Yes?'

'About your relationship with Dominic. It's none of mine,' said Branwell.

'That's right.'

'I just want to say this once, and I won't mention it again, okay?'

'Okay. Fire away,' I agreed.

'No publishing career is without hitches,' he began. 'And there are always points when an author and publisher argue. It's a bit like a marriage. I can't think of one author who has not had cross words with their publisher. You are in the ascendant phase right now, so all is well, but there will come a day — '

'We discuss everything very openly,' I said. 'There's our work, then there's our private life. We don't mix them up.'

Even as I said this, I knew it wasn't true. All aspects of our life were constantly straddling boundaries.

'I just want to protect you. You are not obliged contractually to involve him in every aspect of your publishing life. It's not a problem if you do, but you might find it hard to get out of some of your arrangements, if the day comes when there's a cooling off on the personal side,' Branwell counselled.

'I appreciate your words, but I think I've got that under control. Don't worry.'

'I won't then. And I will not mention it again unless you do. Now, let's get stuck into this chocolate pudding!'

I insisted on paying for lunch, which was a lovely feeling.

As I was leaving, Branwell reached into his pocket. 'Oh! Nearly forgot! There's just one other thing,' he said, handing me a folded slip of paper.

'What's this?' I asked.

'Not sure really. We had a phone call from a lady asking to speak to you, found our number on the internet in connection with you. She wouldn't give her name and didn't want her details on e-mail, but asks that you call her on this number. It's up to you, of course. Might be a lunatic — that'll be the next thing, the crazies who want to get close to you! Don't arrange to meet anyone, okay?'

'Right, okay. What next?!' I sighed.

'I know. You need a nice quiet time now to get on with book two. How's that coming along?'

'No progress of late, but I'm all refreshed and raring to go. Don't worry!' I assured him.

'Good show. Breaks are lovely, darling, but

you don't want to take too much time away from the voice. It's always a bugger to get it going again!'

'Yes, I'm sure.'

As I went back to Paddington in the cab, I looked at the number on the slip of paper, then tucked it into my purse.

82

The Phone Call

I got home about 7pm, and Dominic was curious to hear all about the lunch.

'So, who was the special guest?' he asked.

I had decided what to say. 'Erm, it was a new author Branwell is taking on. He wanted me to give some guidance about social media. Ha! Comical or what?' I lied.

May God forgive you, Daisy Delaney. You are a serial fibber when it comes to men. What will become of you?

★ ★ ★

While Dominic went to read to Minty at bedtime, I decided to try the number on the slip of paper.

I bet it's one of those horrid ladies who spoke to me in the car park at Hay after my event that day. Barbara and Martha.

I keyed in the number, a mobile phone number. I couldn't help shaking as it started to ring.

'Hello,' said a lady.

'Erm, hello. This is Daisy Delaney. Did you call the Branwell Thornton agency asking to speak to me?'

'I did.'

'Right. Can I help you?'

'Daisy. This is Mrs Burton speaking, from the Swan Hotel in Hay.'

I froze. Mrs Burton who told the *Daily Mail* that Dominic and I had shared a 'compact' double room. I said nothing, my brain whirring.

She went on. 'Don't hang up. There's something I need to tell you.'

Again, I said nothing.

She carried on. 'It wasn't me who spoke to the *Mail*. They tried to get me to speak, but I didn't say a word. I swear it. I liked you, and I love your book. I'm not a big mouth. Somebody else must've told them and used my name.'

Should I believe this?

I did believe her. I had thought it strange at the time when Kitty told me about the betrayal. Mrs Burton didn't seem the sort to double cross.

'Mrs Burton, can you remember the name of the journalist you spoke to?' I asked.

'No, but I have his card somewhere . . . let me see. Asked me to call him back, but I never did. Wait a minute. Ah, here it is. Michael Swanston.'

'Mrs Burton, thank you for telling me this,' I said. 'I really appreciate it.'

'I've been up to the ninety-nines about it. You must have been thinking the worst of me, and that bothered me. I hope we'll see you again next year?' she said.

'Well, I don't think my new book will be out by then, but maybe the year after that,' I told her. 'But do stay in touch.'

'Right you are. Oh, I feel so much better. I

really do! Well, all the best in the meantime.'

'And to you, Mrs Burton. Bye for now.'

I Googled Michael Swanston. A freelancer, mostly working for the *Mail*.

★ ★ ★

I slept badly that night. The American man loomed in my mind. The faked sincerity. *Am I up for that level of attention? I was so upset about one tiny leak, how would I manage a whole flood?*

'Everything okay?' said Dominic, rolling round to embrace me.

'Yeah,' I responded. 'Just London stressed. It jangles me these days.'

'I know. Country living is so peaceful. You get used to it.'

'Exactly,' I agreed.

'Maybe you should get used to it permanently. Have you thought about giving up your flat?' he suggested.

'Yes, it's a waste of money when I'm living out here, isn't it?'

He rolled on top of me, looking right into my eyes, the rising sun lending some light to the room.

'Daisy, why don't we — '

'Ssshhh,' I said, kissing him.

83

Pavlova

The researchers on the *Hannah* morning show had contacted Dominic to ask if I'd appear at short notice to discuss following dreams, adapting to change and feminine feminism. They had a gap; someone had let them down.

Seen sense, more like.

'What do you think?' asked Dominic over the kitchen table.

'Sounds like a good opportunity?' I mulled.

'Yes, I asked for the figures. It regularly reaches 1.4 million viewers, mostly in our demographic. They did a feature on *The Hen Weekend* and that trebled sales instantly.'

'So, you will have one finger poised over the 'reprint' button?'

'Yes, but that's happening anyway, Daisy. It's a phenomenon.'

★ ★ ★

The day before the TV appearance, I went up to Primrose Hill to clear out the flat. A truck was due to take all my belongings down to Bluebells. Kitty had decided to stay on — she could afford the rent alone with her modelling jobs. Pippa was living with James in New York and the

359

Hamptons, so it didn't seem likely she'd be living at Rosehip Lane again.

'How's it going with Dominic?' asked Kitty as we sat having tea, me on the Lloyd Loom chair, she on the sofa.

I tried to work out if she was concerned for me or a little sad that I was moving into another stage of life before her. *Maybe it's a bit of both.*

'Don't change, Daisy,' she said.

'I'm not changing, Kitty. I promise. You think I am?'

'No, but don't. Because what makes people love you is the real you.'

Kitty went out for supplies and I stood at the oven, picturing Michel looking in the window, his face alight with excitement when he saw me in the lingerie that Friday afternoon. I sat on the loom chair and sobbed. I didn't want to go back to that day, but with hindsight, it had been the sweetest, funniest, most pivotal moment of my life. I knew the house in Elsworthy Road was empty. It felt to me as though Primrose Hill was empty because Michel had gone. In fact, that London was empty.

If I had only known how short-lived those fun times would be.

I kept thinking of a Shakespeare quote my English teacher, Mrs Murphy, used to say when we were all moaning about our boyfriends. From a *Midsummer Night's Dream*, 'So quick bright things come to confusion!'

I boxed up my make-up, books, trinkets and some clothes. I ditched all the letters from Tom Percy. There wasn't an awful lot to call my own.

After one of our nostalgic tapas suppers, Kitty helped me pick out what to wear for the *Hannah* programme.

'A bit sexy, a bit girl-next-door,' she decided. We opted for a pale green dress with sweetheart neckline and puff sleeves, with hair up and minimal jewellery.

'I look like a nurse, circa 1978,' I said.

'Exactly. Nurses are sexy girls next door,' said Kitty.

We flumped out together in the sitting room with a bottle of prosecco.

'I'm going to miss you, Daisy,' she said.

'Don't. I'm only just holding myself together. Life has got so weird lately. You know how Mrs Burton told the *Mail* that I had slept with Dominic at her hotel?'

'Yeah?'

'Well, she didn't. She contacted me through Branwell, really upset. Claims she said nothing. It was some journalist guy called Michael Swanston who approached her. She thinks someone else spoke to him, and her name was used as a smokescreen.'

'That's awful. Michael Swanston? I think he contacted me as well. Maybe it was on Twitter. I didn't say a word either,' said Kitty.

'What did he say to you?'

'Asked to talk about you. Did I know the status of your relationship with either Michel Amiel or Dominic McGann?' she revealed.

'And?'

'I said I knew nothing about either and that if I did, I still wouldn't speak, at any price. I hate

how they cause suspicion with their hacky ways,'
said Kitty. 'You know how careful I am.'

'I do, of course.'

'We should get to the bottom of this,' said
Kitty.

'I agree.'

Kitty sent a private Twitter message to
Michael Swanston.

Kitty: *Who really told you that Daisy and
Dominic were a couple?*

Michael: *Can I call you?*

Kitty: *Yes.* She typed her mobile number.

The call came through straight away.

'This is Kitty Chang,' she said.

She asked Michael if he could expand on his
story. I watched her nod, gasp, then wind up the
call.

Kitty came off the phone looking ashen.

'Well? Who told him?' I asked.

Kitty looked awkward. 'Are you sure you want
to know?'

'Of course I do!' I exclaimed, heart racing.

'He claims it was Dominic,' said Kitty. 'I'm
sorry.'

I gasped, catching my breath in my throat,
coughing, struggling to comprehend.

'I'm so sorry, Daisy!'

'Was Michael Swanston quite sure?' I pressed.

'Yes, he said it was a direct call with Dominic,
no middle people,' Kitty explained.

'But, why?' I asked.

'Maybe just to get rid of Michel once and for
all — to help you get over him,' Kitty said, being
charitable to Dominic. 'Perhaps he could see at

362

Hay that you weren't over him. That you two might rekindle things. And maybe you would have done were it not for that 'leak' about the double bed.'

I could hardly take it in. I knew that Dominic was a strategist, but this was another level. I went to bed feeling that my new world might be paved with gold, but it was also laced with poison.

★ ★ ★

Early the next morning, a car came to collect me for the TV show.

So much for the minimal make-up — I was taken for a complete masking, and they had another idea for what I might wear. Black trousers and a silky pink blouse, high heels. TV code for successful woman.

Such progress have I made in my life that I no longer get to dress myself. Nice.

Hannah was lovely, very gentle in her questioning, zooming right in on how hard it must be to adapt to such rapid life changes rather than glorifying the success.

'Yes, it has been a shock,' I admitted. 'And I suppose I now need to create some time to reflect on what has been good and what's been not so good and decide on the way I want to live from now.'

'Yes,' she agreed. 'I've spoken to lots of people who've had really sudden changes in fortune, whether it's a lottery win, winning a medal for sporting achievement or being elected into high office unexpectedly. Whatever the case, there are challenges associated with it, and a sense of surreality . . . People don't want to hear that it's not all upsides, but it's hard work being successful, isn't it?'

I nodded. 'I've got some regrets, but when things happen at great speed, that's inevitable, I guess.'

Hannah was getting braver. 'Look, everyone's going to want me to ask about Michel Amiel. They say that love and hate are very close. Is it a case of that?'

I was taken aback. I had been briefed on the questions, but this hadn't appeared in the briefing.

I cleared my throat. 'Michel Amiel has been very important in my story. He has inspired me in many ways, and I learned a lot of my baking skills at his cookery school,' I said.

'But the spats on Twitter — sounds like something went wrong a bit. Would that be fair to say?'

I took a deep breath.

'Well, yeah. It was decided that *French Fancy* would come out under the Lucy Lovecake pseudonym,' I said. 'Largely my own idea.'

'Right . . .'

'And part of making sure that would work as a teaser was that absolutely no one outside the central team should know about it. My identity had to be kept secret until well after launch. The problem was that this made me secretive and even a little treacherous towards people in my life who were not in on the secret.'

'I understand. And Michel Amiel was one of

those people you had to 'betray', as you put it?'

'Yes,' I said, stifling a pathetic sob.

I regained composure.

'I can see that must have been hard,' said Hannah. 'You know you have a potentially life-changing book, you don't want to jeopardise the success of it in any way. Hard situation for you.'

'Yes, and it was the most awful conflict imaginable because he became a more special friend as I was writing the book, and what's more, I was sent to his cookery school in that period. I wanted to be honest with him, and I regret that I was not.'

'Well,' Hannah continued, 'we're going to a break, but when we come back, Daisy Delaney is going to be telling us her secrets of success. How she persevered to get a literary agent and turned around her fortunes — join us for that!'

I checked my phone during the commercial break. Dominic had sent a few messages on a theme. 'Move on from Amiel, ffs.'

After the show, I took out my phone to send a message to Dominic. Branwell's advice about the risks of mixing love and business was ringing in my ears. I didn't want to ruin my career, but I couldn't live with a man I didn't trust:

Dominic, I'm going to spend some time at the flat. Things are moving too fast for me. I'd like to take some time on my own to write the next book. I'm sorry. Maybe I just haven't got Michel Amiel out of my system after all. Thank you for everything, Daisy X

A lot of messages and calls came through from

him after I sent that, but I didn't respond to them. Until, finally, I wrote: *Michael Swanston*. Nothing more after that.

84

Reflections

Before I went back to the flat, I stopped at a supermarket to buy some baking things. The best therapy — making French fancies. I went into the little kitchen and got to work, lost in the processes, producing a plate of dainty iced fancies. After that I walked around the streets of Prim Hill, taking in the sights that had been so familiar for so long. I went into the cookery school to see Catherine.

'Daisy!' she cried. 'Fantastic to see you. Well done! I'm seeing you everywhere. That cake you did at Hay was to die for!'

'Thanks, Catherine. My course here enabled me to try things like that. I don't know how to say thank you.'

'There's no need. Plenty of people learn to bake here. Not everyone has turned that knowledge into a bestselling book.'

'Ach, let's not talk about all that. What's going on with the cookery school?' I asked.

'We're not sure, is the simple answer,' she said.

'Michel never comes now?'

'Never.'

'Is he okay?'

'We've heard he's really depressed. Last we saw of him, he looked rough,' she confided.

'Yes, I agree. He wasn't well at Hay.'

'He's living in Paris, and this place is ticking along okay for now. I think Brasserie Rose is in need of his touch, but the manager does his best. We're all trying to hold things together while he sorts himself out. But we're not at all sure that he is doing that,' Catherine revealed.

'Sad.' I sighed, deep and long.

Catherine leaned forward. 'Let me give you his new address.'

I said nothing but did not object. She went into her desk drawer and produced a small card with Michel's details.

As I walked back to the flat, I felt somehow comforted by the card, but I knew I would be too afraid to get in touch. Too afraid that nothing came back.

I let myself in, forlorn.

'Kitty! I'm back!'

No reply. Kitty wasn't there. However, a familiar scent was.

Sitting in the loom chair was Michel Amiel.

'Kitty told me you'd be here,' he said.

'Michel!' I gasped. He looked fit and well; dressed immaculately. I saw from his tagged bag that he'd just arrived from the airport.

'You came especially to see me?' I asked.

'I did.'

'How have you been?' I wanted to know.

'For a while I was lovesick. But then I thought, no, don't give in to this. I've been running every day, swimming, writing a new book, eating well, staying off the booze, learning some new skills, getting myself ready,' he said.

'Ready for what?'

'For now,' he said, stepping towards me.

'Do you forgive me?' I whispered.

'Of course I do,' he replied, pulling me towards him.

I said nothing as we embraced.

He sat on the sofa and pulled me onto his lap, kissing me tenderly.

'I thought I'd lost you forever,' I said.

'Nobody could be that lucky.' He smiled.

I laughed, messing up his immaculate hair.

'That cost a lot of money!' he protested.

'But I like you messy!'

'Women!' he complained. 'We are too dirty. We are too clean. What's a man to do?'

I kissed him on the lips. He stroked my thighs. 'What, no stockings?' he complained.

'I can fix that,' I said, breaking away to go to my room.

When I returned he said, 'Music, please.'

'What sort?'

'For a foxtrot.' He danced a few steps.

'You learned to dance?'

'*Oui.*'

'Just for me?'

'For us.'

After our dance, he undid my dress and it fell to the floor.

'Can I offer you a French fancy?' I suggested.

'But I am your French fancy.'

We do hope that you have enjoyed reading this large print book.

Did you know that all of our titles are available for purchase?

We publish a wide range of high quality large print books including:
Romances, Mysteries, Classics
General Fiction
Non Fiction and Westerns

Special interest titles available in large print are:
The Little Oxford Dictionary
Music Book
Song Book
Hymn Book
Service Book

Also available from us courtesy of Oxford University Press:
Young Readers' Dictionary
(large print edition)
Young Readers' Thesaurus
(large print edition)

For further information or a free brochure, please contact us at:
Ulverscroft Large Print Books Ltd.,
The Green, Bradgate Road, Anstey,
Leicester, LE7 7FU, England.
Tel: (00 44) 0116 236 4325
Fax: (00 44) 0116 234 0205